THE HOLE
WE'RE IN

Gabrielle Zevin

○ ○ ○

THE HOLE
WE'RE IN

A Novel

Black Cat
New York
a paperback original imprint of Grove/Atlantic, Inc.

Published simultaneously in Canada
Printed in the United States of America

FIRST EDITION

ISBN-13: 978-0-8021-1923-0

Black Cat
a paperback original imprint of Grove/Atlantic, Inc.
841 Broadway
New York, NY 10003

Distributed by Publishers Group West

www.groveatlantic.com

10 11 12 13   10 9 8 7 6 5 4 3 2 1

To Hans Canosa

CONTENTS

CONTENTS

THE HOLE
WE'RE IN

PART I

○ ○ ○

The Red House

Oh baby, baby, how was I supposed to know
that something wasn't right here?

"... BABY ONE MORE TIME"

... that ellipsis tells a tale.

ROLLING STONE, APRIL 25, 1999

A June and Six Septembers

MIDWAY THROUGH HIS son's graduation from college, somewhere between the Ns and the Os, Roger Pomeroy decided that he owed it to himself to go back to school. He was forty-two years old, though people told him at least once a week that he looked younger. Last Christmas, a salesgirl had mistaken his then nineteen-year-old daughter for his wife. Last week, a different salesgirl had mistaken his forty-one-year-old wife for his mother. He knew it wasn't flattery, because in both instances the salesgirls had already made their sales: respectively, a flannel nightgown (wife's Christmas) and a leather fanny pack (son's graduation). And, at work—Roger was an assistant principal at the same Christian high school that his two older children had attended—all the girls flirted with him no matter how much he discouraged the practice.

His wife, George (née Georgia), nudged him. "You're supposed to be standing." Roger looked at the crowd, then past it to the dais. A flag was being raised. Everyone was standing, so Roger stood.

The more he thought about it, the more it made sense to do it now. Roger had completed a master's in education while working full-time, but if he wanted to get really serious (that is to say, a PhD) he would have to take leave. He had three children: Vincent, the son who was graduating; Helen, who would be a college junior the following year; and Patricia, age ten, the baby of the family though hardly a baby anymore. In any case, the kids were mostly grown, which meant two fewer mouths to feed. And if George had to work a couple of extra hours—here, he paused to smile at his wife. The smile was meant to acknowledge the official magnitude of the occasion, A Son's Graduation from College, but George immediately detected the ulterior in it. She grinned back.

Roger lowered his thoughts to a whisper. If George had to work a couple of extra hours, it would ultimately be for the best. With a PhD, Roger would earn more money, which meant the wife could retire altogether. Based on the time it had taken him to complete his master's, Roger estimated three years for a doctorate. He had been a family man for twenty-two years, over half his life. He had never cheated at anything, marriage included. He was an honorary pastor at their church and considered himself to be a better-than-average Christian. He had made sacrifices for others and now, he reckoned, sacrifices should be made for him.

George squeezed her husband's hand. "Earth to Roger," she whispered. "Your son's next."

They called Vinnie's name, and Roger applauded. He had missed his own graduation from college because George had gone into labor with the boy. It seemed fitting and good that he had come to this decision on this day.

Caps flew through the air and Roger's eyes filled with tears. The youngest, Patsy, was standing on the other side of him. He lifted her over his shoulders so that she could better see the show.

"Daddy," Patsy said. She placed her doll hands on his cheeks. "Are you crying because you're still mad at Vinnie?"

"No, I'm just happy, baby."

* * *

FIFTEEN MONTHS LATER, Roger moved his family from Tennessee to Texas and began the PhD program at Teacher's College, Texas University. He loved being full-time and working forms of the word *matriculate* into casual conversation. He was a sucker for anything (mugs, mouse pads, tube socks) with the Fighting Yellow Devils logo, despite the fact that these items were sold at a premium. If he could have afforded and gotten his wife to agree to it, he would have lived in student housing.

No doubt about it, the first year was difficult financially. The move alone had drained a good portion of their savings. But, by the second year, Roger had a decent teaching stipend amounting to fifteen thousand dollars per annum—less than a third of what he had taken in as an assistant principal, but combined with low-interest student loans, high-interest credit cards, a cashed-in retirement plan, and George's job, not bad. And besides, he wouldn't be a student forever. Just three years. Or four. Certainly no more than four.

After a summer of soul searching, Roger settled on a topic for his dissertation September of his fifth year. He would study the differences between kids who had attended schools with a religious component and kids who hadn't. The topic was near to his heart: Patsy, now nearly sixteen, was going to a public school because no acceptable religious one had been found within a thirty-mile radius of Texas U. Roger's standards for such an institution were very high indeed.

For the record, it was not an extraordinarily slow pace at which to complete a PhD. It was on the fast side of average, though it had obviously exceeded Roger's initial estimates.

George asked him if he might consider going back to work full-time while writing the dissertation. Roger declined. He had a lot of research to do, and he believed the whole enterprise would go more quickly if he could just focus. One other thing: upon reading his proposal, his adviser, the distinguished professor Carolyn Murray, had commented, "There just might be a book in this, Rog." He was embarrassed by how many times he'd repeated these words to himself. Despite the comfort he took in them, Roger chose not to share them with his wife. Instead, he imagined the following scene:

Roger, who has not yet turned fifty but regardless looks much younger, *has taken Georgia to the nicest restaurant in town.*

"Can we afford this?" George asks after a cursory look at the menu.

Roger nods and encourages the woman to order whatever she wants.

"Well, if you're certain . . ."

"I am, George. I am."

After dessert is served, Roger casually reaches under the table and pulls a published book out from under it.

"What's this?" she asks.

"It's a book," he says. {Alternatively, he says, "It's all our dreams come true," though this line effectually ends the scene, and Roger prefers to draw it out.}

George looks at the book. "But, it has your name on the cover."

"That's because it's my book, George. It's our book, and it's going to make us very, very rich."

"Why, Roger," she says, "I didn't even know you were writing a book!"

"I wanted to keep it a secret until I was sure," he says, turning back the cover with a jaunty flick of the wrist. "Read this . . ."

George puts on her glasses: "To my family, especially my wife, Georgia, without whom there would be no book. And to our Lord Savior, Jesus Christ, without whom there would be no life." *George clears her throat. {Sometimes, the dedication continues:* And to Professor Carolyn Murray, who supported this book in its infancy . . . *And sometimes not. His wife's hypothetical retort, "Roger, who's Carolyn Murray?" pushed the scene in an unusual and frankly somewhat undesirable direction.}*

"And look"—Roger flips to the back flap—"your name's here, too. I've used the picture you took of me at Helen's wedding for my author photo.

You're a professional photographer, George!" {He considers this to be a particularly nice touch, including her in the process as it did.}

George's voice is husky with emotion. "Come here, you wonderful, wonderful man!"

"Roger." The dream was deferred by Professor Murray's latest assistant: a skinny, pimple-scarred, faux-hawked, gay (or so Roger suspected), overpriced-glasses-wearing, twenty-four-year-old kid, who claimed his name was Cherish. The kid was also at approximately the same place in the PhD program as Roger. "Carolyn will see you now."

Her office was nice enough, but nothing special: furniture made of wood and not the particleboard rubbish that cluttered the offices of the junior faculty and staff; a brown leather chair with just the right patina; a Tiffany-style lamp; framed and matted reproductions by O'Keefe and Gauguin; a photograph of the professor with Laura Bush, the governor's wife; another with Coretta Scott King; a humdinger of a group shot that included First Lady Hillary Clinton, poet laureate Maya Angelou, and Betty Friedan, taken at a women's education summit in Washington, DC; a rather phallic pillar candle scented in cucumber-melon; an Oriental (Roger wondered if the term was offensive . . .) rug on the floor that almost managed to distract from the gray industrial carpet that plagued even the most attractive parts of campus; a first-class view of the university chapel and memorial gardens. *It really is nothing special,* he thought, *but it really should be mine.*

He had the same birthday as Professor Murray: March 12, though she was five years older than him. This fact had been revealed under somewhat embarrassing circumstances during Roger's second year in the program. At the end of one of her famous lecture classes, her inner circle of students, a group that did not include Roger, arranged for a surprise cake. Roger stood when he saw the cake speeding through the door on the borrowed AV cart. *How had they known it was his birthday?* He was giddy with astonishment and pleasure. The cake made its way down the aisle, sweet and white as a bride, and he felt nearly like he had on his wedding day. And then, it passed him by. Roger wondered if he should follow it to the front: *Is that how these things were done?* That was when the singing began. By the third line, it became clear that the cake had never been for him. He clapped his hands and tapped his foot in time to the music as if this had been his reason for standing all along.

"Come in, Rog," Professor Murray called. "Sit."

He obeyed.

She looked him up and down in a manner that struck Roger as not quite professional. "My, you're looking well!"

For the record, Carolyn Murray was a handsome woman, though Roger had never been attracted to the kind of women who were thought to be handsome women. She was ten pounds past slim, but she carried the extra weight well. Her suit was well cut, like her gray, curly hair, and its fabric expensive. It was not the kind of suit that often made an appearance at Roger's church or in his wife's closet. Even Professor Murray only wore the suit on lecture days, a custom in which Roger perceived gentility. At that moment, she had her shoes off and her feet displayed like a pair of knickknacks on the cluttered cherry desk. Roger could see a hole the size of a dime in her black stockings. It was just over the pad below her big toe, and its presence struck him as obscene. He wanted very badly to cover it up but settled for repositioning himself so he could no longer see it.

Although she was an ordinary enough specimen for a liberal arts college, Roger was a bit dazzled by her—that hole notwithstanding. He had spent his education (and, by extension, his life) in religious settings where the native birds tended to be of a different sort.

"So, Rog," she said, "I've been thinking of you."

Roger cleared his throat. He wasn't sure how to respond.

Professor Murray took her feet off the desk and tucked them away from Roger. She laughed a little to herself, then said, "Your work. I've been thinking of your dissertation proposal."

Roger cleared his throat again.

"Are you ill?" she asked.

Roger cleared his throat a third time. "I'm . . . ," he began. "What have you been thinking?"

"Well . . ."—she removed the proposal from her top desk drawer— "I've made some notes." The top sheet was scarred with red ink. Roger couldn't make out the words—Professor Murray's handwriting was indulgently illegible in the style of MDs and PhDs worldwide—but he could see many exclamation points and even more question marks.

"I thought you liked it." Roger tried not to sound childish, but did not succeed.

"I do, Roger. Very much. I think I mentioned to you when last we spoke that there might even be a book in it."

He conceded remembering something of the sort.

"Though the truth is, I think this topic might be broader and require more resources than what your standard dissertation allows," Professor Murray said. "In addition to library work, I foresee you conducting research trips, and you'll probably want several grad students to conduct interviews, and of course you'll need a good statistician. Have you put any thought into a good statistician?"

Roger had planned to run the statistics himself. He had taken an introductory statistics class in college and had recently purchased *Statistics for Dummies* as a refresher. He sensed that this would not be an acceptable response to the eminent professor's query. "I had not," he said.

"Well, I know a good one." Professor Murray made yet another note on Roger's proposal. "The thing is, Roger, I fear you may be a bit out of your depth here."

"Oh." Roger looked at his sneakers. His wife had purchased them in a back-to-school shopping trip that had also included a backpack for his youngest daughter. If worn more than two days in a row, the shoes, which were man-made in China, began to smell.

"Now, don't look so gloomy," Professor Murray said. "I think we can help each other."

Here, the professor took off her glasses and switched her voice to tones normally reserved for the classroom. "You're no doubt aware that there's a growing movement in this country to send children to religious schools. In the seventies and eighties, we saw parochial schools closing in record numbers. And now, for the first time in decades, we're seeing a small but significant number of new ones popping up. What accounts for this? Even in nonreligious settings, they're reintroducing prayer in the classroom whilst removing sexual education and *The Catcher in the Rye,* and, well, I suspect this reflects larger trends in our society, yada yada yada. My point is, Rog, I think you may have hit upon something incredibly fecund here."

Fecund was good. Roger giggled. The professor had a charming bit of Brooklyn in her speech that revealed itself when she was excited and only in words like *fecund.*

"You're smiling. What?"

Oh, what the heck, Roger thought. "Did anyone ever say that you, uh, sound like a lawyer?"

She widened her eyes in mock horror. "No!"

"No, I said that wrong. Not *a* lawyer. *The* lawyer. From the O.J. trial"—the Jewish one, he wanted to say, but he wasn't sure if that was racist—"I don't remember the name."

"Marcia Clark?"

"No."

The professor gathered her curly hair into a loose bun. He considered telling her that he liked her hair that way but decided it wouldn't be appropriate.

"You're a fundamentalist Christian, am I right?" Professor Murray asked.

"Well . . . Yes." Roger furrowed his brow in a way he both hoped and didn't hope would be observed.

"Did I say something wrong?"

"No. It's just, we're called Sabbath Day Adventists."

"So you're not a fundamentalist Christian?"

"I am. It's the same thing really." All at once, he realized he didn't wish to be having this discussion with this woman. "It doesn't matter. Go on."

"Don't ever be afraid to correct me, Roger. If the other term is more precise, that's what I'll use. And before you came here, you taught for twenty or so years in a Sabbath Day Adventist"—she paused to receive the approval Roger was overly eager to bestow—"high school?"

"Twenty-one years," Roger said. "And for half of those, I wasn't a teacher. I was an assistant principal."

Carolyn laughed, though Roger didn't think he'd said anything particularly funny. "How marvelous," she said. "Were you aware that I am a nonpracticing Jew?"

It was Alan Dershowitz, he thought.

"And now I like to call myself a weekend Buddhist, which is to say, I go on a lot of yoga retreats."

Roger wasn't sure if he was supposed to laugh.

"The point is, Rog, I think we'd make a very good team."

"Team?"

"We should write this book together. I can offer you resources and experience and a different perspective and—"

In his mind, Roger crossed Jesus out of the dedication:

Revision 1

Roger casually reaches under the table and pulls a published book out from under it.

"What's this?" George asks.

"It's a book, George," he says. "Mine and this other woman's, Carolyn Murray's. You remember her from the GSE Christmas party? She said she loved your sweater, took great pains to find out where you got it. You thought it was Ross Dress for Less, but you couldn't remember for sure."

"Oh, right," George says. "Her." She cracks the crust of her crème brûlée before taking the tiniest bite. "You know, honey, I don't think she even liked my sweater."

"Well, she said she did," Roger replies. "But back to my book. It's going to make us very, very rich."

"Us and Carolyn Murray," George corrects him.

"What about my dissertation?" Roger asked quietly.

"Oh, well, I imagine you'll write that on some smaller topic relating to this one. But honestly, Roger, we're onto something much bigger here. Do you have a notebook?"

Of course he did. It had a yellow devil gilded to the front and was separated into sections by dual pocket folders—$5.99 at the university bookstore.

Among other things, Professor Murray described how Roger would give up the four classes he was TAing (–$15,000) and become her full-time project coordinator (+$5,000). Roger decided it would be rude to ask her how in the good Lord's name he was meant to make up the $10,000 difference.

"Let me pray on it," he says.

"Seriously?" Carolyn Murray raises an impressively plucked eyebrow.

"What you describe is not necessarily the tack I was planning to take. I'm . . . I'm in favor of a religious education, Professor Murray. I'm a product of one, as are my children. And the book I was planning to write was going to be in praise of—"

"Seriously? Do you know who I am? And do you know who you are? And do you have any idea what I'm offering you? I know you're Christian, but are you also daft?"

"Well, let me at least talk it over with my wife. There are financial matters to consider, and—"

"You mean that woman with the tacky sweater from the holiday party?"

She knew you didn't like it, *Roger thinks.*

"Honestly, Rog, if you don't get on board, and right quick, I'll probably just steal the idea from you and write my own book. And where will you be then? Fifty years old and saddled with eighty thousand dollars in

student loans. You and that tacky-sweater-wearing wife of yours will be working until you're both buried in a hole in the ground. Why don't you just pray on that, choir boy?"

The professor smiled at him, and Roger noticed that she had very nice teeth. "Take as much time as you need to think it over," she said. "It occurs to me . . . I know your work from advising you for the past several years, but you might not know mine." She danced over to the larger of her two bookshelves. "You may have bought some of these for your classes, but just in case . . ." She handed him a stack of her books. They had all been published by major publishers —not a university press, and certainly not a *religious* university press, among them. Her first book, *The Wheels on the Bus Go Round,* was considered the seminal work about school integration and busing practices. *Wheels* was still used in education classes everywhere, but it was the kind of book regular people bought, too. Several years ago, PBS's *Frontline* had devoted an entire episode to the fifteenth anniversary of the work. Roger had turned up the volume when Carolyn's interview came on. "George," he said, "that's my teacher!"

"Unga," had been his wife's reply. Roger had tried to shake her awake, but George would not be roused.

Roger wondered how many copies of *The Wheels on the Bus Go Round* sold each year. All he knew was that it had been used in a half dozen of his classes, and not just the ones taught by Professor Murray either. He contemplated asking Professor Murray to sign the copy she'd just given him, but decided that would irreparably unbalance their power dynamic. If he'd opened the book, he would have discovered that it was already presigned: "Live the dream, Carolyn Murray."

She sauntered back to her desk and took off her suit jacket. "Excuse me," she said. "I don't normally give my colleagues a striptease, but it must be ninety degrees out there today."

"Carolyn"—he had never called her Carolyn before—"Carolyn, of course I know your work. Everyone knows your work. And it would be such an incredible honor to work with you. When you called this meeting, I never imagined . . ." He was rambling. "A product of all religious schools—a religious high school and a religious college and . . ." She nodded encouragingly but also looked a bit bored or impatient. "Of course I want to work with you."

"Good." She praised him as if he were an obedient dog. In lieu of shaking hands, Carolyn stood to hug him. He could feel her breasts through her shirt. He didn't want to be feeling them, but the fact was, he was. They felt strange. They felt strangely . . . buoyant. They felt like they could bounce or maybe even float. Was it possible that the esteemed professor had had a breast job? Or was it the trick of a clever bra maker? Roger knew little about such matters.

"Now, Rog, do you mind if I do something?"

"Um . . . no, I guess not."

She reached her hand under his collar and lifted the back of his still-blond hair out of it. Her hand was cool and surprisingly soft. "That's been really bothering me," she said.

"I guess I need to get it cut."

She didn't disagree. "My husband—ex-husband—used to go to this terrific guy not far from campus. I'll have my assistant e-mail you his name."

"Where do you get yours cut?" Roger had no idea why he had asked that. "For my wife, I mean."

"Me?" She said the name of a place, which Roger instantly forgot and which his wife surely couldn't afford anyway.

The meeting was over, but neither was sure how to end it. Carolyn returned to her burnished throne, and she and Roger beamed at each other a bit. She put her feet up on the desk again. Roger could see a pesky corn pushing through the tear in her stockings. Now that they would be working closely together, he imagined buying her a gift certificate for a pedicure for Christmas. Women liked that sort of thing . . . Didn't they? Did Carolyn celebrate Christmas? In any case, for the holidays. Was a pedicure an appropriate gift for a colleague?

Carolyn had a funny little smile on her face. "What are you looking at?" she asked evenly.

"Your foot. I mean, there's a hole. I mean, your stocking has a hole," he stammered, like it was the first time he'd ever spoken to a girl. "What I'm looking at is the hole." In pointing at the rip, he accidentally grazed her foot with his index finger, but she didn't seem to notice anyway.

"How can you look at a hole?" she mused.

October

THE LEAVES WERE not changing, and the air was not brisk, and there was nothing to indicate October except that was what the calendar said, and sons were playing football, and daughters were being tossed from pyramids, and George's children were older, and George, too, was older, and she still had October bills to pay.

The painters had arrived early. There were only two of them; they were Mexican and related, though George wasn't sure how. Either father/son or brothers. The older one had told her, but George hadn't understood, and at some point in her life she had gotten the idea that it was rude to ask people with accents to repeat things. Both men seemed to be called Ramón, which may have been either their first or last name. She wondered if they were illegals before deciding this was none of her business. She had not personally hired them, after all. She had hired a company who hired them, and this degree of separation removed her from any ethical obligation.

She could not really afford to take two days off from her job as a data processor. George was paid $16.50 an hour and had herself been hired, not by the insurance company where she worked but by a temporary agency that was paid an additional $16.50 for every hour of

George's labor. George wondered about the ethics of that, too. The agency had tested her typing and computer skills, briefly reviewed her résumé, and called her two weeks later with the job she still had. How much was this worth and for how long? She had been working for the insurance company for a year and had accrued neither sick nor vacation days. (Her own health insurance was covered by her husband.) Still, this gig was the best she had ever had. She had never finished college, which meant that her employment history had included smocks (Slickmart; a brief stint as a lunch lady), standing all day, asking permission to go to the bathroom, a machine that sliced off three of her closest colleague's fingers, hairnets, and a blue laminated button that read PULL MY FINGER. At her current job, she got to sit, wear her own clothes, and go to the ladies' whenever she pleased. Paradise.

But the fact was, she could not really afford the time off. Nor could she afford the paint job that had been needed since the too-large house had been purchased. Nor could she afford many of the possessions that had been bought to fill the too-large house, or even, at times, the cost of regulating its climate. She certainly could not afford to get sick or for any of the rest of them to get sick either. Working at a health insurance company from 7:30 to 3:30, five days a week, she thought a lot about getting sick and what a luxury it really was. She harbored particular envy for rich people who could afford mental hospitals— how relaxing that sounded! Alas, such pleasures were out of her stars. Middle-class folks were forced to go nuts in their living rooms; the rich got to do it at spas. George could not afford to lose her mind or even get the flu. According to a recent spreadsheet that had crossed her desk, for a woman her age, forty-seven, it was cheaper to take a cruise to Alaska than to get a case of food poisoning that required hospitalization.

She couldn't afford the wedding she was planning for her older daughter, Helen. The wedding, incidentally, had been the impetus for painting the house. After much lobbying, George had convinced

Helen to have the event at home as opposed to at an expensive venue. At the time, George had thought this would save money, but this wasn't turning out to be the case. Landscaping had to be redone! Wooden floors refinished! Chairs and tables rented! And, of course, the house needed to be repainted. George couldn't help but think that it would have been cheaper to have had it at the downtown Marriott, which was what Helen had wanted in the first place.

The doorbell rang. The older of the two painters wanted to know if George would like to look at the paint before they began applying it. George didn't particularly, but it seemed the thing to do, so she followed the man out to the yard. He opened a can and held it out to her. For a second, she got the idea that she should sniff it like a wine cork, though neither she nor her husband drank. In the can, the hue looked somehow brighter than she remembered from the store.

"Is all right?" the older painter asked.

"Um . . . Well, it looks a bit light," said George.

"Do not worry, missus. Will dry darker."

"It'll honest to God end up looking brick colored?"

Ramón Sr. nodded, though later it would occur to George that he, too, might have been taught that it was rude to ask people with accents to repeat things.

It was ninety-four degrees out, and Ramón the Elder was already sweating. Had October always been this hot? George had spent her childhood in Vermont, but of course it had been cooler there.

"Hot one," she said.

"Missus?"

"Hot," she repeated. She fanned herself by way of demonstration.

"Caliente," he said. He smiled at her and held out the paint can.

"Caliente," she repeated.

"The paint is . . . Caliente . . . is OK?"

"Looks"—the phone rang inside her house—"A-OK," she said. She made a thumbs-up sign then trotted off to answer the phone. She wasn't normally this excited about a call, but it seemed like a good enough way to end the conversation with the elder Ramón.

She was winded by the time she reached the phone and considered not answering. She hated the sound of her winded voice—she thought out-of-breath people sounded unhealthy, fat. She *was* fat and probably unhealthy (she hadn't been to the doctor in some time, so she couldn't say for certain), but the person on the other side needn't know your whole life story.

Despite this, she answered the phone. It was her oldest daughter.

"Mother, you sound out of breath," Helen said.

"I was just outside," George apologized. "They're painting the house today, you'll be glad to know."

Helen said she remembered—*obviously, Mother*—that's why she'd called George at home and not at work. "Maybe I'll stop by to see it tomorrow."

Please don't, George thought.

"Why? Don't you want to see me?" Helen asked.

George wondered if she had somehow spoken her thoughts aloud before realizing that Helen had only been responding to the silence. "It's just if you came tomorrow you wouldn't really be able to see it."

Helen asked her what she meant.

"They've got two more days of work. And also, the paint goes on a little light."

Helen asked her what she meant.

"The color. The painter said it looks light in the can but dries darker."

"Really?"

"Yes."

"Mother, did you even look in the cans before they started putting it on?"

"Of course I did, Helen."

"Are you sure?"

"Yes, I'm sure!"

"Well," said Helen, "I really don't understand why Daddy couldn't stay home with the painters. It doesn't make any sense. You've got to take off three days from work, and he'd only have to miss an hour or two of classes. Plus, he's better with these things."

"What things?"

"Maintenance things."

Where in the world had her twenty-five-year-old daughter gotten that idea? George had been "maintaining things" for as long as she and Roger had been married. "Why are you calling, anyway?" George asked.

"I wanted to make sure you called the invite place with the credit card number. You did, didn't you?"

"Um," said George.

"Because they won't start making them till you call with the number. You know that, right?"

"I—"

"And if they don't start making them now, we aren't going to be able to send them out on time."

"I didn't know they needed to start so soon, Helly. We're still eight and a half months out."

"Well, they do. You said you would call last week, remember?"

George did remember but decided to pretend she didn't. "How much is it going to be again?"

"Three hundred now and three hundred on delivery."

"Honestly, Helen, that seems a little pricy. Couldn't we maybe make them ourselves? I saw these kits at Craft Barn—"

"No, Mother, we cannot make them. We *cannot* make them. We absolutely cannot. We've . . ." Helen sighed. "Why are you doing this?"

"Doing what?"

"Making me feel bad about something we've already discussed and settled a million times."

"I'm not trying to make you feel bad," George said.

Helen, a speech therapist, switched into her patient, professional voice. "Mother, do you need the phone number again?"

"OK, Helen. How you doing otherwise, babe?" George asked.

"I'm fine. I'm just fine, but Mother, I am begging you. Please don't forget to call the engraver, all right?"

"I won't."

"Because if the save-the-date cards don't get mailed, it's like Elliot and I haven't claimed the date. And any one of our friends or family could, like, swoop right in. Plus, we'll both have a ton of people coming from out of town—"

"Save-the-date cards?" George asked. "You mean these aren't the actual invites?"

"You are losing it, Mother, I swear. I've only told you this about a million times." Helen sighed. "Do you want me to have someone from the invitation place call you? Because I can do that."

"No, Helen, I'll take care of it," George promised. "In fact, I'll call as soon as we hang up." George said this in order to get Helen *to* hang up.

But George did not call. She wasn't sure where she had written the phone number, and there was no way she was calling Helen back to get it.

In George's mind, this wedding could not come at a worse time. Next year would be a wonderful time. Next year, Roger would be done with his PhD and back at work, and she would be able to breathe again. This year, Roger was making only five thousand dollars for reasons George still did not completely understand. "I got a promotion," he had announced a little over a month ago.

"A promotion," she said. "How wonderful!"

"The thing is, Georgie, I'll be making a little less money than I was. But that's only temporary, and then I'll be making so much more."

Then he kissed her hard on the mouth. Her husband might be almost fifty years old, but he was still dashing. Roger had blondish brown hair, and he was slim and tall. He wasn't handsome like an actor or model. His features were less tortured and more regular than those kinds of men. He was handsome in a placid way, like a weatherman. All the ladies flirted with him. It used to bother her, but Roger had never strayed, and now those flirtations amused her more than anything. George still believed that if you lined up all the husbands at their church, hers was the handsomest.

This wasn't to say she had been fooled by the kiss. George knew there was no universe in which a ten-thousand-dollar pay cut somehow represented career advancement. No. The point of Roger's kiss (or so George thought) had been to say something along the lines of, *Please let this be all right with you because there's nothing I can do about it now.* So George tasted her husband's mouth and thought to herself, *Whatever has happened has happened, so I may as well enjoy this kiss and then we'll just get on with it, whatever it is.*

Sometime after lunch and a nap, George checked the mail. There were bills, of course, and three college admissions pamphlets for Patsy, two credit card offers for Vinnie though he had never resided at this address, a notice that Señor's teeth needed to be cleaned (Señor was Helen's cat who had died last year), the September issue of *Christian Educator Monthly* for Roger (it always seemed to arrive a month late), and a specialty catalog catering to the mature, full-figured lady who could appreciate a high-quality caftan. *Who in the world is this supposed to be for?* George wondered, flipping the catalog over to look at the mailing label. *Of course,* she realized. *Me.*

Lacking the serious mental preparation required for bill opening, she stuffed the bills in the kitchen "bill" drawer. She was about to toss most of the kids' mail into the trash when one of Vincent's credit card offers caught her eye. It was preapproved with an introductory APR of 0.0%. George decided to set this one aside. Maybe her son could use a better credit card? She knew he had at least one already, but he could always do a balance transfer or something. She decided to call him to ask but as usual only got his voice mail. "Hi Vinnie.

It's Mommy. There's a credit card offer here . . ." George always felt awkward leaving messages, like the recording was somehow draining the life force from her. *Keep it light,* she coached herself. *Sound normal. Don't ramble. An answering machine is not the place for a heart-to-heart.* "Really, it's a better deal than any of Daddy's and my credit cards at this point. So . . . so, just give a call back when you have the time. Love you, honey."

George paged through the fat-lady catalog, pausing to admire a red empire-waist dress with a matching multicolored quilted jacket. She was wondering whether the color was too bold to wear to Helen's wedding when the phone rang again. She dog-eared the catalog page.

"Good afternoon, Mrs. Pomeroy. This is Laine Philips from the Paper Trail, Highland Mall location."

"Who?"

"We're doing the invites for your daughter's wedding," said Laine. "Helen," she added, as if George could possibly have forgotten the name of the daughter who was getting married.

"Oh. OK. Nice to meet you."

"Helen asked us to call for your credit card information, if that's all right."

"Um, just a minute." George dug through her bottomless purse. Over the years, her purses had grown in proportion to her hips, and this one was starting to become one of those epic old-lady bags, the kind she had said she'd never have. The kind her grandmother had carried. Her grandmother who used to carry around a five-pound marble ashtray even after she had quit smoking. Even after the woman had been diagnosed with lung cancer, for Pete's sake.

"Mrs. Pomeroy?"

I told Helen I would call, George thought.

"Mrs. Pomeroy?"

"I'm just trying to find my credit card," George apologized.

"No problem," said Laine. "So, it must be super exciting having your daughter get married?"

"Yeah. It's truly"—George paused—"something. Oh, I just found it!" She was about to read the numbers when the phone beeped. Maybe it was Vinnie? "I'm sorry, someone's on the other line. Can I just take this real quick?" As she clicked over, George felt slightly annoyed with herself for asking permission.

"Hello, Georgia, this is Kate Johnson, Janet Johnson's mother, from the cheerleading team." *The only time this woman calls is for money,* George thought. When Patsy had joined the cheerleading team two years ago, she had had no idea it was such an expensive pastime. George's notions of cheerleading had come straight from her own 1960s high school where color coordinated skirts, pompoms, and the occasional ponytail holder had been all that was required. "How y'all doin' today?" Mrs. Johnson drawled. The more money she wanted, the more Texan her accent got.

"Um, could I call you back? My older daughter's getting married—"

"Congratulations!"

"Well, I'm not the one getting married, Kate," George joked.

"Well, a daughter's wedding is like your own, though, isn't it?"

"Sure. The thing is, could I call you back? I've got the engraver on the other line."

"Why don't I just hold?" Mrs. Johnson offered.

George clicked back to the Paper Trail. "Sorry about that." She read her credit card number, then returned to Mrs. Johnson.

"The reason I'm calling, Georgia . . . do you go by Georgie?"

George answered the same way she had answered every other time Mrs. Johnson had posed this question, "You can call me whatever you like."

"So, Georgie, the girls are having a fund-raiser, which of course means that we're having a fund-raiser for them . . ."

And blah, blah, blah. George tuned Mrs. Johnson out. Eventually, she'd come to the point.

"So assuming the bikini car wash goes well, which it always has in years past, each girl only needs to sell one hundred rolls of wrapping paper . . ."

More than anything in the world, George hated selling that stupid crap. Over the course of three children, George had sold magazine subscriptions, chocolate bars that tasted like soap, raffle tickets, prepaid calling cards, potted plants, greeting cards, gourmet baskets, cheese, encyclopedias, personalized Bibles, and a variety of baked goods. As she was not a natural salesperson, she had never gotten the knack for asking her colleagues and neighbors to buy this crap either. Besides, a sale to a neighbor or colleague contained an unspoken promise that she would buy whatever their kid sold in the future. Consequently, she herself had usually ended up buying the majority of whatever her children were meant to be selling. And *whatever* sat in the garage until it ultimately rotted or was given to Goodwill. She wished they would just ask them for the money flat out.

"But if the bikini car wash doesn't go well, probably one hundred fifty rolls. In any case, that should leave plenty of money to pay for the girls' airfare to nationals in San Diego and team boxer briefs."

"Boxer briefs?" George asked.

"They're boxer shorts that are tight, like underwear. Boxers and briefs at the same time."

George knew what they were. She was just wondering why exactly the girls' cheerleading team would need them. "Aren't boxers for boys?" she finally asked.

Mrs. Johnson laughed. "The girls like them, too. It's sort of a thing. It's sort of a—"

The phone beeped again, and the tone was sweet to George's ears— deliverance. She apologized to Mrs. Johnson and asked if she could call her back later.

"Oh, that's all right, Georgie," Mrs. Johnson said. "I really just wanted to give you the heads up that Patsy should be bringing home the catalog with the wrapping paper samples this evening, OK?"

"Now I know," George said.

"Because you know how the girls can be about remembering to give things to their moms. My Janet, God love her, but her backpack's like the Bermuda Triangle."

"Mmm-hmm, I've really got to get the other—"

"Sorry, hon. I'll give you a call some time next week. Buh-bye now!" George clicked over to the other line.

"Hello, Mrs. Pomeroy. This is Laine from the Paper Trail again."

"Hi there," George said.

"Um, well, the credit card you gave me . . . I was wondering if you had a different one."

"Is it not . . . ," George began, but at that moment, Patsy came through the kitchen door. The youngest left her gym bag in the middle of the kitchen, waved at George, and headed straight for the fridge.

"Hey, Mom," Patsy whispered. "Who you talking to?"

Patsy's accent always surprised George. The family had moved from Massachusetts to Tennessee when Patsy was one month old, and Patsy was the only one who had developed the voice of the region. Roger, whose mother was Southern, had a little Tennessee from time to time, but then, he was a bit of a mockingbird. He had gotten the long *a*'s of a Kennedy when they had lived in Massachusetts, too. "Someone for Helen's wedding," George whispered back. "Sorry," George said to Laine, "My youngest just got home from school. So, do you want to run it through again?"

"Yeah, the thing is I've already done that. Twice actually. This happens pretty often, though. You might want to call your credit card company or something."

"Right," George said. "I'll definitely have to do that."

"So, in the mean time, the easiest thing might be if you just have another card."

But that's the one that works, George thought. While George was fishing through her massive purse for a different credit card, Patsy sat down across the table from her with a snack that included two Twizzlers, a handful of Cheetos, and a Coke. George suspected she ought to pester Patsy to eat something nonsynthetic, but she didn't feel up to an argument.

For lack of any other reading material, Patsy picked up the fat lady catalog, which sprang open to the dog-eared page.

"Mom," Patsy whispered, "what in the world is this?" She pointed to the rainbow jacket.

"I was thinking I might wear it to Helen's wedding. Or, you know, the rehearsal dinner or something," George whispered back.

"Yeah," Patsy said. "Or you could wear it to clown school?"

"Is it that bad?" George covered the mouthpiece of the phone. "I thought all the colors were sort of pretty."

"Why don't you just cut a hole in the middle of the bedspread and wear that?" With a cheese-stained finger, Patsy cut a circle in the air, then left. George could hear the television come on in the den.

"Mrs. Pomeroy," Laine asked, "are you still there?"

George made a note to clean out her purse. "Oh, um, I just found it." George produced the second credit card and read the numbers to Laine.

"Why don't you stay on the line while I ring it through?" Laine suggested.

An endless ninety seconds later, the card was approved. George apologized for the trouble and hung up the phone.

Hell, George thought, *now I have to deal with whatever's wrong with the good credit card.*

Though not mentally prepared for such a task, she opened the bill drawer and found the statement in question. It turned out there was nothing wrong with the credit card except the obvious—its eight-thousand-dollar limit was all used up. Most of the charges were familiar to George—groceries, the cable bill—but then there were a few larger ones that Roger must have made without telling her. Things like airplane tickets. Airplane tickets to New York.

All was easily explained. The tickets, it turned out, were a research trip Roger was taking to New York in February for his dissertation. It was the only expense he had to take care of—the rest of the trip was being sponsored by his faculty adviser. "It's OK, isn't it?" Roger asked George that night in bed.

"It's fine. It's just better if you tell me first. So I can plan," George said.

"Maybe I can get the department to reimburse me for the travel?"

"That would be good."

"I doubt they'll do it, though," Roger said. "They're already being really aboveboard to cover the hotel."

"Fine."

Roger turned to look at George in bed. "Are we OK?"

George nodded. "We're fine." And then she sighed. "We'll be better when Helen's wedding is over and you've got your PhD."

"Do I need to worry?"

"No." There was no point in him worrying. One of her designated marital responsibilities had always been worrying. "Roger?" She tried to say this as gently as possible. "The next time you make reservations, it might be better if you flew coach. For the time being, I mean."

"You're right. It's just that Carolyn"—he began, then corrected himself—"Professor Murray, my adviser, always flies business class, and she thought we'd be able to get some work done on the plane."

George considered this argument. "That makes sense," she said after a while. But Roger was already asleep.

Despite the fact that she was overweight and they were in debt, their sex life was really very good. Or at least regular. Around 3 AM, George woke to the feeling of her husband atop her. "Is it all right if I go in?" he asked.

George wasn't really in the mood, but as the question had been put so politely, she consented.

He lifted up her nightgown and crawled under it. She couldn't see his face. It was like having sex with a pink nylon ghost.

The question of contraception was not considered. Roger had always been against it on both Christian and pagan principles, and George's periods had lately become irregular enough to make the issue moot.

After sex, George couldn't sleep. She went downstairs and prayed for a bit: *Dear God, let us all stay healthy. Dear God, let Roger finish his PhD this year. Dear God, let us not have to declare bankruptcy. Dear God, dear God, dear God.* In the end, she threw in something about *the poor children in Africa* and *innocent people with AIDS* and *sinners everywhere* just so her prayers didn't seem completely narcissistic.

But she really only meant the first part.

She went into the kitchen. The answering machine light was blinking. It was Vinnie. He apologized for calling so late—the hours in the graduate film program he was attending were very long—but he was interested in the credit card offer and asked George to set it aside for him. He'd get it at Christmas or the next time she had something to send him or whenever.

George thought she had left the application on the counter, but it wasn't there. It had gotten mixed up with a rough crowd: the bill drawer bills. She was awake and had nothing else to do, so she filled it out for him. Like any mother, she knew his name, his date of birth, his social security number, and even the way he signed his name: the extravagant upstroke of the capital *V*; the tightly packed, indistinct lowercases; the *P* with its oversized, arrogant loop; the final *y*, which ended in a flourish, not unlike his father's.

November

LAST PRACTICE BEFORE the last game of the year, and the football team was distracted. Basketball tryouts in the gym had forced the cheerleaders to hold practice on the sidelines.

Harland Bright, the wide receiver, watched the girls form a three-level pyramid. He was known for his great eyes and his even greater speed, and he saw before anyone else that the little blonde at the top was about to fall on her head. He started running.

"*Bright, where you going?*" Coach called out.

Harland didn't answer. That was his great gift as an athlete. He never felt like he had to explain himself. He just got it done.

He arrived at the pyramid just as the little blonde was about to crash into the gravel. He caught her, but a moment too late. The back of her head bounced briefly against the ground then her neck twisted causing her temple to skid across the gravel—a fumble—and then she passed out.

"What's her name?" he asked her teammates.

"Patsy Pomeroy," someone told him.

"Pomeroy," he repeated. *Like the apple,* he thought.

* * *

HE DIDN'T SEE the little blonde for another week, but he thought about her. About the way her head had felt in his hands—silky and clean and smaller than a football. About the way she had smelled— sweaty and bloody and a little sweet. He wished he had another chance to run the play. If he'd just been a little faster or taken a slightly more efficient route to the sidelines, she wouldn't have hit her head at all. Harland Bright was a perfectionist.

And then, there she was in the flesh, standing in front of his locker.

"Hear you saved my life," she said. Now that she was standing, he could see that she was more than a foot shorter than him.

"Not quite," he said. He nodded toward the neck brace she was wearing.

"Aw, that? That's nothing. I could be in a wheelchair or like, dead, you know?"

"S'pose."

She narrowed her bluish green eyes at him. "Yeah, maybe I should be pissed at you," she said. "I have to sit out the whole rest of the cheerleading season."

"Hadn't heard that," Harland said.

"You're not too talkative," she commented.

"Sorry, ma'am."

The bell rang, and the little blonde turned to leave.

"Is it a tragedy, Patsy?" he called out.

"So, the big football star knows my name," she said. "Is what a tragedy?"

"Sitting out the rest of the cheerleading season."

"Not really. I pretty much hate it."

"Where's your team spirit?"

Patsy shrugged. "Guess they'll just have to find some other five-foot-tall blonde girl to drop on her head."

She wasn't beautiful. He corrected himself. She wasn't his idea of beautiful. When he dated (which was not very often), he preferred leggy, dark-haired girls. But there was something appealing about her. And, in a way, she belonged to him. She was his game ball.

"Let me give you a ride home," Harland said.

Her house was easy to find: it was painted stop-sign red. "A mistake," she told him, though beyond that, she did not specify.

She asked him inside, where they watched *Oprah* on mute and told each other all their secrets.

He told her how he was waiting to hear from Harvard, but his mother thought he should go to a Big Ten school instead. That way, he had a better chance of playing professionally. And she told him how her brother had gone to Yale and how it had caused this big rift. "Basically the same as going to hell, my dad said, though I guess he recovered before Vinnie's graduation because we all went to that. Kinda last minute. Just told us to get in the car, and twenty-three hours later we're in New Haven. My dad's still crazy religious, though."

"Crazy religious? What's that mean exactly?" Harland wanted to know the likelihood that Patsy's father would end up, say, hanging him from a tree.

"Um, different things, I guess. Depends on his mood. We don't eat meat. And my dad occasionally goes on these fasts to be, like, closer to God or, like"—she pumped her hand in a jerking-off motion—"but really it's just 'cause he thinks he's getting fat. And I get in trouble for all sorts of things."

"Aw, come on," Harland said with a grin. He had concluded that this was the amusing (and not the fatal) kind of crazy religious after all. "A good girl like you, I bet you don't do nothing wrong."

"Well, my dad thinks so. Like a couple of months ago, I got punished for wearing too much makeup."

"So do my sisters."

"Yeah, but my dad wouldn't let me shower for a week. It was supposed to prove to me that my body is a temple, but whatever. Mainly it was gross."

"But he doesn't mind those little cheerleading skirts?"

Patsy shrugged. "Guess not. Probably just hasn't noticed yet. He hasn't ever been to one of our games or anything, which is probably a good thing. But yeah, when he's paying attention, he's, like I said before, crazy religious and he thinks we should all go to schools within the faith."

"Why you going to school with us sinners then?"

"Well, the only Sabbath Day one's in Wyattville and . . . I guess my dad thought that was a bad part of town."

"That's where I used to live, you know," Harland said. "Before I could drive, they used to bus me here."

"Yeah."

"Wonder what your dad would think of me?" Harland asked.

Patsy smiled so sweetly he could hardly stand it and then she shrugged. "S'pose the only question should concern you is what I think of you."

Harland laughed. Her little Southern accent made her sound kind of . . . well, dumb . . . but he could tell she wasn't dumb at all.

"They were gonna homeschool me, but I was, like, *no way*. My mom told my dad it would be fine for me to go to a public school as long as it was close to home and they could keep watch over me and if every summer I went to Bible camp." Patsy rolled her eyes.

"Bible camp. That sounds pretty hard-core."

"Yeah. It's pretty much the highlight of my year," she said. "You honestly would not believe how crazy horny the kids at Bible camp are. All that repression, I reckon." Patsy started to undo her neck brace.

"Hey, are you allowed to take that off?"

For short times, she told him. To shower and to swim three times a week for physical therapy. "And how else am I gonna give you a blow job?" she added.

She looked at his face. He didn't look nearly as stunned as she'd hoped. A big athlete like him probably got offered blow jobs "for real" all the time. She had thought she was going to sound worldly, but she had just ended up sounding stupid. She rubbed her neck with the meat of her palm. "Just kidding. First of all, I can't, 'cause my neck's totally screwed up. And secondly, I wouldn't, 'cause I'm not that kind of girl."

"I know you aren't, little blondie," Harland said. He ran his fingers along the smooth, white skin of her neck. "What time do your folks get home?" he asked.

"Late," Patsy replied. "My dad's in school, and my mom works two jobs."

Around seven o'clock, Harland left, and Patsy put her neck brace back on.

As she watched him back his car out of the driveway, it occurred to her that this was probably the first time a black guy had ever been in her parents' house.

PATSY WENT UPSTAIRS and called Magnum French, her long-distance boyfriend. He was from Buckstop, Tennessee, Patsy's hometown, but he had moved there after she'd left. Bible camp in Alabama was where they had actually met.

"Magnum," she said, "this can't go on."

There were tears, threats, and words not found in the Bible. It took nineteen hours of long-distance calls at the Pomeroy's one-rate plan of ten cents per minute, but Magnum finally got the message.

"I just want you to know one thing." His voice was thick with snot.

"All right," she said.

He was sobbing. "Every . . . day . . ."

"I can't understand you, Magnum. On account of you crying so much and all."

"I said, every day you're not"—deep sniffle—"with me"—another deep sniffle—"you'll be thirst."

"Thirsty? Why am I gonna be thirsty?"

"Cursed!"

"OK. Whatever." She hung up the phone. He called her back, but she didn't pick up. For the first seventeen hours, she had felt sorry for him, but in the last hour or two, she'd really started to despise him.

Outside, a car horn. Harland was waiting to drive her to her swimming lesson.

"Hey, little blondie," he said.

"Hey."

"Where's your neck brace?"

"I'm all better now," she said.

"A miracle."

Patsy's swimming therapy took place at the Olympic-size swimming pool at her dad's college. While she worked with the therapist, Harland liked to watch from the bleachers. He had nothing else to do: football season was over, classes required no effort, and well, he liked seeing Patsy in her swimsuit. She was a bit thick-waisted and a bit small-breasted, and as he often liked to remind himself, Altogether Not His Type. On the other hand, she was really sturdy from all that cheerleading. Nice oval calves. Cute dimples for elbows. Cute dimples for dimples. An ass like an apple. Blonde eyelashes. He'd never known anyone with blonde eyelashes before. Not personally, at least. Not up close.

Patsy's class ended at five o'clock, at which time the pool was declared open for free swim.

"Come in," Patsy called.

Harland shook his head. "Naw."

"Why won't you ever come in with me?"

The reason should have been obvious. Harland couldn't swim, but he hadn't wanted to admit it to the little blonde.

"One of these days, I'm just gonna pull you in, Harland Bright," she said. She pulled herself up to the edge of the pool and rested her elbows on the side. She reminded Harland of a seal.

He kneeled down by the side. His full lips were practically touching her thin ones. "I'd probably drown," he said.

"Then I'd have to save you." She pushed herself out of the pool with short, strong arms.

"You'd like that, Little Blondie."

"At least we'd be even." She dried herself off, then wrapped the towel around her body.

"We're already even," he said.

"How do you figure?"

Harland took her hand, and they walked out to his car. Her hand felt pruny from the water, and a strange notion popped into his head. He imagined that he was holding hands with Patsy, only she was a very old lady and they had been married a very long time.

Someone would ask, "How did you two meet?"

And he would always answer the same way: "She fell from the sky."

"Hey, Harland," Patsy said. "I could teach you to swim, you know."

"Mmm," he said.

"Seriously. You ought to know how before you leave for Hahr-vahrd."

He laughed. A Boston accent sounded ridiculous layered atop her Tennessean one. "You worried I'll drown?"

"Maybe I am." She dropped his hand. "Maybe I just want to leave a mark on you."

Four Novembers later, Patsy will be a US Army Reservist stationed in Baghdad, and she'll have bribed a pal of hers with candy and cigarettes for the use of his satellite radio. Her purpose should be obvious enough—she wants to hear a football game starring Harland Bright. It's the big Harvard-Yale game, and the announcer will mention that "Bright, the famously disciplined wide receiver" swims every day as part of his conditioning. The little blonde will wonder if this is to be her sole contribution to society, the lone evidence that Patricia Pomeroy ever existed.

Toward the end of the third quarter, she will hear a small-to-average-sized explosion somewhere nearby. She will ignore it. She's got the afternoon off, and no one's screaming, so it can't be that bad. She will simply turn up the volume on the radio and imagine Harland Bright in a crimson jersey, clutching the ball to his chest. Does he know she's married? Does he know she's in Iraq? Does he think of her when he swims?

December

"JUST PULL THE tip of your tongue over your teeth, then push it out. *Th. Th,*" Helen repeated for the two hundredth or so time in the last half hour.

"*Sl, sl,*" said her patient.

"Almost there," she said brightly.

Violinist, Helen thought. *I could have been a violinist. They said I had a real ear when I was young.*

"*Sluh.*"

"Definitely getting better, Mr. Thayer. Push the tongue even harder. *Th.* It's a thwack. A thwack."

"*Sluuuuuh,*" said Mr. Thayer.

Helen wiped the spit from her forehead. She had considered wearing a visor to work but ultimately decided that it would be too demoralizing for the patients.

"Imagine a golf club just as it hits the ball. The-whack."

Or a gymnast. I was so flexible. I could turn more cartwheels than anyone.

Helen realized that Mr. Thayer had not spoken for several minutes. She looked up at him. He was crying quietly, so she handed him a Kleenex.

"It's going to get better," she said.

He shook his head.

Or a lawyer. I'm terrific in an argument.

"You're already doing so much better," Helen said.

He shook his head again.

Or anything really. Anything but this.

She smiled at Mr. Thayer and clapped her hands together. "What do you say we work with the straw for the rest of today? Really get those sucking skills down."

Mr. Thayer was forty-six years old, younger than Helen's dad. Until his stroke last year, he had been an opera singer and a music teacher. An interesting case, as much as any of this could possibly be interesting to Helen anymore. He'd recovered physically and could write well enough, but his speech was still pretty much nonexistent. Helen suspected it was embarrassment more than anything that was holding him back. But the truth was, Helen didn't much care. He was just her Thursday five o'clock. Last appointment of the day, thank you, Jesus.

She handed Mr. Thayer a straw to put in his mouth. He wouldn't take it, so she stuck it in his mouth for him. He let it fall to the floor. This was annoying to Helen. She'd rather be thinking about the things she'd rather be doing than playing pickup sticks with Mr. Thayer. She stuck the straw in his mouth again. "Blow," she said. Mr. Thayer shook his head and let the straw fall to the ground.

"Mr. Thayer, what's wrong?"

He removed a notepad from his pocket.

"Will I always be like this?" he wrote.

"Only if you give up," Helen replied.

"I'm so in love with you," Mr. Thayer wrote.

Helen nodded. Out of the corner of her eye, she checked her watch.

"You've got the tightest little ass I've ever seen."

"Mr. Thayer!" Helen shook her head and laughed, not unkindly. "I'm getting married, Mr. Thayer. And besides, I'm half your age. And you don't even know me. And if you did, you'd know I was awful." A bell rang. Hallelujah, time was up. "We're done for today," she said. "Hopefully, when next we meet, you'll be ready to work."

On the drive home, Helen stopped at the mall to do some Christmas shopping. She hated the mall, mainly because it reminded her of her credit card debt and of all the things she would like to buy but couldn't afford. This bottomless wanting had started from her first breath; the debt, more recently in college. On registration day, in point of fact. A free glow-in-the-dark Frisbee and a student credit card with an eight-hundred-dollar limit. The debt just continued on from there. Use up one credit card, replace it with another. She told no one—not her mother, not her fiancé, no one. It was her secret.

For Helen, holiday shopping was a completely joyless affair. She selected gifts based on how large and expensive they appeared, but she didn't particularly care if the recipients would enjoy them. For her mother, a towering basket of gingerbread-scented bath products; her father, slippers with built-in massagers; her sister, a terry cloth bathrobe with a terry cloth patch of a cow jumping over a moon; her brother, a seventy-five-dollar gift certificate to a record store. For her fiancé, she bought a wallet. She got Christmas ornaments for the secretaries at her office. And more bath products for her fiancé's siblings and mother. And then a couple of generic, unisex emergency gifts for people she hadn't thought of yet: the odd patient who unexpectedly brought her a present; the office secret Santa that she'd surely forgotten. By the time she finished shopping, she had spent almost fifteen hundred dollars, which brought her total debt to just over nineteen thousand dollars.

Helen was flushed with spending and even a bit pleased with herself. She had spent all that money in less than two hours.

She sat down in the mall food court, where a Muzak version of "Smells Like Teen Spirit" blared over the loudspeaker. Despite herself, she thought about Mr. Thayer. Nothing was working, and it depressed her how little she cared.

Across the food court, she spied a little blonde girl kissing a tall black guy. It took Helen a moment to realize that the blonde girl was her little sister. *Christ, couldn't she be more discreet?* Helen wondered if her parents knew about this. It wasn't that they were racists exactly. Like, they'd had black friends and known black people at church. They had just always made it perfectly clear (without actually saying anything specific) that none of them should date a black guy. Helen had known, the same way she had always known exactly who her father had voted for (Dole, Bush, and Reagan) without him having to say.

OK, so they probably were racists.

Helen watched Patsy for a moment. For as long as she could remember, Helen had been the good one in the family, and as the good one, she had always been the family informant. She was about to take out her cell phone to do her job when a strange thrill shot through her typically selfish heart. *Patsy's in love,* she thought, and then she tossed the phone in her bag and turned her back on the couple. This, not that pointless terry cloth monstrosity, would be Helen's real Christmas gift to her sister: pretending she hadn't seen a damn thing.

Helen's fiancé, Elliot, arrived at precisely eight o'clock. "Hi, babe," he said.

Per her religious upbringing, they had not yet had sex. This was not to say she hadn't had any sex. She had had anal sex with her high school boyfriend. It might have been rape, though not because Helen had said no. She had definitely thought no, but the word had never made it out of her lips. Not the first time or the six and a half times that followed, either.

And once, she had fallen asleep in the arms of another girl in a minivan on the way back from a community service retreat. Nothing sexual had happened, but Helen felt it counted somehow.

And in the two years she'd been with Elliot, she'd given him forty-eight blow jobs. For Christmas, in addition to the wallet, she planned to give him his forty-ninth.

They were in premarital therapy at their church. During their last session, the therapist had asked them to complete the following sentence, "When I look at you, I . . ."

"Say the first thing that pops into your head," the therapist had implored her.

"When I look at you, I . . ."

"Don't think, Helen!" Elliot and the therapist had determined that Helen's main flaws were thinking too much, secrecy, and trying to control every situation.

"When I look at you, I feel . . ." *Nothing* had been what she wanted to say. Nothing, nothing, fucking nothing. "Content."

Helen had tried surprising herself with the same question several times since it had first been posed to her: at church ("When I look at you, I feel lonely"); at his parents' house for dinner ("When I look at you, I feel like a liar"); waiting for him to exit a public men's restroom ("When I look at you, I feel pretty repulsed"); and now, at the mall food court ("When I look at you, I feel like I lack the ability to love anyone or anything. When I look at you, I feel broken").

Elliot kissed her on the cheek. "My Christmas present in one of these?"

"None of your business," she said.

"You know you don't have to *buy* me anything." He winked at her. *When I look at you, I wish I was dead.*

"Actually, babe, could I borrow your credit card?" Elliot asked. "I left my wallet in the car, and I wanna pick up my brother's present while I'm here."

"Sure," said Helen as casually as possible. "What are you getting Darryl anyway?"

"Speakers," he replied. "Big ones." As Elliot led her to the stereo store, Helen calculated how much "big ones" cost and if she would have enough credit left on her card.

Helen considered trying to convince Elliot not to get the speakers today. She could, for instance, suggest they have dinner, and then maybe by the time dinner was over, the mall would be closing. She tried this tack just as they were about to enter the store.

"Hon, I'm real hungry," she said. She stuck out her lower lip in a manner the bathroom mirror had told her was both pouty and sexy.

"OK," Elliot replied, "this'll only take a sec. I know exactly which ones I want."

Elliot selected the speakers. They were $299.99. It would be close. She set her card on the counter.

She knew that he wouldn't pay her back, and she also knew that she wouldn't mention it to him, either. For some time, this had been her role in their relationship. Helen was the one who paid for things.

Not that Elliot was poor. Quite the contrary. His family owned a Christian home health-care business. They had houses in Florida, Texas, and California, and it probably went without saying that they were far, far wealthier than Helen's family. It was just . . . well, Elliot didn't think about money in the same way Helen did. Helen knew this, and in order to act as though she did think about money the way Elliot did, she had to do things like pretend it didn't matter to purchase speakers and not be paid back.

"It's taking a while," Helen commented to the cashier.

"I should have asked you before, but would you like to apply for a store charge account while you wait? Save ten percent today if you're approved." The clerk handed Helen a shiny pamphlet. Helen could feel her heart grow two sizes too large in her chest, buoyed by the refrain SAVE 10 PERCENT, SAVE 10 PERCENT.

"Could I . . . ," Helen stammered. "Would the stuff I just purchased count? For the ten percent, I mean."

The clerk said that he didn't see why not. They could just return Helen's current purchase, which shouldn't take more than five minutes. Then ten minutes for the application. Then another five minutes to ring the original purchase through again. It was all starting to sound too difficult to Helen. And she probably wouldn't be approved anyway. "Forget it," Helen said.

Across the store, Helen could see Elliot examining an electronic massager that looked suspiciously like a sex toy. A pretty salesgirl approached him and offered to show him how to use it, wink wink. The salesgirl looked to be about Patsy's age, but Helen didn't feel at all jealous. Massager girl could have him. Helen only hoped that he wouldn't want to put the tawdry massager on her credit card, too.

The other reason Helen paid for everything was because Elliot was still in dental school. She hoped things would be different when he graduated next June. The plan was this: get married, get pregnant, take a maternity leave, never go back.

"Is there a problem with the card?" Helen tapped her fingers on the glass counter. Bitchy masked worried.

"No," said the clerk. "Just Christmas. Makes all the machines run slow."

If the card didn't go through, Helen decided that she would tell Elliot that she must have reached her limit while Christmas shopping. She would pass it off as a silly little nothing. Of course, she'd also imply that she would be paying off the balance at the end of the month. Elliot wasn't the type of person who could even comprehend the idea of credit card debt.

Finally! The cashier passed a little slip of paper across the counter. "Sign here," he said.

Helen signed, then took her copy from the back.

"Aren't you the professional shopper?" the cashier commented.

"Yeah, I've bought a few things in my life."

In the front of the store, Elliot was zoning out as the salesgirl massaged his neck.

When I look at you, I feel—

Helen's phone rang. It was the store that was printing the invitations for the wedding. Apparently, her mother had forgotten to pay them again. *Oh, for God's sake,* Helen thought. First the save-the-dates and now the actual invites, too. You'd think her mother didn't want her to get married. Helen apologized profusely to the printer and assured her it would all be straightened out by tomorrow.

Elliot tapped Helen on the shoulder. "Those my speakers?"

Helen handed him the bag. She'd been planning on a little good-natured bitching about the salesgirl with the tawdry massager, but now she was too annoyed and distracted by the invite situation. "Merry Christmas," she said brusquely.

"Hey, it's not my Christmas present."

But it kind of is, Helen thought. She pursed her lips.

"What?" Elliot asked. "You think I'm not good for the money?"

IMMEDIATELY AFTER DINNER with Elliot, Helen called her mother. Without judgment and in a calm, professional voice, Helen explained to George how her conduct with regard to the wedding had been completely unacceptable, how imperative it was that Elliot's family didn't get the wrong idea about them, etcetera. Helen finished by saying that she'd made an Excel spreadsheet with a timeline detailing when all amounts were due. "I'll e-mail it to you right now, so we can go over it together."

"I can only check my e-mail at work," George said.

"Well . . ." This annoyed Helen. This was 1998. What kind of people didn't have e-mail at home? Old people. Dated people. Poor people. "Well, when you get it tomorrow, you'll see that I've left column H blank. That's for you to fill in as you make each payment, all right?"

"Sure, Helen, that seems fine."

"And as you make your entries, I'd appreciate you e-mailing your changes back to me. Just so I can keep track of it all."

"OK," George said.

"Now, let's talk about the invitations. We owe another six hundred dollars to the Paper Trail."

"I thought we were all done with that," George stammered. "The thing is, Helly, money's a little . . . With Patsy getting hurt. And Christmas. And your dad's schooling. And . . ."

"What are you saying?"

"I'm just saying . . . I'm just wondering . . . Couldn't Elliot's family maybe pay for half of the invites? They wanted the vellum thingy, most of the guests are theirs, and they're so much . . ." George's voice trailed off.

"No, Mother, that is simply not an option. The bride's family pays for the wedding." Helen's throat constricted and she could feel her eyes begin to tear. She just hated every single damn person in her life so much.

"It's fine, Helen. I just need to move some funds around. Don't worry about it, OK? Forget I said anything. It's done. I'll figure something out."

THE NEXT MORNING at work, George called the Paper Trail. She read sixteen brand-new digits to the printer.

"All right, Mrs. Pomeroy, I just need the expiration date and the cardholder's name."

"August 2001," she replied. "Vincent Pomeroy."

January

STEINBECK WAS BEGINNING to seem like a mistake.

A year ago, Steinbeck had been just the thing. A year ago, Vincent had been in the twenty-four-hour used bookstore on East Seventh Street. He was feeling lonely as hell—Christmas alone and classes hadn't started up again and things had gone to total shite with Cassandra for the last time and it was too early to go to breakfast and too late to go to the movies—when he spotted a first edition of *The Pastures of Heaven*.

The copy was a bit battered: a bent spine and a coffee stain on the original jacket. It was inscribed cheekily, regrettably, "To Dogboy, I'd like to see your pastures of heaven . . ." These wounds, in combination with the fact that the work was considered one of Steinbeck's lesser, accounted for the reasonable price of eleven dollars.

Vincent could not explain why he was drawn to the book. He had read and appreciated, if not enjoyed, *The Red Pony* in high school. He had seen the film version of *East of Eden*. But this had been the extent of his knowledge of John Steinbeck. And eleven dollars was not insignificant to Vincent. Eleven dollars could buy fifty-five packets of ramen noodles (nearly two and a half weeks' worth of meals).

He read it that night in bed. (Although what he slept on was not technically a "bed" but an air mattress purchased from the local Kmart—at some point, he will have a one-night stand that will cause the "bed" to pop and slowly leak air until he is left sleeping on a flat plastic mat.) It wasn't a novel at all. It was a collection of short stories based around a single place. Most of the stories were structurally and thematically identical. Someone tried to do something good for someone else, and then it all went to shit. The one Vincent liked best was about two sisters who open a Mexican restaurant. At first, business is terrible, but then they start sexually pleasuring the customers, and business responds accordingly. The sisters don't think of themselves as prostitutes as long as the men understand that they're paying for food, not sex. Eventually they get shut down for running a house of prostitution, at which time they leave for San Francisco to become actual prostitutes.

Vincent liked the sisters—he had two sisters of his own—and he decided that he would make a short-film version of "The Lopez Sisters" for his second-year graduate film school project.

It was really the perfect thing for a student film. Only two characters (give or take). One set (and very few exterior locations). And the characters were poor, so although it was a period piece, it wouldn't necessarily require a lot of expense.

He drafted a letter to the Steinbeck estate asking for rights to make a student film of chapter 7 of *The Pastures of Heaven*. He drew up a prop list (phonograph, donkey, statue of the Virgin Mary, tortilla stone, etcetera) that seemed challenging but not impossible. He wrote a screenplay, which came in at a tight twelve pages. As for the budget? Vincent supposed five thousand dollars, which was the sum his program recommended students spend on producing their ten-minute graduate film shorts. The program did not, incidentally, specify how the students were to get the five thousand dollars.

Vincent took the usual steps. He applied for and received a grant from his film program in the amount of $750, which would mostly cover the crew's meals. The rest he decided to obtain in the form of an additional student loan. He had heard from his peers that they were easy to get. No cosigner necessary if you were over twenty-one with decent credit. Everyone was approved. In three weeks (or less!) he would have his money.

Vincent didn't have three weeks. Preproduction on "The Lopez Sisters" needed to commence immediately. He spent in anticipation of his windfall, which wasn't as insane as it sounded—these were the heady days of 1998, when banks were loaning money to dogs and babies and the homeless and anyone who could make an X (or stamp a paw or drool a bit) on the dotted line. Vincent quickly racked up two thousand dollars on his one credit card.

At the end of four weeks, he received a letter from the financial aid company. His application had been rejected. Vincent was sure there must be some sort of mistake. He called the company, where a representative assured him that there had not been a mistake. Vincent's application had been rejected because of a delinquent credit card.

"That's impossible," Vincent said. "I don't have a delinquent credit card."

The representative, who had the careful voice of a black woman trying to sound like a white one, told him to check his credit report. "If it's a mistake, it can be cleared up, Mr. Pomeroy. And then you can get your money. That's what we all want, of course. To give you your money."

Vincent continued preparing his film. He was an optimist. Mistakes happened, but they could, *they would,* be fixed.

The credit report arrived in the mail the day before he was to begin shooting. He was crazed with last minute preparations and crises: cheap hotel rooms for the crew in upstate New York (which they would fake for Salinas, California), the prizewinning donkey that the lead actress was to ride was too robust, the sound guy had quit, the 1st AC wanted more money, etcetera, etcetera. He didn't have time to look at the report until that night in bed when he curled up with it on his rapidly deflating mattress.

As a personal history, Vinnie's credit report was significantly more whimper than bang.

Yes, those were his student loans—all scrupulously paid on time.

Yes, that was the car loan he had in high school: for a 1986 Honda Accord.

Yes, that was the Sears card he had opened several Christmases ago in order to buy presents for his sisters.

Yes, that was his regular credit card, which was getting disturbingly near its limit thanks to the sisters Lopez.

And then he saw it. A new credit card opened in October of last year. The limit was ten thousand dollars, and it was already sixty days overdue. Vincent smiled. He knew for certain that this card was not his, which meant, of course, that it was a mistake. Mistakes could be corrected.

Before turning off the light, he made a note to call the credit card company as soon as he returned from the shoot.

The film shoot went as such things go. Crews complained and stole to make up for their imaginary grievances. Actors cried. Props were broken. Food was horrible no matter how much was spent. Everything cost more than initial estimates.

It took Vincent nearly a month to get around to calling the credit card company, and then another two weeks for him to receive copies of all the statements, including the address to which the bills were being sent.

That address was familiar, of course.

Vincent called the credit card company again. "There's been a mistake," he said. "This is my parents' credit card, not mine."

But the credit card company insisted that there had not been a mistake. The primary card member was Vincent Pomeroy.

"But I am telling you, this is their address, not mine! I've never even lived in Texas!"

The credit card company told Vincent to stop raising his voice, then courteously offered to start sending the statements to Vincent's address in New York.

"That's not what I want! I want this, this blemish, removed from my record! I want this transferred to the responsible parties!"

The credit card company said that it was not—pause, pause, pause —unfeeling to Vincent's situation, and then it said a phrase that Vincent had never before heard: identity theft. If Mr. Pomeroy thought he had been a victim of identity theft, the only thing to do was take the appropriate parties to court.

"To court?" Vincent asked.

But the credit card company wouldn't recommend that course of action. It would probably cost more than the debt itself. The best thing to do would be to settle the—pause, pause, pause—situation without resorting to legal intervention. "I'm assuming you do know the responsible parties, Mr. Pomeroy?"

Vincent hung up the phone. He decided to go to the movies. He watched *Shakespeare in Love,* which he had already seen, then snuck in to *Rushmore,* which he had also already seen. By the time the second film was over, he decided that he had overreacted. The relationship with his parents had certainly been strained, but no one in his family would *on purpose* open a credit card in his name, then not even bother to keep up with the minimum payments. And if this were a mistake— and how could it be anything but? If this were a mistake, his mother (for she was the one who managed the household's finances) would undoubtedly be willing to do whatever it took to correct it.

That night, he called Helen on the phone. The usual, of course. Helen hated her job and was only fifty-fifty about her fiancé.

"Are Mom and Dad having financial problems?" Vincent asked after they'd turned over the usual nothing for a time.

Helen paused, paused, paused, and then said, "Not that I know of."

"What? What is it?"

She cleared her throat. "It's just . . . Dad's been in school an awfully long time, I guess."

"They're . . . they're not . . . poor, though?"

"No," Helen replied.

"I mean, they're still, like, middle-class," Vincent insisted.

Helen considered the question before answering. "Yeah. Definitely. Why do you ask?"

"No reason," he said, not wanting to impugn his mother if it all turned out to be the mistake he'd been hoping for. "How goes the wedding planning?"

According to Helen, planning a wedding was not unlike producing a short film. Everything cost more than you expected, the vendors were crooks, and the food was likely to be awful.

For a week, Vincent tried calling his mother, but she was conspicuously unreachable. Vincent left messages that he tried to make sound friendly, nonthreatening, and, more to the point, vague. Eventually, he gave up calling his mother and started calling his father's cell phone instead. It took several tries to get his father, too, and he was in class the morning Roger finally did call back with the following message: "Coming to New York City next month on business. Catch up then. Miss you, Son. Dad." The message's lack of personal pronouns put Vincent in mind of an old-fashioned telegram sent by someone who was conscious of being charged by the word.

February

MY GOD, BUSINESS class! People spoke of first-class as if it were the only travel dream worth having. Trade in those frequent flyer miles for a first-class ticket to Hawaii! Contestants, pack your bags: you've just won a trip to Europe with all first-class accommodations! But, business class . . . Maybe it wasn't the dream, but by God, there were unspeakable charms to business class, too.

For his entire life, Roger Pomeroy had flown coach and presumed that this was the only way to travel. First was out of the question for a family of five or even a Christian high school administrator/honorary pastor traveling solo. First was out of his stars, and it had never once occurred to him to try business until Carolyn Murray had suggested it.

Sitting in the business class cabin, Roger felt at home or, at least, among a party of like-minded individuals. A peerage of men his age or thereabouts clad in permanent-press Dockers, navy blue sport coats, white polo shirts bearing their various coats of arms, and good-quality, if unflattering, glasses. Their two carry-ons: a garment bag and a sturdy rolling computer case in either black nylon or leather. These were family men, churchgoers like himself. They bought tacky souvenirs for their children and silk scarves for their wives. They were certainly not the hedonistic spendthrifts you found in first, but they were willing to pay a little extra for a bit more comfort, a bit more civility, a bit more decency. Yes, Roger thought, these were folks you could get behind. If the plane went down—Roger often entertained apocalyptic thoughts while flying—if the plane went down, he would be proud to be counted among these men.

And one woman, of course. In the seat next to him was Carolyn Murray. Roger had already decided that she was an excellent traveler. Unlike his wife, Carolyn checked nothing! Her lone suitcase was a creamy brown leather, a bit battered but glamorously so, the sort of thing a reporter carried to cover a war or a fashion show. She had a tiny spray bottle that she used to hydrate her face. "Would you like a spritz?" she asked Roger just before they were told to put away their electronic devices. He accepted and felt instantly transported to a tropical rainforest. Why didn't George have tricks like that?

About fifteen minutes after they had reached the cruising altitude, Carolyn pulled out a paisley silk, lavender-scented eye mask. "If I don't get rest now, the whole day will be lost to me," she said. She put on the mask, propped an ergonomically designed buckwheat pillow behind her neck and fell asleep like the travel pro she was.

The stewardess came by with breakfast. Courteous of the quiescent woman beside Roger, she whispered, "Something for your wife when she wakes up?"

Roger considered saying that Carolyn was not his wife, but what was the point of that? He would never see the stewardess again and it would be too complicated to explain about the book they were working on, how she was half his boss, half his partner and all that. So, he left it at, "No, thank you." Carolyn had informed him when they were waiting to check in that she never ate plane food, but instead packed her own fruits, vegetables, and bottled water. "Don't worry, Rog," she had assured him, "I brought enough for you, too."

* * *

AT THE AIRPORT in New York, a driver waited for them with a sign: MURRAY. Roger spotted it while Carolyn was in the bathroom freshening up. He went up to the driver. "I think that's my sign."

"The Plaza?"

Roger nodded. "I'm just waiting for Ms. Murray," Roger said.

"No problem, Mr. Murray," the driver replied.

Roger didn't bother correcting the driver, either.

"How long you here?" The driver began his usual small talk.

"We fly back on Monday."

"Romantic weekend in New York City with the wife, eh?"

"No," Roger said. "Just business."

"Well, you better not forget it's Valentine's Day this Sunday, or you'll be in big trouble," the driver joked.

Valentine's Day? Indeed, Roger had forgotten. He reminded himself to call his actual wife.

Finally, Carolyn emerged from the ladies' room. "There she is," Roger said to the driver.

"Your wife's a striking woman," the driver said.

This "wife" business had gone on long enough. "For the record, she's not my wife," Roger said.

"I hear you." The driver winked and raised his eyebrow. Roger was not a fan of this sort of joking, but before he had a chance to set matters straight, Carolyn had arrived and once again it seemed too late to explain.

AT THE HOTEL, a problem with Roger's reservation. The computer had him scheduled to check out on Sunday, but they weren't flying home until Monday. And there weren't any other rooms available on account of the Westminster Dog Show, which was happening that weekend and would conclude the following Tuesday. Carolyn blushed and apologized, but it really wasn't her fault—her faux-hawked assistant had made the reservation. Luckily, she always took a suite when she traveled to New York City. She knew it was silly and extravagant, but it was her little gift to herself, hee hee, and of course, she'd be glad to offer Roger the use of the couch. "It's only for one night," she said. "You can tolerate me that long, I hope."

In point of fact, Roger was uncomfortable with the idea, but he didn't wish to spoil their trip or the important work they would be doing. "It's fine," he said through teeth imperceptibly gritted. "Just one night."

Carolyn handed the desk clerk a twenty-dollar bill and her business card. "This has my cell phone number. Call me if anything opens up between now and then."

"Really, it's fine," Roger said. "No biggie."

After checking in, they walked to midtown to meet with Carolyn's publisher. The first half of the meeting took place in a book-lined conference room and concerned the publicity tour for Carolyn's new (finished) book, which was an updating of *The Wheels on the Bus Go Round* called *Big Wheel Keep On Turning: The Wheels on the Bus Go Round Twenty Years Later.* Carolyn would go on National Public Radio, *Charlie Rose, Good Morning America,* and about fifteen other shows to promote it. They had, the publicist reported, their fingers crossed for *Oprah.*

"Eeee!" Carolyn squealed. "Could that really happen?"

"Well, your book touches on all those themes Oprah loves—race, education, yada yada yada. But one never knows," was the publicist's reply.

Though none of this really concerned him, Roger wasn't the least bit bored or impatient while the publicist was going over these details. He was busily imagining himself on a similar book tour when his (and Carolyn's) book came out.

An impossibly bright soundstage.

Roger, who has just turned fifty but could easily be mistaken for forty, sits at a 120-degree angle from African American talk show host Oprah Winfrey. During the commercial break, Roger touches Oprah's arm and

*makes a series of Extremely Incisive, Memorable, and Downright Uproari-
ous comments about race and religion in America.*

"And you're still getting new color publicity shots done while you're
here, right?" the publicist asked. "'Cause the ones we have are a little
bit . . ."

"Dated! Old! You can say it!" Carolyn laughed. She picked one of
the pictures up from the table and showed it to Roger. Young Carolyn
was dressed in an almost-sheer peasant blouse and had her long, frizzy,
light brown hair parted in the middle. "I was going for a sort of Carly
Simon thing," Carolyn said. Everyone laughed, including Roger.
Truth be told, he couldn't conjure an immediate picture of Carly in
his head. He had never kept up with popular music very much, pre-
ferring to listen to "Christian" music when he bothered to listen at
all. "I loved that shirt," Carolyn said, "but it was a real disaster. They
ended up having to retouch my nipples."

Following the publicity meeting, Carolyn's editor took them out
to lunch to discuss the New Book.

"Karen, I honestly think this book has the potential to be every
bit the touchstone work that *Wheels* was," said Carolyn.

"Well, it sounds wonderful," said the editor. She looked at Roger
to see if he had anything to contribute.

Roger wasn't listening. He was busy with the waiter. "Does the
ravioli special have meat in the sauce?" he asked.

"We can make it either way," said the waiter.

Roger requested it without.

"Good for you," Carolyn's editor said. "I've been meaning to give
up meat forever. It's so much healthier."

"It *is* healthier," Roger conceded, "but that's not why I do it. My
religion doesn't permit the consumption of meat."

"Oh my!" Carolyn's editor opened her eyes very wide—restricting
one's diet for health reasons was one thing, but doing it for God seemed
a bit bizarre, tacky even. "Are you Jewish?"

"He's a Sabbath Day Adventist," Carolyn said. "That's what makes him my perfect partner on this book." She reached across the table to squeeze Roger's hand.

SATURDAY MORNING, THEY visited a Catholic school in the Bronx that had been rocked by a sex scandal involving a—what else?—priest. They interviewed parents and students, an impatient nun or two, and the new priest who was trying to put it all back together. This was the only research Carolyn and Roger did during their New York trip, and Roger wasn't even completely sure how it fit with the book they were writing.

Carolyn explained in the cab back to Manhattan: "When people think religious school, their minds leap to priests having sex with choir boys. We have to start there if we're to make a truly thorough survey. Now Rog, let's talk about something serious . . . You still need a haircut. And don't worry about the cost. It's on me." She leaned forward to address the cabbie, "Driver, could you take us to Bleecker between Sixth Avenue and Seventh?"

At the salon, Carolyn instructed the stylist, a bald homosexual man, to cut it really short with spikes.

"Oh, I love that!" said the stylist. "That'll really bring out his cheekbones. What do you say we add some bronze highlights, too?"

"Well, Rog, what do you think?" Carolyn leaned coquettishly against the side of the haircutting counter.

"Well . . . it won't be too obvious will it?" Roger asked.

"No," the stylist assured him, "it'll just brighten up your face a bit. You'll look like you just got back from vacation."

"Come on, Rog! Go for it!"

So, Roger agreed. After going to the back room for the shampoo (which to his delight included a neck rub!) and color, Roger returned to the stylist's chair.

The stylist ran his fingers through Roger's hair. "I'm just getting a feel for your head before I start. You've got a lot of hair, but my God, it looks like it was cut in the dark with a hunting knife! Who's been doing this to you?"

"My wife," Roger said.

"Certainly not *that* woman!" The stylist gestured toward Carolyn, who was sitting in the waiting area reading a book.

"No, not that woman. We're just . . . colleagues."

"Aren't they all, doll face?"

ON SATURDAY NIGHT, they attended the opera. (The story Carolyn told Roger was that an old friend, a lighting designer, had given her free tickets to *Madame Butterfly*.) It was Roger's first time and he was moved nearly to tears by the spectacle of it all. It felt religious, like being in church. Why had no one ever told him that these kinds of churches existed, too? Men wrote operas, yes, but operas were so grand that one had to believe that the men who wrote them were merely vehicles for God. Cio-Cio-San was busily stabbing herself in the heart, and Roger wondered if he would have been a better Christian if someone had taken him to the opera as a boy. Maybe he would have had an opera in him. Maybe everything would have been different for Roger—his wife, his house, his job, his life.

NOTHING WAS PLANNED for Sunday, so Roger arranged to meet Vincent for brunch downtown. Carolyn offered to accompany him.

"You really want to meet my son?" Roger asked.

"Why not? I like sons," was her reply.

Roger knew he should probably tell Carolyn no. Things had been strained between him and Vinnie for some time. Roger wasn't sure what he had done, only that Vinnie seemed completely convinced of his father's guilt. It had had something to do with Yale and the graduation, he supposed, but hadn't all of that been so long ago? If anyone, Roger was the aggrieved party—his son had disobeyed him to go to a secular college, and even after Roger had made extraordinary overtures by attending Vinnie's commencement, Vinnie still played the injured party and rarely called or visited and would have nothing to do with church. So, really, who cared if Vinnie had specifically said he needed to talk to him about something important? *Something important* didn't necessarily mean *alone*. Carolyn wanted to come, and that was the end of it.

Besides, it would be awkward to tell her no after he'd already told her yes. Maybe it was because she was still kind of his superior, maybe it was gratitude, maybe he was just your garden variety coward . . . but whatever the reason, Roger hadn't acquired the art of saying no to Professor Carolyn Murray.

They encountered traffic on the way to the restaurant and what should normally have been a seven-minute cab ride took twenty-five. Vinnie was waiting inside by the time they arrived.

"How you doing, Son?" Roger asked. He shook Vinnie's hand and patted him on the back.

"Good. Good." Vinnie spotted Carolyn over Roger's shoulder. "Dad, who's that?"

"I'm Carolyn Murray." She extended her hand. "Your father and I are writing a book together. I'm terribly excited to meet you."

Vinnie nodded, but said nothing. He took a moment to consider Carolyn: her tailored wool suit, her well-cut hair, her leather bag that probably cost more than his monthly rent (which was not inconsiderable), her perfect teeth. He reached out his hand. "Nice to meet you," he said.

The topics of conversation were as follows:

- *film school experience, Vinnie's*
- *short film, Vinnie's*
- *book, Roger and Carolyn's*
- *books, Carolyn's*

- *Howard University, Carolyn's daughter, who attends*
- *business-class travel, merits of*

The topics of conversation did not include:

- *George*
- *credit cards*
- *estrangement, Vinnie and Roger's*
- *politics*

Carolyn was good with young people, having spent most of her life studying them, and Vinnie would have been charmed by her, had he not been completely disgusted with Roger for bringing her in the first place. To get back at his teetotaler father, Vinnie, who was not much of a drinker, drank two dirty martinis, a glass of red wine from a bottle Carolyn had ordered, and a Blue Hawaii, which the bartender had to research on the Internet before mixing.

After they had ordered dessert, Carolyn excused herself to go to the bathroom.

"You're drunk," Roger said.

"I'm not that drunk." Vinnie shrugged. "Meal's on you, right?"

"It's embarrassing," Roger said.

"You're embarrassing," Vinnie said. "What the hell, Dad?"

"I don't like your language," Roger said.

"Oh, excuse me. I meant, what the fuck, Dad? I told you I had something to talk to you about, and you bring a . . . a woman."

"Well, we're alone now. Talk, Vincent, if you can manage it civilly."

"Are you sleeping with her?" Vinnie asked.

"Of course not! Don't be vulgar."

Vinnie took a manila folder from his messenger bag and pushed it across the table toward Roger.

"Mom's been stealing from me."

Roger looked at the folder, but would not touch it.

"Take it," Vincent said. "Fucking take it, Dad."

Roger obeyed. He smiled at the table next to them. "Everything's fine."

But Vinnie was not done. "I have never asked you for anything in my life. I did not ask you for help with college when I wanted to go to Yale. I was not mad when you didn't speak in my defense when the church excommunicated me. I was glad when you guys came to my graduation even though you hadn't lifted one damn finger to help me. I'm not mad that you're at a secular college now, even though that same act got me tossed out on my—"

"Apples and oranges. This was the only suitable program for me. This was—"

"Fine, Dad. All I ask—"

"Vincent, lower your voice. We're in public."

"This is New York City. No one cares about us, Dad! You could have sex on the table with your old-ass girlfriend and no one would care."

"She's not my girlfriend."

"Whatever! Just let me say this. I don't ask you for anything except that you and Mom don't make it harder by stealing from me."

"I'm not going to discuss anything with you while you're in this condition and certainly not in front of . . . ," he nodded toward Carolyn, who had just emerged from the bathroom.

"OK, Dad, I'm done." Vinnie stood. "Give me a call after you've read this. By the way, your hair looks gay."

Vinnie brushed past Carolyn on his way out.

"What happened to Vinnie?" Carolyn asked.

SUNDAY NIGHT, ROGER called his wife to wish her a Happy Valentine's Day, then slept with Carolyn Murray.

No other room opened up at the hotel, so Roger was forced to move his things into Carolyn's room. Carolyn helped him open the convertible couch before telling Roger that she was going out for the evening. Old friend, but Roger was welcome to join.

Roger shook his head. He was a bit tired. His plan was to call his wife, then hit the sack.

The conversation with George was not exactly pleasant. She seemed annoyed that he was in New York City for Valentine's Day, though the trip had been in the works for months.

"Did you see Vinnie?" George asked.

"Yes." Roger did not mention the manila folder, which he still hadn't opened anyway.

"How is he?"

"He looked well. How are things there?"

"The usual. Helen says we should sue the painter for painting the house the wrong color. She says there's no way she's getting married in a red house. Patsy ran up about two hundred and fifty dollars on our phone bill. I guess she's broken up with Magnum. I don't know. I'm trying to increase my part-time hours at Dillard's," George replied. "Things will be better when you're out of school."

"They will, George. They really, really will."

"I sometimes wish . . . ," George began.

"What?"

George sighed. "I sometimes wish you'd never gone back to school."

"Well, there's no point in wishing that now, is there?" Roger replied. "Good-bye, George."

He had always despised that about George. Her tendency to look backward. They had both made the decision for Roger to go back to school. It had been for both of them. It wasn't his imagination. She had wanted, too. She had wanted more money. She had wanted a better life. Those things did not come without sacrifice.

And besides, what would she have him do? Should he remain an assistant high school principal until he was in a hole six feet under? Roger had lived his whole life for other people. Wasn't it good and fair and right that he finally take something for himself? Because

Roger knew—he just knew—he had great things in him. He had a gosh darn opera in him if anyone would bother to open up their ears and hear it. And now, when he was so close to getting everything he'd always wanted (*they'd* always wanted), for George to express doubt just seemed plain wrong.

He was still turning all of this over in his head when Carolyn returned from her evening out. Her dress was sparkly black and made the most of her figure. She smelled clean and sweet, like pine trees and lavender.

"Are you all right?" Carolyn asked him.

Her voice was so gentle that Roger was afraid he couldn't answer without a mortifying deluge.

Carolyn embraced him. "What is it? You can tell me."

"I have an opera within me," he whispered.

She didn't ask for an explanation. She just laughed. "Of course you do. That's why I chose you, Roger."

Roger liked her words. He liked having been chosen. And so he grabbed her breast.

March

BIRDMAN, KATHERINE C., is twenty-seven years old and has breast cancer. She'd like to freeze her eggs before beginning chemotherapy and requests that her health insurance provider, Human Wellness Partners, pay for 50 percent of the procedure.

George rubber-stamped a red ink NO. She placed Birdman, Katherine C., in the OUTGOING bin.

Orwell, Leroy B., is thirteen years old and his front adult teeth were knocked out in a car accident a year ago. He'd like dental implants now that he's starting high—

NO.

Rothschild, Edna L., is eighty-four years old and would like to get a home health-care worker to come to her house three times a week so that she—

NO.

The official unofficial policy at Human Wellness Partners was to reject every "extraordinary" claim at least once. In George's opinion, the definition of "extraordinary" was pretty darn ordinary insofar as she could easily imagine most of what was considered extraordinary happening to her or her children and she had never thought of herself as having a particularly vivid imagination.

About two months ago, George's responsibilities at HWP were augmented from data entry to actual insurance claims processing. "But I'm just a temp," she had said at the time. "I don't know anything medical."

"Do you know how to work a rubber stamp?"

In this way, the matter had been decided.

George went into the break room, which always smelled like microwave popcorn, though she'd never actually seen anyone eating microwave popcorn at HWP. Ellen, her one friend at HWP, was already there. Their work friendship was based on four factors: (1) identification: they were the same weight, more or less; (2) circumstance: they were the only temps on floor eight; (3) isolation: none of the perms would talk to them; and (4) like-mindedness: a shared appreciation for Orange Crush and Betsy Ross brownies from the snack machine. Ellen was twenty years younger than George and her dream was to open a knitting store. George knew this because on Ellen's first day, last December, the girl had asked her, "What's your dream?"

"What do you mean?" George had replied.

"Well, you can't actually want to be a temp the rest of your life."

You can't?

"Me? What I want to do is open a knitting store. Like, I'd have . . ." Then, she had gone on to describe the kind of high-end yarns she would stock (no synthetics!) and the space she would leave open for mother-daughter sewing circles and the shade of stain she wanted for the maple floors. Maybe a separate space for quilting? Though Ellen was not at all sure about the wisdom of inviting quilters at all—quilters, with their disorderly, patchwork existences, tended to attract a bad element.

"My mother used to quilt," George had said.

"Oh, well, not your mother. It's just my experience with quilters in general."

George hadn't been offended. The truth was, her mother's life *had* been patchwork—a series of piecemeal jobs and men and venues and choices. Naming her daughter for the state in which she'd been conceived. Leaving that same child to be raised by a series of increasingly distant relatives, who had usually made it clear that it would have been preferable for the pretty almond-eyed girl to die or disappear than to consume their precious food, clothing, air. Returning unexpectedly with a fixer of a husband who knew a thing or two about using a belt. But all this was beside the point.

The more recent truth was this: George had been relieved—Ellen hadn't really wanted to know about George's dreams at all; the girl had only wanted to talk about her own.

But the question had stuck with George. It occurred to her that she hadn't had a dream for a very long time. She had dreams for her children, yes, but the only real dream she harbored for herself was to owe nothing to anyone. She imagined writing checks that erased decades-old debts. She could feel the pen in her hand and the giddy, jaunty way she spelled out the numbers—the immature bubbles of a child who had just learned cursive. She imagined placing those checks in envelopes and the taste of the sealant on her tongue and going through an entire roll of American-flag stamps and her creditors opening those envelopes and shaking their heads and saying, rather paternally, "We never thought she'd make good. You done real well, Mrs. Georgia Pomeroy from Big Rock, Texas." This was the most vivid and sweet dream George could conjure. The dream of zero.

"Worst of the day?" Ellen asked George as she took out her knitting gear.

"Girl wants to freeze her eggs before chemo."

Ellen nodded. Her knitting needles began to clack. "Aw, I got that beat. I got a kid with brain cancer. He'll probably be dead before the parents figure out HWP won't pay for the experimental treatment."

"Yeah, yours is better."

"So, you gotta pay up. You owe me a brownie, Mrs. Pomeroy."

On her way to the snack machine, George was suddenly overcome with heat and nausea. She ran over to the garbage can, but then the feeling subsided.

"You OK?"

"I think I'm getting the flu," George said. "I feel all hot. And just weird, I guess."

"Menopause," Ellen said decisively. "My mom started going through it last year. When was your last period?"

"Oh!" George considered this question. "I'm not entirely sure."

"You need to go to the doctor," Ellen said. "You need to get some hormones, pronto. You don't want to start growing hair on your face or something."

No, George certainly did not want to have a beard *and* be fat at Helen's wedding. She changed the subject. "What are you working on today?"

A sweater, Ellen reported. Her college roommate was having a baby. "I'm using the most amazing blend of alpaca and cashmere," she said. "I almost hate to think of my roommate's dumb-ass baby throwing up all over it."

After making an appointment with Helen's gynecologist for Friday morning, George went into her supervisor's office to request the necessary time off. Yes, of course, it was fine. As a temp, George wouldn't be paid, but it was fine, fine.

Then, her supervisor did something rather extraordinary. He made her an offer. "How would you like to become a member of the HWP team?"

"Huh?"

"How'd you like to become perm, Georgia?"

"Perm?" George squeaked.

The supervisor's name was Philip Throne. He had a BA from Dartmouth, an MBA from Wharton, and needless to say, this—a middle management position at a midsize Texas health insurance company—was not where he saw himself five years postcommencement. The best part of the job was the number of hours he could devote to looking at Internet porn. "You're an awesome worker, George, and you'd basically be doing the same thing you're doing now only you'd get a kick-ass benefits and retirement package. We've got a great dental/vision/hearing plan, too. We'd give you Sylvia Klein's old office on seven and the title of junior claims processor. So, what do you say?"

George was so surprised by this turn of events that she had to sit down on Throne's couch. She had long ago given up the idea of having a real job. The kind with an office with a door and a plastic sign on the window that read MRS. GEORGIA POMEROY and a pair of Hummels from home and pictures of her children (and grandchildren, if any of her children should ever make any) and a shallow bowl of wrapped Brach's peppermints on the MDF desk and a framed Thomas Kinkade lithograph on the wall and an ergonomic chair of her very, very own and a modicum of dignity and security, even if Roger never finished his PhD, and George herself—sans PhD, sans MA, sans BA even—having the power to start digging them out of the hole they were all in. It seemed like too much to even dream of.

"Will there be any kind of pay increase?" George asked.

"Well, not at first," Throne explained. Because George had begun her employ with HWP as a temp, HWP would be responsible for paying George's temp firm a finder's fee, which amounted to a percentage of George's new salary. The fee would be amortized over the first year of George's work. George ran the numbers in her head: $37,500 minus the finders fee (20 percent) minus whatever benefits cost minus . . . "I don't think I can," George said.

Throne reminded her that she would be eligible for bonuses and pay raises if she accepted the new position.

It made no difference, of course. George needed every penny she could squirrel away.

"The pay cut would only be for a year, Georgia," Throne said. "And it's not really a pay cut, because you'd be accruing retirement benefits, too. Don't you plan to retire someday?"

George laughed, but Throne didn't. "Oh," she apologized, "you weren't kidding."

* * *

FRIDAY, GEORGE WENT to Helen's gynecologist, which was located in the same medical complex that contained Helen's office. After the appointment, George and Helen had lunch at the Fuddruckers next door. Neither woman was happy with the restaurant choice—George considered it rather pricey, and Helen considered it rather tacky. Both women lamented the lack of vegetarian choices, as the Fuddruckers menu consisted mainly of hamburgers. And George hated the name of the restaurant, too—the jokey, vile way it tried to get you to accidentally say a dirty word. But proximity won as it usually will. Helen ordered an iced tea (lemon, no sweetener), the Caribbean chicken salad (minus the chicken), and on the side, a loaded baked potato (minus the load). George ordered a vanilla milkshake and a side of onion rings. She had actually been pretty good about watching her weight in the months leading up to Helen's wedding, but she felt like she needed a treat on this particular day.

Predictably, Helen disapproved. "Mom, you're gonna give yourself a heart attack if you keep eating like that."

After their beverages were served, Helen took a printout of her wedding spreadsheet from her purse. "So, this is what we have left to do," Helen began. The list was exhaustive. George had seen it before, but she'd always managed not to consider it too closely, literally holding it at arm's length while she barely let her eyes pass over it. With Helen going through it point by point, it was impossible to take this tack and George started to feel like she might throw up.

"So, you'll be glad to know I've finally got to the bottom of it," Helen said.

"The bottom of what?"

"The red business," Helen replied.

George looked at Helen blankly.

"The house!" And then Helen explained. "It was a mix-up. The paint we selected was number two-three-oh-two Candy Apple Red. The paint they used was number two-three-oh-*one* Caliente Red."

"Oh," said George, taking a small sip of her milkshake.

"The painter—Ramón somebody—told the company that he told you it was Caliente on the day, but I doubt it. He, like, barely speaks English. If he'd shown it to you and said Caliente, you would have said something. In any case, it's their mistake and they'll have to fix it."

George remembered the day the painters had come. She had thought he'd been talking about the weather, but it was somehow impossible to explain this to Helen. And the thought of spending more time at home (not working) with painters who would probably be pretty darn unhappy to be there was intolerable. So George lied: "I . . . well, I'm kind of getting used to the color."

The waitress delivered Helen's salad, which still had chicken in it. "This chicken salad wasn't supposed to have chicken," Helen informed the waitress.

George marveled at how easy it was for Helen to complain. If it had been her salad, George would have just silently borne the chicken and picked out the pieces. She would have been afraid of people spitting in her food or something worse, but Helen obviously didn't possess this fear. Her daughter was a bulldozer.

"What, Mom?"

"I was just saying, I think I'm kind of used to the color now. It's faded in real nice, and I'd almost call it brick now, I really, really would."

"Mother, I cannot get married in a Caliente-colored house. That just isn't a question. It's tacky. And when you and Daddy go to resell it, no one's gonna want to buy it that way, trust me, so you might as well deal with it now. And it's not what we paid for. And it's *their* mistake. Why should we suffer for their mistake?"

Helen's argument was solid enough, and George wasn't at all up to offering a rebuttal. Instead, she silently concocted two strategies for dealing with the house situation: (1) lie: about two weeks from now, tell Helen that the painters repainted the house, but don't actually have anyone repaint the house, or (2) willfully evade: ignore Helen on the issue of the house until it was too late for anything to be done about it anyway. In any case, the only thing to be done at the moment was to placate Helen.

"It's good you got to the bottom of it, honey," George said. "I never would have figured it out myself. You've turned into a real thorough young woman."

Helen's eyes brightened a bit. All she ever wanted was for someone to appreciate her efforts. "Oh, it was no big deal," she said. "How was the doctor?"

"It was fine," George said. She dipped an onion ring in the milkshake.

"Forty-seven," Helen sighed. "So, I guess I know about how old I'll be when I get menopause."

Across the restaurant, a little boy threw a hamburger at his mother's face. The mother wiped the ketchup, etcetera, off her brow, then put the hamburger back in the bun. George could read the woman's lips: *Now. You. Eat. It.* "Well, you never know, Helen."

"But as a gauge," Helen insisted. "If you started menopause at forty-seven, then I'll probably start around then, too."

"Maybe." George looked at her daughter, at her de-chickened, possibly sputum-coated chicken salad. "We aren't exactly the same person, you know."

BACK AT THE office, there were several messages on George's work voice mail: from the accountant at her church ("Just wondering if there might have been a bookkeeping error regarding yours and Roger's tithe. Give a call."); from Throne (about the job); from the phone company (the bill was overdue . . . again); from the catering company for Helen's wedding (needing the first third of the deposit, and a reminder that the second third was due in a week); from that awful Janet's mother from the cheerleading team (wondering if George had the check for the wrapping paper despite the fact that Patsy hadn't been on the team since October); and from Vincent (something about a settlement). She deleted all the messages, then headed for Throne's office.

"I'm going to need Monday off," she said. "I have to go to the doctor again. But don't worry, I'll be back Tuesday."

"Hope nothing too serious," Throne replied.

"No."

"If you took the permanent job, you'd be getting paid for Monday," he reminded her.

"Yeah, about that. I can't work it out. I wish I could, but I can't. Thanks a lot for thinking of me, Mr. Throne. I really, really appreciate it."

MONDAY, GEORGE WENT to the doctor, and Tuesday, she was back at work as promised.

Ellen set a brownie on George's desk.

"What's this for?" George asked.

"I'm going perm," she said. "I know you turned down the job first, so I figured I owed you a brownie."

"What about your knitting shop?"

Ellen shrugged. "Oh, I'll still do that, too. One doesn't exactly eliminate the other, you know."

"And the pay cut doesn't bother you?" George asked.

"I negotiated the temp agency down. It's not that bad."

"Smart girl," said George. She took the brownie out of the cellophane wrapper and split it in two, offering the larger piece to Ellen.

"No thanks." Ellen shook her head. "I'm trying to get my weight down before my health insurance exam. I'm psyched to finally be covered. It wouldn't have been that big a thing for you, but not all of us have husbands with insurance, right? You know, reading about sick people all day was turning me into a total hypochondriac."

April

THAT SPRING, THE song playing everywhere was "... Baby One More Time," the elliptical debut of a seventeen-year-old pop tart, and one of the places it was playing was the Texas U pool where Patsy Pomeroy was teaching Harland Bright to swim.

"Do you like this?" Harland asked Patsy.

"It's all right," she said. "Nothing special."

"I like it," Harland said. He sang a few bars along with the radio. "Oh baby, baby, how was I supposed to know that something wasn't right here?"

"It sounds way better when you sing it," Patsy said.

"Yeah, I bet it does." Harland raised an eyebrow, and Patsy kissed him on it. "The thing is, she reminds me of you a little."

Patsy swatted Harland on the shoulder.

"What? I thought that was a compliment."

Patsy swatted him again. "Well, it ain't."

"Damn, I didn't know you were so violent." This time, Harland dodged before she could hit him. "She's kind of hot."

"Kind of slutty, maybe."

"Slutty hot," Harland said even though he didn't find the pop tart in question to be at all slutty. Just young and sweet and maybe a little silly.

"Slutty hot," Patsy agreed.

Patsy pushed herself out of the pool.

"You've got pretty feet," Harland commented. "Perfect toes."

She put her hand on Harland's forehead. "You feeling OK?" she asked.

"What?"

"First with Britney Spears and now with my feet. You've just been saying some mighty unusual shit, Harland."

Harland shrugged. "It's all good."

THE SONG WAS playing in the women's locker room as Patsy toweled off after her shower. She caught a glimpse of her foot reflected in the mirror at the end of a row of lockers and paused to consider it. The foot was neither wide nor narrow. There were five toes and no calluses or other defects worthy of commentary. It was well-arched—no military would (or will) disqualify her on the basis of it

She was still looking at her feet when a gray-haired woman in a beige waffle-weave bathrobe approached her.

"I'm Carolyn Murray," the woman said. She then went on to explain that she worked with Patsy's father and that they (Carolyn and Patsy) had met before. "At the ed department family picnic. Two years ago, I think it was. You were a lot smaller then."

"Oh, right," Patsy said, but she was just being polite.

Carolyn laughed. "You don't remember me at all, do you?"

"Not really," Patsy admitted.

"Well, I pass your picture on your dad's desk almost every day. Nice to meet you in the flesh." When they shook hands, Carolyn's robe opened a bit and Patsy got a good look at Carolyn's breasts. They were round and youthful, incongruous with the woman's hair and face, and, most intriguing to Patsy, lacking nipples. It was like looking at a face with no eyes.

Carolyn readjusted her robe as she stood back up. "Do you swim here often?" she asked.

Patsy wondered if Carolyn had seen her with Harland at the pool and if she would mention it to her father, because obviously that could cause trouble. Patsy thought about asking her to pretend they hadn't run into each other. Jedi mind trick. *You didn't see me. I'm not here.* But that wouldn't work and would probably just arouse suspicion. So, she only said something about having hurt her neck.

"You hurt your neck? Your father never mentioned that."

"Uh-huh. Well, nice to meet you again."

Later, after everything had been revealed and all navigations had been irrevocably set, Patsy would contemplate the best lie she might have told at that moment. She could have said that the black man was her physical therapist. She would shake her head and imagine the inflections she might have used and how it all would have been so obvious and simple and believable really.

IN THE CAR on her way to work, Helen called George.

"What's all the noise?" George asked.

"It's called music, Mother," Helen replied. "I'm driving."

"Oh, hang up, Helen! It's not safe to talk and drive at the same time."

"I can handle it," Helen said. "I'm very capable."

"Just call me when you get there. I don't want you to get into an accident."

"I won't have any time to call you once I'm at work." Helen sighed and turned down the radio—it was no sacrifice; she didn't care for the song or the girl who sang it anyway—before stating her real reason for calling. It had recently occurred to her that the wedding venue

lacked a certain something. A certain ambience. Helen had been thinking that the addition of live swans might be just the thing.

"Swans?"

"Swans or, you know, it could be geese or something, too. You rent
them for the day, then give them back. I think Canadian geese are
the cheapest, but it might not be worth it 'cause they . . . you know . . .
a lot, too," Helen said. "And I was also thinking it might be nice if
there were a pond in the backyard. Just a little one."

George said she didn't know anything about building ponds.

"How hard can it be to build a pond?" Helen asked. "You hire a
couple of Mexicans to dig a hole. Or maybe Daddy could just dig the
hole himself."

Postgraduation, Helen had had several places where she might have
begun her speech therapy practice. She had chosen Big Rock because,
of those options, Big Rock had the largest population. That her father
had chosen to go to school there had not been a factor in her decision.
However, when she first met Elliot at the local Adventist church, she
had told him that she had chosen the city to be near her family. She
had wanted to seem like the kind of girl who would choose a job based
on its proximity to home. More to the point, she wanted to be that kind
of girl; she wanted to understand what it was like to want to be near
home. Having a backyard wedding (or at least consenting to it) had
been a chapter in the story Helen wished to tell about herself.

Sometimes she suspected that something inside her was a bit broken.
She related to documentaries she had seen about autistic people. She knew
how a person was supposed to react to things—love, for instance, or
excitement or delight—and could put on the appropriate show of those
feelings, but she never felt any of them. The only emotion she truly
experienced was mild annoyance, and she felt that most all the time.

At the office, her nine o'clock, Mr. Thayer, was late. She had the
secretary call his house, and it turned out he was dead. He had hanged
himself over the weekend.

Since she had a good forty-five minutes to spare, Helen called her brother. She could hear that darn pop song coming from her brother's side of the country.

"Gosh," Helen said, "that song is on the radio twenty-four-seven."

"I'm watching the video actually."

Helen told Vincent about Mr. Thayer hanging himself and how she wondered if it was the speech therapy that did it, and Vincent laughed at her. "Honestly," she said, "I ought to be the one hanging myself, having to listen to people like him all day." She had meant this as a joke, but it hadn't come out that way.

At some point, Vincent asked her how long it had been since she checked her credit history.

Her credit was absolutely none of her brother's business. It was no one's business. That's personal, she wanted to say. She could feel her sternocleidomastoid muscle constrict and she rotated her neck in the same way she would have instructed a patient. "Why?" Helen asked.

According to Vinnie, their mother had been stealing from him. Helen wasn't shocked by this news, though she very much wished it was something she could un-know. She wondered how much of her wedding had been put on Vincent's purloined credit card. Then she decided that she couldn't think about that anymore. Her mother was a grown-up, and Helen certainly hadn't asked her to steal.

"In terms of my credit report, my only real option is to sue her," Vincent said.

"Sue who?"

"Mom." But he wasn't going to do that. He couldn't do that to Patsy or Helen. And it would probably cost him more to take his mother to court than what she even owed him. Since trying to contact his mother had borne no fruit, Vinnie had decided that the best thing to do was appeal to his dad's better angel and get him to pay what he could. "But in any case, you really ought to check your credit card statements. And I'm going to tell Patsy to do the same the next time I see her."

Helen said she'd check, but she knew there really wasn't a need.

Her credit had been ruined for years, of course. Somewhere—maybe in that hunter green Rubbermaid tub with her old college papers, maybe in the netted bag in the garage with her ragtag collection of sporting equipment—was the free Frisbee that had started it all.

A cute guy in a polo shirt had thrown it at her. "Yours," he had said. "All you have to do is fill out the application." He had smiled at her, and Helen had picked up the pen.

CHERISH FLIPPED THROUGH a *Rolling Stone* and waited for the boss's return from lunch. As Roger suspected, he had not been born Cherish. Cherish was the name he had given himself for his eighteenth birthday—he had taken it from a Madonna song.

"What're you reading?" Carolyn asked upon her return.

Cherish held up the magazine. On the cover lounged a polka-dot-underwear-clad Lolita on a pink satin bed, talking on the phone and hugging a Teletubby.

"Hmmmmm." Carolyn's left eyebrow rose slightly: The picture wasn't particularly shocking to her, though the use of the child's doll did strike her as needlessly tawdry. Otherwise, this was just one in a very long line of blonde, overly sexed/sexualized, too young, usually tragic, female icons. The picture put her in mind of an auction at Christie's that a colleague had convinced her to attend the prior year. The auction, arranged to coincide with the thirty-fifth anniversary of Marilyn Monroe's death or some such, had consisted of the star's books, garments, household goods, and ephemera. The pièce de résistance was *that dress,* the one Marilyn had worn to sing "Happy Birthday" to President Kennedy, the one they'd famously had to stitch her into. For the bidding, they had placed the garment on a Marilyn torso (cut to her exact proportions, but of course), while a recording of Marilyn's birthday serenade had played in the background. "Can you believe this?" her colleague had whispered. Carolyn could see that the friend was already mentally drafting the essay on the event she would write, ideally, for the *New York Review of Books,* but acceptably, for the *American Journal of Semiotics* or *Daedalus.* As Carolyn wasn't planning to bid, she just tsk-tsked appropriately and excused herself to go to the bathroom. She had never been a Marilyn Monroe person, yet she still found the whole thing enormously depressing. That sad, faded dress with the sequins falling off. It looked old and smelly and putrid. Carolyn went into the stall, locked the door, sat on a toilet, and for the first time since her own mother's death, wept.

"Who's that?" she asked Cherish, though of course the image had already told her all she needed to know.

"Britney Spears." The cover story for the April 25, 1999, issue of *Rolling Stone* was "Britney Spears: Inside the Heart and Mind (and Bedroom) of America's New Teen Queen." Cherish didn't think all that much of Britney. He thought she was basically a Madonna wannabe. Slightly better voice than early Madonna maybe, but no Catholic guilt or dead mother to make her interesting. Of the new girls, Cherish definitely preferred Christina Aguilera. He liked a girl who could sing, a girl who could Work. It. Out. Musically speaking, that is. Most of the time he preferred boys, though he referred to himself as bisexual and would continue to do so for the next fifteen years. In theory, though, he didn't think it particularly mattered what hole you were in.

Carolyn took the magazine and squinted at it a bit. "She looks like Sandra Dee." Cherish looked at her blankly. "Well, you're too young to remember her. Is she popular?"

"Yeah, you've probably heard her song. It's, like, totally ubiquitous, Carolyn." Cherish sang a couple of bars, then, by way of punctuation, stuck a finger down his throat.

Carolyn didn't think she'd heard it.

Cherish told her that she might be interested in the article because it talked about how the girl was this odd mix of God fearing and provocative, not unlike the country, not unlike Carolyn's (he did not think of it as Carolyn and Roger's) book. "Like, in her video, she's wearing this Catholic school girl uniform, but the song's all about S and M, basically. And she's in her underwear on the cover of a magazine, but she says how she's gonna be a virgin until she gets married. I'm *so sure*. And there's, like, a burning bush outside her house." Cherish rolled his eyes. "But mainly it's all just the writer being a smarty pants. The kid's just a cute little robot sex doll. Here, take it," he said. "I'm so done."

Carolyn took the magazine and went into her office. She kicked off her shoes and removed her jacket and made a doctor's appointment (she had found a small lump under her armpit, but it might have just been razor burn or a pimple) and called her publicist and left a message for her daughter Allegra at her dorm. Around five o'clock, after Cherish had left for the day, Roger stopped by, and they spent fifteen minutes on the topic of the book they were sort of writing and forty minutes having sex.

A funny thing about sex with Roger. She had worried about him seeing her breasts, because of her decision to not have nipple reconstruction—it had seemed like too much bother to get a skin graft or tattoos, and she was perfectly fine nipple-less, thank you very much, and wasn't half the point of most bras to conceal nipples? In any case, Roger had never once taken off her bra. He was equal-opportunity on this point as he had never removed his shirt either. In any case, if he'd noticed that she didn't have nipples, he'd certainly never mentioned it.

"I ran into your daughter," Carolyn said as she put her underwear back on.

"Oh?" Roger pulled up his boxers.

Carolyn stuck one foot into her panty hose. "At the pool." And then the other foot. "She's adorable, Rog."

Roger put on his pants, but stopped short of zipping up his fly. "What was she doing there?"

"Swimming, I imagine." Carolyn made a face. "Something about a neck injury?" Carolyn slipped her skirt over her hips.

"Oh, right." Zip. "Cheerleading."

"She was with her boyfriend."

"Her boyfriend's in Tennessee." Roger tied his left shoe.

Carolyn ran her fingers roughly through her tangled hair. She was in desperate need of a cut. "Maybe she has a new one?"

"Hmmph," Roger said. "I don't think so." As he was saying this, it occurred to him that he couldn't even remember the last conversation he'd had with Patsy. "What did he look like?"

"Handsome," Carolyn replied. "Tall." She sniffed under her armpit and decided that she didn't have the scent of sex on her. She wondered if she smelled like cancer. "African American."

"African American?" Roger laughed.

"Black. Whatever." Carolyn presumed he was laughing at her use of the politically correct term. Since it had entered parlance, the term had made her uncomfortable—how could you assume that any black person you met was African or American? But that wasn't why Roger was laughing anyway. Her beau, it turned out, was just a little bit racist. Not the white-sheet-wearing kind, but still. And so the conversation continued and the revelations kept coming: Roger knew *African American* people at his church and claimed to have several *African American* friends and acquaintances, but, all things considered, he would still prefer that his daughter not date an actual *African American*. Though she would hate herself for this later, Carolyn tried to calm him down by backtracking—"Maybe I saw wrong"—but it was too late. Just like that, Carolyn's 1998–99 School Fling had become substantially less fun.

They had been planning to have dinner that night, but Roger claimed to have some calls to make and Carolyn didn't try to stop his leaving.

Oy.

She could only come up with clichés to describe her motivations in choosing Roger: easy conquest, self-esteem boost, abuse of power, quick fix. Maybe she had simply liked his looks. He reminded her of

Sam Champion, the New York City weatherman she'd become somewhat obsessed with during a recent stint as a visiting professor at Barnard. She suspected Roger might be a closeted homosexual, but that didn't really bother her. Carolyn had always liked a project and she didn't mind anal sex either.

When she got home from school, she called her daughter on the phone and this time, she actually got her. They talked about whether Carolyn would be able to come to Washington, DC, to see *A Raisin in the Sun* (Allegra was playing Beneatha Younger) and they talked about Allegra's new girlfriend, Grace, and they talked about Carolyn's love life.

"You seeing anyone, Mom?"

"I was," Carolyn replied. "But it's just about kaput, I think." She knew how she'd do it, too. It would all be very aboveboard or as aboveboard as it was possible to be under such circumstances. She'd tell him that the book project wasn't working out and that would be that. She would encourage Roger to write his dissertation over the summer and fall semester. For her part, Carolyn would arrange for a sabbatical, in theory, to promote *The Wheels on the Bus 2*. The college would grant it — she was the star of the department and everyone knew it. By the time she came back, Roger would be gone, restored to the racist, God-fearing backwater from whence he came. She felt around her armpit to see if that bump was still there (yes) and thought to herself, *I'm getting too old for this shit.*

In Allegra's dorm room, someone turned up the volume, and Carolyn could hear a chorus of rowdy, young females singing along to a pop song: "Give me a sign, hit me baby, one more time!"

Allegra shushed them. "Guys, I'm talking to my mother!"

"Sorry, Allegra's mother!" one of the girls called in a singsong voice.

Carolyn listened to the music. She could hear it more clearly now that Allegra's suite mates had stopped singing. It's familiar. It's . . . "Oh, I know this! I *know* this!" Carolyn delighted in recognition. "The girl in the underwear."

April II

"APRIL FIFTEENTH," THE preacher intoned. "Shakespeare should have called it the Ides of April. *Beware* them nasty, lowdown, good for nothing Ides of April."

A titter from the congregation.

"Oh, come now? Is that the best you can do? I give you Shakespeare and a joke, and what I get is these doomy, gloomy faces. And y'all been coming to see me all week with these same doomy, gloomy faces. Telling me about your troubles. How you can't pay this, and you can't buy that, and you don't know how you're gonna make ends meet. Pastor Paul, you say, I just don't know how we're gonna make it. I ain't been on a vacation in Lord knows how long! And hubby's La-Z-Boy's got holes in it! And little Billy wants some of those Michael Jordan sneakers and all we can get him is the Wal-Mart kind! And those mean little kiddies at school, how they'll laugh at him. It ain't fair, Pastor. It ain't right. It ain't even Christian." The pastor shook his head and bulged out his eyes. "I said, it ain't even Christian!"

Big laugh.

"Now, that's more like it. But, some of you come to me with more serious problems. Lost jobs. Missed mortgage payments. Credit card debt. 'Pastor,' you say, 'if I can just get out of this hole I'm in, if I can just find the money to dig me out of this *turrrrrible* deep hole.' And what I think to myself is, money ain't gonna save you, Brother, but I know someone who can, and He's been there all along.

"It's time for a brand-new bookkeeping. It's time for a brand-new mathematics. A spiritual mathematics. The world tells you that all these secular debts matter, but my whole reason for being put here on this earth is to tell you that they do not. The only debts that matter are spiritual debts. And by spiritual debts, I mean what you owe to Him who died so that you might live . . ."

In the pew, Roger took George's hand. "Amen," he whispered.

He looked at Patsy, so sweet and pretty with her white blonde hair pulled back in a blue gingham headband. Last Friday night, he had confronted her about the black boyfriend, and Patsy had denied it. She had admitted running into Carolyn at the pool but claimed that Carolyn must have seen her "swimming near a black guy and not *with* a black guy." George hadn't heard anything about Patsy having a black boyfriend either, and as Roger had never known Patsy to lie, he decided to let the matter drop. "I don't see what the big deal would be if I *did* have a black boyfriend," Patsy had said. Roger told her that she missed the point. "And what is the point?" Patsy wanted to know. The point was that Patsy was supposed to introduce all her boyfriends to her parents. And the second point was that Patsy was supposed to date people from the church. "So, it would be fine if I dated a black guy as long as he were Adventist?" she asked. Roger told her she was parsing his words too carefully and cursed Carolyn for having bad eyesight and for sticking her oar where it didn't belong in the first place.

He looked past Patsy to Helen: Helen's eyes were closed and she was nodding rather fiercely in time to the pastor's words. "Amen," she said.

On his way out of church, Roger was stopped by Pastor Paul. The pastor shook Roger's hand, and Roger congratulated him on a stirring sermon. "Would you be able to stop by Wednesday afternoon around five?" Pastor Paul asked. "I need your help."

"Nothing serious, I hope?"

"Oh no, nothing like that"—the pastor laughed—"just some regular old church business"—then stopped laughing—"Wednesday."

"I have class on Wednesday," Roger said.

"How about Friday, then?"

Roger arrived at the church fifteen minutes early and the pastor's secretary directed him to a rickety wicker loveseat, which struck Roger as embarrassingly feminine. Its cushion was stingy with a thin, useless layer of floral-print-covered cotton batting, and the frame wheezed every time Roger made even the slightest move. The sofa made him feel like he was in trouble, and he wondered if he was.

For instance . . . what if George had somehow figured out that he'd been sleeping with Carolyn Murray? And instead of confronting Roger directly, what if George had told Pastor Paul, and now Pastor Paul was planning to have a "talk" with Roger about his conduct? Even the thought of it was completely humiliating.

Pastor Paul came out of his office. "It's good to see you, Roger. Come in, come in." Roger rose and the chair gasped, as if it were relieved to be rid of his burden.

"That was quite the sermon you gave last Saturday," Roger said.

"I'm glad you liked it," Pastor Paul replied. "Cup of herbal tea?" Roger declined but Pastor Paul placed a teacup on the desk in front of him anyway. "Have one," he said, pouring hot water over the bag. "The sermon. Well, I don't have to tell you it was from the heart. This time of year—tax season, you know?—people spend a lot of time thinking about finances and not too much time thinking about God. I like to do what I can to remind people that the big guy's still around.

"It's funny you should bring up the sermon. Because, well, one of the people I was especially speaking to was you."

"Me?"

"In a way, yes. There's a problem with your family's tithe, Roger."

Pastor Paul took a spreadsheet from his top desk drawer. The title was "Pomeroy Tithings, 1998–1999," and it was a record of his family's earnings and 10 percent payments to the church. "Neither you nor your wife is currently employed by the church, which means that your family is responsible for sending in the ten percent payments at the end of each month. As you can see, the last payment we received from your family was in August 1998. So, that would be eight months ago."

Roger quickly glanced at the spreadsheet and ascertained a long row of zeroes. He pushed the document back across the table. "I wouldn't really know about any of this, Pastor. George takes care of all the household finances. The person you should really be speaking to is her."

Pastor Paul nodded. "We tried that, Roger. We've been leaving messages for her for the last six months. Several times after church, I personally appealed to her to come see me. She hasn't, which is why I'm forced to bring this matter to your attention, Roger."

Roger cleared his throat. He tried to speak but found that he could not.

"Have some tea, Roger."

Roger drank, but his throat didn't feel any less desiccated. "I've been so busy trying to finish school . . . I know money's been . . . somewhat tight . . . George would never . . . but I'm sure it's just some kind of mistake . . . I can fix it . . ."

"When you don't pay your tithe, you're robbing God." Pastor Paul took Roger's hands in his.

"I know," Roger said. This was all so humiliating. It was actually worse than being confronted about the affair.

"I just thought you'd want to get all of this straightened out before Helen's wedding."

* * *

AFTER MEETING WITH the pastor, Roger drove back across town for his afternoon meeting with Carolyn.

En route, he calculated the amount he'd spent on gas driving to and from the school and whether his total driving expenses (gas plus car insurance) were more or less than he'd made as Carolyn's teaching assistant.

This office should be mine.

"Roger," she said. "How are you?" She offered him her hand. The gesture struck Roger as curiously formal considering what their relations had been like for the last two months.

Roger shook her hand. "What's this?" he asked.

Carolyn laughed a bit too loudly, a bit too long. "Sorry. The thing is, Rog, I wanted to talk to you as a colleague today and not as that other thing. Have a seat," she said.

"Fine," he said. "I've been wanting to talk to you, um, that way, too."

"Please," she said. "What's on your mind?"

"Well, I could use a loan," he said. He looked at Carolyn to see how this request was being received. Her face revealed nothing. "Or a raise. It could really be either one." And then Roger explained how he had had to take a pay cut to come work for Carolyn and how his daughter was getting married and how consequently his family had fallen behind on some of their household expenses, like, for instance, paying their tithe.

"Tithe?"

"I pay ten percent of all my earnings to the church."

"Oh, right, that kind of tithe. That's"—she reminded herself that she could not afford to sound condescending—"I didn't know people still did that. The church is like your agent."

"Um . . ."

"That was a joke," she said. "Well, the thing is, Rog, I've got some news, too." She told him about her plan to take a sabbatical next year.

"Where does that put our book?" he asked.

"On hold for a bit, I imagine," she said. "I was thinking you could take advantage of my absence to finish your dissertation and then we'd reapproach the idea of our book when I got back."

"Are you saying you don't want to work on the book anymore?"

"No. I'm just saying I need a break. That's all. I've got my own book to promote next year. My daughter's graduating from college. You know, I'm going to be very busy."

Roger felt that his head could very possibly explode.

"Actually, Rog, you know what you should do? You should write the book without me. You can have all the research we've done. Just be sure to dedicate it to me, right?"

"Carolyn." Roger cleared his throat. He stood up and leaned over the professor's desk. "Carolyn, I can't stress to you enough how much I need this book to happen. How much I was counting on this book happening. The book, it was my redemption, it was my—"

"Calm down, Roger. It was just a thought."

"Carolyn. Carolyn." Roger hoped he wasn't crying. "I'm in trouble. I'm in deep trouble. I need help."

"Money, you mean." Carolyn's voice was even and cool.

"Help! I mean, help. If I could just get a little help . . ." Roger dropped to one knee, and for one awful moment, Carolyn worried that he was about to propose. Her first husband had not proposed in this manner. The year had been 1971, and she and Clarence had been on a bus on the way back from a protest rally. "Sister," he'd said, "I've been thinking we should cohabitate."

"I would never live with someone I wasn't married to," Carolyn had replied, though strictly speaking, this hadn't been true.

He'd scratched his scalp and a few dandruff flakes floated down. *Like snow,* she had thought. (She had really been ridiculously in love with the man.) "Hadn't taken you for a square," he had said.

"Well, I'm not," she'd said. "Except in some things."

A month later, they had been married at city hall. They moved in together that same day.

"Carolyn," Roger said.

While she'd been reminiscing, her soon-to-be ex-lover had wrapped his hands around her calf.

"Please, Roger. I need my leg now." Carolyn pulled her leg out from his hand and walked to the bookshelf where her purse lay. She took out her wallet. "I want to help you with this tithe business. You made five thousand dollars last semester, which means you'd owe five hundred dollars to the church, right? I'll write you a check for seven hundred and fifty dollars, OK? I hope this helps." In the memo section, she wrote, "Research Reimbursement," but she said that was just for tax purposes.

"I'll pay you back," he said. Roger took the check and put it in his pants pocket. He felt a bit calmer knowing the money was there.

"No need."

"Is it over between us?"

Carolyn returned her wallet to her handbag and zipped it shut. "The sabbatical doesn't have anything to do with you, if that's what you're asking. It's all just lousy timing, Rog." She didn't think Roger would ever sue her—she'd known all along that his piousness was her protection in all of this. His interest in appearing to be a good Christian was too strong to willingly expose himself as having had an extramarital affair, and this had been one of the most compelling reasons for choosing him. But she also knew her conduct had been morally ambiguous at best. So, in order to make Roger feel better about things, she told him about the lump under her armpit and blamed everything on that.

"Let me see it," he said.

Carolyn found this to be a remarkably strange request, but she lifted her gray cashmere sweater, unfastened her bra, and raised her arm. "You can't really see it," she said, "but you can feel it."

Roger put his fingers under her arm. "Like a BB," he said.

"It might be nothing."

She lowered her sweater and fastened her bra. It was the first time he'd ever seen her without one, and the last time, too.

*   *   *

AFTER STOPPING AT the check cashing place, Roger drove home. No one was there. George was still at work; Patsy was God knows where. While he waited for George's return, he decided to search the house for all their current financial paperwork. He found unopened bills in the bill drawer, in shopping bags in the garage, in shoeboxes in George's closet, in a plastic bin under the guest bathroom sink, everywhere, just everywhere. He found endless and seemingly contradictory paperwork for his daughter's wedding, which, based on the invoices, was still more unpaid than paid. How had he failed to notice that he had been living in a paper house? Light a match and the whole thing would burn to the ground in an instant.

He was just about at the end of his hunt when he came across a legal-size envelope with his son's return address on it. Roger unhooked the brad. Inside was a Post-it note affixed to a credit card statement dated March 22, 1999. Vincent had written, "Your latest. I've canceled this one, too. Mother, this must stop."

Roger looked through the charges on the statement. He'd once heard someone say on television (*Frontline? Maury Povich?*) that a family's secret history was written on their credit card statements. Because, honestly, where had all their money gone? It was not as if they had been living high on the hog. And the money hadn't been going to the church. And his wife had apparently been stealing from their only son. So, where had it gone? Where the H-E-double-hockey-sticks had it gone?

$300.00 to the Paper Trail Highland Mall.

$72.89 to Time Warner Cable.

$249.14 to Central Energy.

$275.00 to Planned Parenthood of Central Texas.

$35.17 to Fuddruckers.

He stopped.

And then, he read it again:

$275.00 to Planned Parenthood.

Planned Parenthood.

Planned Fucking Parenthood.

Patsy with a black guy at the pool.

Patsy fucking a black guy at the pool.

Patsy fucking some, excuse my French because I'm really not that kind of person, nigger at a pool.

Patsy fucking some nigger at a pool.

We're all good Christians here.

Patsy at Planned Parenthood.

George putting it on a secret credit card to hide it from ME.

At Vinnie's graduation, I lifted my little girl in the air so that she could better see the show.

Patsy at Planned Parenthood having an abortion.

My little girl is lost to me.

My little girl is dead.

My little girl is going to hell.

My little girl is lost.

He hoped his wife got home first, because he worried he might kill his daughter.

We're good Christian people here.

He sat in the kitchen. He didn't turn on a light even after it was dark. In the blackness, he came to see how he had brought all this on himself. Patsy's sin and George's sin—their sins were really his. His selfishness and vanity in trying to get his PhD and in taking his family away from Tennessee and his daughter from her good Christian school. And his poor wife, whom he had betrayed and abandoned. The financial weight he'd forced her to carry alone. His inattention, distraction. The adulterous affair with Carolyn Murray—the snake, how she flattered! What a fool he'd been. He saw now. Oh, how he saw! God was punishing him, and he deserved it. "Oh!" His groan was bestial, toneless. "Oh! I am a sinner! God forgive me!" He got down on his knees and prayed and wept and then he prayed some more. "Tell me what to do, sweet Lord! Give me a sign! Help me out of this hole!" He repeated this and variants for the next eleven minutes. In the twelfth minute, he heard the voice of Jesus Christ and saw a halo of light around the stainless steel refrigerator door.

REPENT

CAST OUT YOUR DAUGHTER

DEVOTE YOUR LIFE TO ME AND MY WORD

"I will, Lord. Thank you, thank you."
The light went out as quickly as it had come on.

ALMOST AS IF there had been a switch.

IT MIGHT HAVE been, for instance, the Gita family who lived next door. The prior summer, Mr. Gita had installed a floodlight over the side garage entrance. It worked on a movement sensor so that he could move the trash cans inside and back without having to set them down and fumble about for a light switch in the dark. The impetus had been an incident with rotten ground lamb.

OR NOT.

WHEN GEORGE GOT home, she turned on the kitchen light and found Roger on his knees with his lips pressed up against the refrigerator door. He had scratches on his hands and his eyes were red and awful.

"What's happened?" George asked.

"Where's Patsy?" His voice was gone, just squeaks and whispers.

"She's sleeping over at a friend's house. She'll meet us at church tomorrow morning."

"Where were you?"

"I've been working nights in the plus-size section at Dillard's since

November. I told you." George noticed the financial ephemera that was scattered everywhere. From this evidence, she could instantly concoct several possible narratives. None was appealing, and she decided she didn't care to know what Roger knew.

She helped her husband to his feet and led him up the stairs to their bedroom and put him to bed. She dabbed a cotton ball in hydrogen peroxide and cleaned his hands.

"I'm sorry," George said. "Whatever it is, I'm sorry."

The next morning, Roger rose before dawn. He took a shower and felt an almost pleasure at the sting of soap against his sore body. He shaved his face carefully, as if his life depended on not nicking himself. He combed his blond hair and applied his usual pomade. He looked at himself in the mirror: he was still young, strong, and healthy. He had failed God and his family, but he would make amends.

He put on his best suit. Then he sat by George's bedside and waited for her to rise.

The moment her eyes opened, Roger took her hand and said, "I know about the tithe. I know about Vinnie's credit cards. I'm starting to get a pretty good picture of the financial . . . uh, situation."

"I can explain—"

Roger interrupted her. "Don't. It's my fault as much as yours. What I need to know . . . What I want you to tell me about is Patsy's abortion."

"Patsy?" George's voice was thick with sleep.

"Don't try to protect her. I know about it, George. I saw the charge on Vinnie's credit card statement. I know what you did: how you tried to cover it up."

George sat up in bed. Her body felt heavy. Her breasts felt tender, almost like she was getting her period. Her nightgown was blue flannel with sheep on it. It was incredibly soft because it was incredibly worn. There was a tear in the fabric near her pubic area, and the hole embarrassed her. She was embarrassed to be having this conversation while dressed this way. "Please, Roger, can't I just take a shower first?"

Roger shook his head.

"I'll tell you anything you want to know. Just let me take a shower first. I smell weird."

George tried to stand, and Roger pushed her back onto the bed. "I need to know now. When did she tell you she was pregnant?"

George sighed and covered the hole with her hand. "She didn't."

"What do you mean she didn't?"

"I noticed." George curled her knees up to her chest and put her head between them down the neckline of her nightgown. She inhaled, and got a whiff of her own vagina. She exhaled, and the gown billowed around her like a hot air balloon. When her children were still children, she would take them under the blankets and tell them stories by flashlight. She found it easier to spin a tale with conviction when it didn't have to bounce around an entire room, an entire house, an entire world.

"I noticed," George repeated, her voice muffled by the nightgown. "When she was getting fitted for her bridesmaid dress. She'd gained an inch in the waist. At first, I thought it was because she wasn't cheering anymore, but then somehow I knew. I just knew." George lifted her head out of her gown and looked at Roger to see how the story was playing. She began to weep. "I just knew . . . I asked her . . . And she told me she wanted to have an abortion . . ."

Roger slapped George across the face with the back of his hand. "How could you let this happen? Do you want our daughter to go to hell?"

"What was I to do? We've got no money. I'm a forty-seven-year-old temp; you're in school and you're never home. I was all alone. I did the best I could."

"And the boy . . . Who was he?"

"Some guy from school."

"The black guy?"

"Huh?"

"The one Carolyn—my boss—saw her with at the university swimming pool. I asked you about it. Remember?" He grabbed the collar of George's nightgown and pulled her toward him.

"Yes, Roger. That's him."

"Why did you lie when I asked you about it?"

"I don't know! I don't know! You tell one, you have to keep telling them. Please, Roger, you're choking me."

Roger released George's gown and she fell back against the headboard. The skirt was flipped over her head, exposing her stomach. She didn't bother to right it.

Roger went downstairs and came back with a bag of frozen peas for George's face. "Come on. We're going to be late for church."

In the car, Roger said to George, "She'll have to be sent away."

"Shouldn't she finish out the school year first?"

"No."

"But Roger, what's done is—"

"No."

George sighed. Her cheek hurt. Roger had never hit her before. Her cheek hurt, and the pain made it uncomfortable to move her jaw very much. "Where will you send her?"

"Back to my mother's in Tennessee."

"You won't tell your mother about the abortion, will you?"

"Of course not. I never want it spoken of again."

"What will you say to her, then?"

"I'll tell her that Patsy's been running wild and needs discipline."

"Let me be the one to tell Patsy," George said. "You're too upset. And what's happened is as much my fault as hers. I shouldn't have let it happen. It'll be easier coming from me."

Roger considered this request as he made a right turn into the church parking lot. They were running late, so all the spaces were filled. He'd have to make a U-turn and park at the strip mall across the street. The strip mall had recently made it known that they would prefer the Adventists not use their parking lot, as Saturday was their busiest shopping day. Sunday would be one thing, but these crazy Saturday Christians were an incredible inconvenience. "Yes," he agreed. "You should be the one to tell her." He drove across the street and said a prayer that he wouldn't get towed.

May

May 23, 1999

Harland,

Well, by now you've no doubt noticed that I'm not at school. Ha. And I don't know what all you were told about my leaving, if anything. But it obviously was not by choice. I just wanted to let you know that I'm thinking about you. I wish I could have called you or gone to see you in person, but Mom told me I was being sent away and next thing I know I'm on a Greyhound bus to Buckstop, and that's that. And like, the whole time my dad won't even talk or look at me. The only thing he says is he hopes I'll have some time to reflect over what all I've done and to pray.

I don't want to burden you with my troubles, but things haven't been all that great for me here. I'm staying with my grandmother in Buckstop as aforementioned, and I never really liked her all that much to begin with. Like, when she tried to hold me as a baby, I'd cry. She smelled funny and her clothes were always scratchy or something, I don't know. But I swear to God, I never noticed how crazy she was till just now.

So I get to her house and the first thing I notice is the smell. It smells like the special wing at school. Like microwave popcorn and ammonia. So basically, like piss or like someone trying to cover up piss.

And the first night I'm here she's all like, "Patsy, your daddy says you've been flying too high and getting too big for your britches in your fancy city school."

I had a laugh at that, 'cause it's not like Texas is exactly Vegas or wherever.

She's all, What're you laughing at? And I say, Nothing, ma'am. And she says, Your face is smiling so you must be laughing at something. And I'm like, No. And whatever, it goes back and forth like this for a while. And then she sends me to my room without dinner, which is ridiculous . . . I mean, I'm an adult for God's sake. So I wake up hungry in the middle of the night and I take a Polly-O string cheese and a yogurt from her fridge and the next morning, she says, "Patsy, we need to have a serious talk about your morals." And then she calls me a thief! And that afternoon, this big-ass padlock shows up on the fridge. But the hilarious part comes the next day. She forgets the combo and then the old bitch has to break off her stupid lock with a crowbar.

I laughed at that, too. (Inside, this time. I'm learning.)

But then the day after that, she forgets that she broke the lock and she accuses ME of breaking the lock. And she chases me up the stairs with her creaky bad hip and she locks me in the bedroom. And that's the first time I notice that there's a lock on the OUTSIDE!!! of my freaking door. And well, so it goes.

She burned all my clothes in a metal bin in the backyard, 'cause apparently I was showing too much arm and boob (like I even got that much to show!). And then the next day, she's all like, Why don't you have anything to wear?

There's no television here, just a single radio that's usually tuned on choir music or, like, people yelling. Once, when I thought she was asleep, I tried to change the channel to something decent. But the next thing I know something hits me in the back of the head. It's an apple! She threw a Red Delicious at me! The old woman's got pretty good aim, I must admit.

Well, I finally got to talk to my mom last Friday. And it don't look like they're going to let me come back anytime soon. Maybe for Helen's wedding, but I guess you'll most likely be graduated and gone by then.

I'm not ashamed to say that I cried a little when I was talking to my mom. I basically begged her to let me come back, but whatever, not gonna happen. So yeah, I don't even know if I'll ever see you again. Unless you come to Tennessee or something, but even if you did, I'm being kept on a pretty tight leash. Like, the only time I've gone out is to church and that's about it.

I don't want to get all dramatic about it, but yeah, I miss you. And I hadn't gotten a chance to teach you the backstroke yet so I hope you'll manage to pick it up somewhere or other.

Love,
Patsy

P.S. I really hope you're not going to prom with freakin' Janet Johnson —I know for a fact she's had her eye on you all year.

P.P.S. If you're considering it, you should know that I cheered with Janet for two years, and she gets BO something fierce, and also her mom's a total bitch.

Patsy put the letter in an envelope and sealed it, but Grandma Fran wouldn't give her a stamp and Patsy didn't have the money or the freedom to buy one of her own. For the first but not the last time, she wondered how it was that life could seem so expansive one moment and so infinitesimal the next.

On Saturday, Fran took Patsy to church. Marcus, the son of the minister, was there. He was best friends with Patsy's old boyfriend and had basically known Patsy her whole life. He smiled at her. Patsy nodded because, since coming to Fran's, she had learned that not smiling was usually the smartest choice.

After church, Fran spoke to the minister about something dull and liturgical, and Marcus was able to get Patsy by herself.

"Heard you were back in town."

"Apparently," Patsy said.

"Well, can you come out with us?"

Patsy shook her head. "I'm being punished."

"What'd you do?"

"I was dating this black guy," Patsy said. "And I lied about it, I guess."

"Aw, that doesn't seem all that bad," Marcus said.

"Reckon my dad thought so." Patsy shrugged. For the last fourteen days, she'd gone without television, privacy, and regular meals, and consequently she'd had plenty of time for the prayer and reflection that her father believed her to so desperately need. So she'd prayed and reflected and what she'd come to was this: people did what they could live with; all sin was relative.

June

AT THE WEDDING, the groom's lips were chapped; the bride's shoes hurt; the napkins were embossed; the pastor was paid off; the signing board was warped; the bridesmaids' dresses were wrinkled; the house was still Caliente; there were neither swans nor a pond; the bride's brother wasn't speaking to the mother of the bride; the father of the bride wasn't speaking to the maid of honor; the bride would have preferred not to be speaking to the mother of the bride, but couldn't avoid it; the mother of the bride wept for reasons both apparent and not; the bride wept, too, but no more than most; the grandmother's dress had an insidious watermark; formal photographs were organized like military campaigns; and the wedding was, in general quality and overall effect, like most any other wedding in the history of weddings.

The week after the blessed event, the mother of the bride put the house on the market:

1205 SHADY LANE. BRING YOUR SUITCASE AND MOVE RIGHT IN. VIBRANTLY HUED 4 BR, 2½ BA HOME ON LARGE, LANDSCAPED LOT. SHORT, TWENTY-MINUTE DRIVE TO UNIVERSITY. EXCELLENT

PORTER ISD SCHOOLS. HOUSE PAINTED AND FLOORS FINISHED IN LAST YEAR. GREAT FOR A LARGE FAMILY OR ONE JUST STARTING OUT. OWNER WILL CONSIDER ALL REASONABLE OFFERS. LET'S MAKE A DEAL.

July

AT HER MINISTER'S suggestion, Grandma Fran paid for Patsy to be sent to Christian Soldiers Bible Camp in Alabama again.

While there, Patsy made a leather wallet, rode horses, threw a pot, swam, and spent an awful lot of time on her knees praying. She felt like someone in an ad for herpes medication minus the herpes. Still, it beat being at Fran's. Bible camp people might be crazy, but at least they were consistent.

Her ex-boyfriend, Magnum, was also in attendance as a counselor in the boys' division. He avoided her for the first three days but sidled up to her after the Wednesday Night Abstinence Rally.

"You look skinny," Magnum said. "What're you, like, anorexic now or something?"

"My grandmother's starving me," Patsy said.

"Ha. What happened to your new boyfriend?"

"You ask a lot of questions," she said.

"What happened? He dump you?"

Patsy shrugged. "Nothing happened."

"So, I was wondering if you wanna be partners on the trip to Wildwater Theme Park?"

"You gonna cry if I say no?"

Patsy agreed, mainly because Magnum was a counselor, which meant he'd get to ride in the air-conditioned minivan as opposed to the rented school bus. And the truth was, she'd always found time spent with Magnum to be pleasant if not exactly earth shattering. He was no Harland, but Harland wasn't around. Magnum was sweet and a bit dumb. He had nice hair and round shoulders and soft hands and he would probably make some girl a perfectly acceptable husband some day.

The second-to-last night of camp, Magnum took her to an abandoned cabin in the woods behind the mess hall. He offered her a joint, which she accepted.

"You going back to Buckstop Academy next year?"

"Yeah, I guess so."

"You're pretty, Patsy," he said, while stroking her hair.

"Rub my neck," she said.

He did.

Somehow, Patsy's shirt came off. And then Magnum's pants. And then Patsy's skirt. And then his hand between her legs—soft and damp and the slightest bit sticky. And then she slipped off her underwear. And then he slipped off his. And then Patsy asked him if he had something. And Magnum said yes. And Patsy lay down on a cot that had dead leaves stuck to one end. And Magnum asked her if she was sure. And Patsy said yes. And Magnum asked if she was worried about God. And Patsy said, "No, I'm not sure if I even believe in him anymore." So, Magnum climbed on top. And Patsy moaned a bit. "Go slower," she said. And Magnum did his best to take note. And the whole thing was over in 113 seconds, which Patsy knew because she'd been counting.

"Poor Patsy, you're bleeding," he said. Magnum kissed her stomach and her thighs.

"It's my first time," she said.

"You didn't do it with that other guy?" Magnum couldn't help smiling at his conquest.

"He wouldn't," Patsy said. "But you needn't look so pleased with yourself, Magnum. I wanted to, but he thought we should wait."

Magnum kissed Patsy on the mouth. "I'm gonna marry you, Patricia Pomeroy."

"Sure you are." Patsy laughed at him, though his words made her depressed beyond belief. The cabin felt too small. She felt like she was shrinking, like she might wake one morning and find that she'd disappeared. She would have cried, but she didn't want Magnum to think it was about the sex, or worse, about Jesus. *I could marry him,* she thought. *I could marry him, and if I did, I wouldn't want him to be thinking how I cried that first time every other time we did it.*

Jesus, she thought, *I really could marry him.*

"What are you thinking?"

"It's crazy," she said.

"What is?"

The connections, she thought. Or the lack of them. The discontinuity. How it was impossible to understand how a person got from point a to point b, even if you were that person and you had been there for every, every step. How there were unseen and mysterious forces beyond yourself. How you ran into a woman with no nipples and two weeks later you found yourself on a Greyhound bus bound for Nowheresville. How your father stopped speaking to you. *I am sixteen years old. An ex-cheerleader and an outcast. My parents are bigots. I'm not sure if I believe in God, not my dad's God at least. I just lost my virginity to a boy I don't love, and the way things go in this part of the world, I'll probably end up married to him. I'll probably have three kids before I'm twenty-five. I probably won't ever see anything but the back room of a Slickmart.*

"Uh, Patsy? Still there?"

"I fell from the top of this pyramid last year and everything since then's felt sort of like a dream," she said with a giggle.

"You're really baked, aren't you?"

"Pretty much," she said.

August

Like Patsy, Roger had spent most of the summer in prayer, though his prayers were a bit more adamant and significantly more specific than hers. He prayed for Patsy's soul and the soul of her unborn baby and the souls of unborn babies everywhere; he prayed for George who had allowed Patsy's sins to happen and who had stolen money from their son and, even worse than that, the church; he prayed for Carolyn Murray and himself (though murder/abortion and thievery were far worse than adultery in Roger's moral universe); he prayed that he could somehow find it in himself to forgive his wife and daughter; he prayed that the house would sell; he prayed that they could pay all their bills; he prayed to earn enough money to return to Tennessee; he prayed, in short, for a miracle.

Then, one came.

While Patsy was away at Christian Soldiers Bible Camp, Roger's mother fell down the stairs, lapsed into a coma, and died. (It turned out, as Patsy certainly could have guessed, that Fran had dementia and what may have been early-onset Alzheimer's.) Roger was named the executor of Fran's estate. Fran had left $15,000 to each of the grandchildren, with a month-old codicil on Patsy's specifying that

to continue the religious education that this
ch deep need of." To Roger, Fran left every-
uded her house and a $75,000 life insurance

ed with the sale of the Texas house, was enough
rge back to zero. It didn't leave any extra, but

nish his dissertation from Tennessee. He in-
her jobs and pack up a U-Haul, and it was as
ened at all.

od and his mother, Roger decided to give up
become a full-time preacher. When he had
spair, he had received the calling from Jesus
ill provide," he said to his wife on the thresh-
old) house in Buckstop. He liked the sound
words so much, he said it twice, like someone in a movie:
"God will provide."

George nodded. She went into the foyer, where it smelled like
mothballs and urine (or someone trying to cover it up). The house
was not air-conditioned, so George opened up all the windows to let
the air in and the scent out. Then she went upstairs and did the same.
Some of the window sashes were stuck to the stools, as if they hadn't
been opened since whenever they had last been painted. George banged
on the window frame with her fist and recalled how much she had
always disliked her mother-in-law and, by association, this house.

The last window was over the bathroom sink. George opened it,
then locked the door behind her. She sat down on the toilet. Her
breasts had felt tender when she woke that morning and it was as she
suspected: she had her period.

George looked under Fran's sink, but all she found was an ancient
box of menstrual pads, the kind that involved a belt and skinny strips
of double-sided tape. "Fucking hell," George said and then she started
to cry.

September

IN SEPTEMBER, PATSY transferred to the same religious high school where her father had once been vice principal. The school determined that Patsy was academically advanced but morally behind (pants too tight, mouth too loose, etcetera), and she spent most of her senior year in one form of trouble or another. It was not, for instance, a popular act to entitle one's science term paper, "Creationism for Dummies."

The college counselor, who was also the girls' gymnastics coach, suggested the same college he suggested for every student at the high school: Tennessee Adventist University. Patsy thought, *No way in hell*. She wanted to major in African American Studies or Eastern Religions, topics that did not even exist at TAU.

She ignored the coach's advice and applied to ten secular colleges, using money she'd saved from working afternoons at the local snack cake factory to pay the application fees. Her essay was a six-hundred-word tract about bigotry and God, the hard-won life lessons of a seventeen-year-old girl who'd seen some things. It impressed its intended audience enough that, despite a somewhat patchy academic record, she received several thick envelopes in the spring, complete with welcome brochures and applications for financial aid.

By summer, she was rejected by all the major student loan companies. It turned out that there was already a flag on her embryonic credit history. March of 1999, someone had opened up a credit card in her name, then gone on to make several late payments. Until this cleared up, Patsy was seventeen years old and a high-risk candidate. Her parents (more specifically, her father) wouldn't cosign either. For the most part, Patsy and Roger had passed her last year at home peaceably enough. This truce had been accomplished by scheduling their days so that they rarely met. Still, Roger had found it necessary to break their uneasy accord to weigh in on Patsy's plan to go secular. "I've been there," he said, not quite looking her in the eyes (he never looked her in the eyes), "and nothing good can come of it." She had expected such a response and had nearly trained herself not to care.

She saw the army poster

MONEY FOR COLLEGE
BE ALL THAT YOU CAN BE

inside the financial aid office of the state university, wedged between flyers for the Miss USA pageant, which billed itself as a scholarship competition, and for an ambiguously worded job opportunity that claimed to pay ten thousand dollars to any woman over five feet four in exchange for an unspecified service. *My eggs?* Patsy wondered. *Kidneys?* At five feet one, Patsy wasn't qualified for the vague position anyway, so she briefly considered the Miss USA pageant instead. She concluded that five feet one was probably too short for Miss USA as well. She was pretty enough, but she looked squat in a bikini. In contrast, the military didn't care what she looked like in a swimsuit, and, after speaking with a recruitment officer, she decided that organ donation and scholarship pageants both involved more significant

time and moral commitments than becoming a reservist. The pitch
went down like cough syrup, easy enough if a bit thick: basic training, *you'll get in awesome shape,* one weekend a month and maybe a
couple of weeks a year unless there's a war, *and darlin', we're living
in a period of unprecedented peace, don't you know?*

PART II

What's a Nice Girl Like You Doing in a War Like This?

Six Years Later

November 2006

Patsy at the Airport

SHE DID NOT consider herself to be a political person. She hadn't even voted in the last election, on account of being overseas at the time and then a misunderstanding with regard to the absentee ballot process. Something about postmarked vs. received by, or maybe it had been ink vs. pencil—she had never been entirely sure. Had her vote counted, it would have been cast for the gentleman who won anyway. At the time, she had found his directive to "stay the course" compelling—to do or believe otherwise would have been the same as saying that the last several years of her life and all its accompanying hardships had signified nothing. And how could a person think that and keep lacing up her boots and strapping on her gun day after day? No, a person could most definitely not believe that and go on. But she hadn't managed to vote for the gentleman from Texas anyhow, and she was somewhat comforted by the knowledge that, in terms of the bigger picture, if such a thing even existed, her one idiot vote wouldn't have changed a damn thing. She had also heard, though she didn't know if this were true, that absentees weren't counted unless the election was close; she had been told that the election had not been close.

She was not a political person, but had she been or even known anyone who was, the first or second thing on her agenda most certainly would have been The State of American Airports.

Though it was not a major holiday, nor was the weather notably inclement, the security line stretched all the way to curbside check-in. In two hours, she had gone through the usual spectrum of emotions that a person waiting in a long line experiences: the degradation of being in the back followed by the elated, irrational superiority of those who had waited their way to the front. She was a mere eight people from the X-ray machine (and only two from taking off her shoes) when she began to feel rumblings that she would, in all likelihood, be throwing up in the not-too-distant future. She debated: should she attempt to get through the line first and then vomit, or should she immediately shift her focus to exit strategies? Ahead of her: a pair of old-timers in matching sweat suits and a girl near her age with five little children. (*The girl had been busy,* she thought.) Neither party was built for speed. She decided that her stomach wouldn't make it. She flagged security and asked in the same deferent voice she had once reserved for girlhood prayers, "Would it be possible for me to go to the bathroom and then return to my same place in line?"

NO.

"'Cause I'm not feeling all that well—"

NO.

"'Cause my plane's in, like—"

NO.

"'Cause I'm not wearing my uniform, but—"

NO.

Over and eff'n out, y'all.

The last several times she had flown domestic, she'd been in uniform. This time, having been discharged, she was dressed in civilian attire, and she suspected that her civvies might have made a difference in her treatment.

Missing her flight was not an option, so she began to consider throwing up right there, in media res and ideally on security's shoes. But she couldn't bring herself to do it. She had had to do jobs like that herself—i.e., the management of the ungrateful masses in exchange for a minimal amount of compensation. And besides, she hadn't been reared that way. Which is to say, she had not been reared to make a spectacle of herself in public.

She asked the man behind her in line if he'd save her place. He reminded her of her father, and this was not necessarily encouraging. He had thinning blondish gray hair and Perma Press khakis, and there was something about the eyes, too—clear and blue, but the hue not very deep, perhaps.

"I can't promise you nothing, sweetheart," he said. "If the line moves on, I go with it."

Though it was the best she could do, she suspected his commitment level would not be sufficient to get them down the aisle. She was right. By the time she returned from the bathroom, her mock dad, along with everyone else she'd been with, including the jerk from security, was gone and replaced by a whole new generation of anxious waiters and security jerks, who didn't know her from Adam and who were most definitely not going to let her cut.

Basic goddamn clusterfuck, she thought. *Back of the line for Patricia Pomeroy French.* She had been there before.

Eventually, it got so late that they started pulling people from her flight to Chattanooga to the front of the line. Again, it had been a while since she'd flown domestic, and she was not completely familiar with all the protocols. (It did occur to her that no one else, including the people running the show, seemed all that familiar with the protocols either . . .) But she did the dance as best she could: duffel on the conveyor, plastic Baggie of products into the bin, etcetera, etcetera. She took off her boots and her belt, which caused her pants to slip down a little. They were low-riders, and she was thicker through the middle than whenever she had bought them. As she shuffled through the metal detector, she thought, *Airport's turning into a goddamn strip club.*

BEEP BEEP BEEP.

"STEP ASIDE."

She tried to explain how she had a little shrapnel in her foot, and sometimes, but not consistently, it set these things off.

"TAKE OFF YOUR SOCKS."

Apparently she was supposed to have documentation—which she thought she may have known about at some point, but maybe not. Lacking such documentation, they had to see the injury.

"YOUR SOCKS, MA'AM?"

This has gone too far, she thought. She had served her country, and people who had served their countries should not be forced to have bare feet in public! On or about the same time she had gotten the shrapnel in her foot, she had ended up losing her second toe, the long one, the supermodel of the foot. While she knew there were people— good men, men she had served with—who were far more screwed than her, and that she was one of the lucky ones, the absence of toe still looked odd, or more precisely, remarkable. To strangers, a missing appendage was a story, and she was not always in the mood for telling that story. It would almost have been her druthers to have had a more heroic injury, not something she could have gotten from a mildly intense day of gardening. The point was, she didn't like to call attention to her toe (or lack thereof).

And yet, she didn't want to make anyone's job or her life harder, so she took off the socks. Security ran the handheld metal detector over her foot, and they all concluded that it was exactly like she had said in the first place.

"You're lucky you don't have a limp," security said.

"Sure." *It'd be luckier still if I had my toe,* she thought.

"How'd you lose that toe, anyhows?"

She had saved up a few stretchers for situations like this: (1) "born that way," (2) "stubbed it real bad," and (3) (her favorite) "What? I lost my toe?" But she wasn't in the mood for an impromptu round of grab-ass. What she was in the mood for was making security feel as bad as possible about harassing an amputee. So she told the truth. "In the war," she said, as she was pulling her sock back on.

"You a soldier?"

There wasn't time for her to answer because a different member of the Department of Homeland Security was standing over her duffel.

"This your bag?"

"Yessir, something I can help you with?"

"We just need to open it up."

As they rifled through her bag, she was put in mind of the time she had been accused of shoplifting at the mall in Big Rock, Texas. Though she had been guilty of nothing but being young and looking something like a particular girl who *had* been a habitual shoplifter, she had felt like a criminal. Seeing the innards of her backpack spilled out on the concrete floor—crumpled note papers and a waterlogged history book and gum wrappers and fuzzy mints and pens chewed on one end and permission slips she hadn't given her mother—she felt exposed and inclined to confess. She had actually begun to doubt her own innocence. *Was it possible,* she wondered, *to steal something and not even know about it?*

From her duffel, Homeland Security produced a tiny glass snow globe. The globe had been a token from a war buddy and was of sentimental value. Inside the dome was a pile of rocks, and instead of snow, there was sand. On the dome it read, WISH YOU WERE HERE? and then something else on the back in Arabic, which she had never bothered to have translated. She had speculated that it was an answer to the question WISH YOU WERE HERE? Something like, 'CAUSE WE SURE AS SHIT DON'T.

"You can't take this on board."

"Why?"

"'Cause of the liquid. Snow globes aren't allowed on planes."

"Well, this ain't the liquid kind," she said. "Just rocks and sand."

Procedure was procedure. No snow globes over a certain size on planes. There'd been a snow globe memo. There'd been a directive:

Stay the course, folks: no snow globes on domestic flights. They weren't heartless, though. They were willing to make accommodations. They would let her take it aboard if she was willing to find a way to unscrew the dome from the base to prove there wasn't water. That was the best they could do.

"I'm no engineer," she said, "and there's no time on account of that course I just took in remedial line waiting, and eff that anyway—it would destroy the thing."

But that was the best they could do.

She decided to abandon the sand globe in security. "Use it in good health, shitbags," she muttered as she ran to her departure gate. No one heard her. In point of fact, she hadn't really wanted anyone to hear her.

She needn't have bothered rushing. By the time she got to the gate, they'd announced that the plane was delayed, and they didn't anticipate leaving for at least another four hours. In the service, they referred to such a situation as *a serious case of hurry up and wait.* She nudged the man sitting next to her. "A serious case of hurry up and fucking wait, you know?" she said.

He smiled noncommittally, nodded, and turned back to his laptop screen. With his blue chambray button-down, the kind that had enjoyed its heyday around 1994, and his black rolling suitcase, he, too, reminded her of her father. "Sorry about the cussing," she said.

He nodded again but still said nothing.

She felt like buying something to read so she asked him if he would watch her duffel bag.

"Um," he said, "I think that's against the rules. You know." He scanned the room to see if anyone was listening then whispered a single word: "Terrorists."

"Come on, man," she implored. "I'm no terrorist. I'm a soldier, if you want to know."

She went to the gift shop, but all the books were about dying, loving, screwing, or fighting, subjects that had ceased to hold any entertainment value for her. She finally bought an *Us* magazine, which she considered below her intellectual pay rate but sufficient to meet her meager needs: kill some time, stop thinking.

"Thanks for watching my bag," she said upon her return.

The second man who looked like her father nodded and said nothing.

She began reading the magazine. "Jesus," she exclaimed, "Britney Spears is getting divorced!"

"Seems so," said the man.

"Jesus, I have the same birthday as her—December second, same day though I'm two years younger—and we're both from the South, so I, like, feel this girl, you know?" And she did. She liked to hear her news, the same way people appreciated occasional updates about the homecoming queen from high school.

"Uh . . . ,"

"God, poor Brit. Married to some shitbag and two kids and divorced and not even twenty-five yet. Makes me wonder what the hell I've been doing with my time, you know?"

"I'm kind of doing something here," said the man who looked like her father.

"Uh, hey, sorry!

She turned back to her magazine, but it only took her about a half hour to finish the whole thing. She decided to tell the man who looked like her father about the situation back in security. "You know the really funny thing? I was also packing a Twin Towers lighter. You ever seen one of those? OK, it's in real bad taste, so of course all of us who were over there had to have one. The Twin Towers are engraved on the front and when you flip the top to ignite it, it looks like the buildings are on fire. I could have done a hell of a lot more damage with my lighter than with my sand globe, right? Fucking clusterfuck is what it was."

The man closed his laptop screen. "Um, it was . . . nice talking to you." He placed the computer almost lovingly into his black vinyl valise, then zipped the bag shut. "Good luck." He rolled his suitcase into the men's room. She didn't notice when or if he ever came out.

She was still ruminating over Brit and her troubles when they announced boarding.

She was on the two-seat side of the coach section, and for the longest time, it looked as if no one would sit next to her, which would have been ideal. She was having some trouble being among people back then—bizarre moments of intimacy and confession alternated with long, sullen retreats—and when she was in the latter part of the cycle, she didn't like people getting up in her business or questioning her or touching her too much.

Just before the plane doors were locked, a man sat down beside her. He looked like the first man who looked like her father, though it wasn't him. She was beginning to wonder if all business travelers of a certain age looked the same, if her father was *of a class,* a type hopelessly general and forgettable to anyone but the specific children they traumatized. "Whoa," he said, "barely made the flight."

She said nothing. His timing was wrong. She was through with these men who looked like her father. She was through talking for the day. She closed her eyes and rested her head against the plastic window shade.

"So, honey, tell me your life story."

"I'd just like to get some sleep, if you don't mind," she said.

"Aw, come on. You're no fun. I need some entertainment."

"I was born in some shit-kicking town you never heard of, and I went a million miles to some other shit-kicking town, and now I'm going back to the first shit-kicking town. The end."

He didn't take the hint. He thought she was being clever, flirtatious even. "What's the name of this shit-kicking town, darlin'?"

"You never been there," she said.

"Try me."

"What difference does it make?" she asked. "They're all the same."

"Just being friendly," he said.

"I never met a person on a plane who became a lifelong friend, have you?"

"S'pose not," he said. He realized that she hadn't been being clever or flirtatious, so he put on a pair of headphones.

By then, she was no longer tired. She attempted to read the airline's in-flight magazine, but the only thing that struck her fancy was the Sudoku puzzle, and someone had already done it. She snuck a sidelong glance at her seat mate's pouch to determine if he was in possession of a virgin copy. That was when she noticed a woman in a burka sitting across the row and promptly passed out.

Patsy had been having similar episodes for the last two months. It wasn't like she thought the woman was a terrorist. It was just stress, she supposed. And fatigue. And a stomach that had suddenly turned weak on her. In any case, the blackouts had been pretty damned inconvenient when she was driving a truck in a war zone, but they were fine and even good while a passenger on a plane. When she woke up, she was in Chattanooga, a mere thirty minutes from good old Fort Living Room AKA home.

Patsy on the Road

HER HUSBAND WAS waiting for her just outside arrivals in the penlike area reserved for the nonticketed mob. The first thing she noticed was how fat he looked, and she wondered if he was thinking the same about her.

"You look good, babe," he said. "Healthy."

She presumed that meant fat.

"You look like shit, Mags." She swatted him on the ass.

He came in for a kiss, but at the last second, she couldn't. She just couldn't kiss or even consent to be kissed. She dodged him and asked him where he had parked.

"You wanna drive, Patsy?"

"Nah, I been driving for months."

"You're limping a little," he observed.

"Not too much."

"Car's on level B of the garage," he said. "Stairs or elevator?"

"Elevator," she replied. "No, stairs."

"Well, I wanna take the elevator," he said upon arriving at the parking garage. "Your bag's heavy as doomsday."

"Fine, I'll meet you up there."

She opened the door that led to the stairwell while Magnum pressed the UP button for the elevator. The door swung shut behind her, and though he did not follow, Magnum yelled, "Why're you always making things so difficult for yourself, woman?"

ON THE PASSENGER seat was a basket of Betsy Ross snack cakes. "What're those for?" she asked.

"Aw, you know, in case you get hungry. It's a long ride back to Buckstop."

"Damn, Magnum, you know how I feel about Betsy Rosses!" She despised the Betsy Ross Snack Cake Company. Her grievances included their so-called "health" granola bars, which contained 67 percent fat, and their use of animal by-products, which she found completely hypocritical in a company that was run by a sect of Christians who advocated a vegetarian lifestyle.

"Yeah, I know, I know. But I got this friend who's working there now, so I get a lot of free stuff."

She looked at his belly. "I can tell."

"Yeah, reckon I put on a few."

"A few? You're gonna be one of those fat-ass gym teachers all the kids are laughing at behind their backs." Her husband was indeed a gym teacher. When she told people what he did for a living, she usually omitted the word *gym.*

"All right, Patsy."

"Magnum, I could be on a mother eff'n desert island, and I wouldn't eat that crap."

"OK."

"Lord, it's making me queasy even looking at 'em."

Her husband picked up the snack cake basket and set it tenderly on the backseat. He was chuckling in a way that had always annoyed her—softly as if asking her permission to laugh.

"What's so damn funny?" she asked.

"Before, you said dessert island. Like, an island filled with desserts, you—"

"Yeah, I get it."

"Thought you might appreciate the word play is all." Magnum nodded and started the car. She told him she wanted to rest, and that's what she pretended to do until they were almost back to Buckstop.

In all the years she had lived in Buckstop, she had found precious little to recommend it. The town's only attractions were the Buckstop Church of Sabbath Day Adventists, three schools (all run by the church), a handful of government traffic lights, the Betsy Ross factory, which was also owned by the church, a sign that let you know when you'd arrived, and another sign saying you'd left. She didn't think the church owned the signs, but she wouldn't have been shocked to discover the opposite was true, either. The first sign said YOU ARE ENTERING BUCK-STOP: IN GOD WE TRUST and featured a carving of a deer's head and antlers. The sign to leave looked nearly identical except it depicted the deer from behind, and its message was YOU ARE LEAVING BUCKSTOP: DRIVE CAREFULLY, LIVE PRAYERFULLY. While the leaving sign did not specifically mention God, she had always felt that the implication was *God help you if you are so foolish as to leave Buckstop.* Besides Christians, the other thing Buckstop had was deer, which of course had been the inspiration for the town's name.

She knew everyone there, and everyone knew her. And if they didn't know her, they certainly knew her father, who had become the town minister five years earlier, following the death of the old one and after Roger's own epic midlife crisis. The church was the big show in Buckstop, and her father was a rock star. Not long after his appointment, she had begun referring to him as "Pastor Dad."

They were just driving past the YOU ARE ENTERING BUCKSTOP sign when a deer ran out in front of the car.

"MAGNUM!" Patsy yelled.

"What?"

She could tell he didn't see it. It was late and maybe he thought it was part of the sign come to life; she didn't know and there wasn't time to figure it out. She reached over Magnum and grabbed the steering wheel. Her instincts were quick from all those months driving in the desert.

Magnum pulled the car the rest of the way over to the side of the road, and they sat there without saying anything for a spell. The deer regarded them, and they regarded the deer. As it lacked antlers, Patsy decided it must be a doe. She thought it might have been with child because it looked rather thick through the middle. She didn't get a long enough look to be sure, because Magnum turned off the headlights and the doe bolted.

"Deer in the headlights," he said. "You know, Patsy? *Deer. In. The. Headlights.*" He laughed. It was probably nervous laughter, but she took it the wrong way. Maybe she was just in the mood for fighting.

"You're a fucking idiot," she said to him.

"What?" he said.

"You think it's a goddamn laugh riot to nearly kill a living creature?"

"Aw hell's bells, Patsy-cake. You know I don't think that. I was only trying to release tension, right?"

She said nothing.

"The thing is, Patsy, there's an overpopulation problem. It's throughout the whole county. You wouldn't know it, 'cause you've been gone a long time. And people are even allowed to shoot them, but no one'll shoot in Buckstop, 'cause your father and the SDAs won't allow it. So, all the deer are coming to Buckstop."

"That ain't no excuse, Magnum. You ought to be watching for them!"

"Yeah, it was that dumb sign that confounded me."

"Who's your friend?"

"What? What friend?"

"The friend who's working at Betsy Ross? The one who's trying to fatten you up like a goddamned Thanksgiving turkey."

"No one you would know," he said after a pause she considered noteworthy.

"I know everyone you know."

"Not everyone. Not anymore."

"Mm-hmm."

"You been gone a long time, Pats."

He was about to restart the car when she realized she had to throw up again. She got out of the car and christened the Tennessee soil.

As she was vomiting, she thought about Britney Spears and whether the girl felt like an asshole for having married that jerk in the first place. Like all her friends and her family saying he was bad news and all of them having been exactly right. This line of thought led right back to her own husband. How he was probably having an affair with someone who worked at the Betsy Ross factory, the pride of Buckstop, Tennessee, the fifth-biggest snack cake factory in the US of A. He was probably having an affair with someone who wore a hairnet for at least eight hours a day. But whatever—she really had been gone a long time.

"You OK?" he asked.

"Motion sickness," she claimed. "FUCK! FUUUCCCKKK! I FUCKING HATE THROWING UP!"

"When'd you start cursing so much?"

She shrugged. "Always cursed a lot."

"Yeah. S'pose it just never bothered me before."

Back on the road, Patsy considered the question *Had her years in the service made her foulmouthed or had she always been foulmouthed?* In trying to answer it, she was put in mind of a certain man with whom she had served. They had called him Smartie because he'd gone to West Point and, even more suspicious than that, could often be found reading. Worse, his selections had never been on the Typical (Male) Soldier Reading List, which she had observed to be limited to pornography,

the Bible, and *Tuesdays with Morrie*. The first time she noticed his pre-
dilection, for instance, he was reading *Tristram Shandy,* which wasn't
something they read in her part of the world. The title had sounded
clever to her, like ivy on a wall or bare skin under a pleated woolen
kilt. When she asked him what the book was about, he replied, "How
we can't escape the circumstances of our birth." She'd liked that phrase,
"the circumstances of our birth," and had often repeated it to herself.

"You're quiet. What you thinking about, Pats?" Magnum asked.

"Nothing," she said. "Well, you ever read a book called *Tristram
Shandy?*"

Magnum shook his head. "Was I supposed to?"

Smartie had been in Special Operations, and she had sometimes
shared a truck with him during her second tour when she had started
working as what they called a lioness. (Muslim women didn't necessarily take to being handled by American male soldiers, so Patsy's
job had been to act as a female go-between.) Her first or second night
partnered with Smartie, he had said to her, "You're one of those girl
soldiers who likes to show how tough she is by cursing up a red
storm, am I right?"

She couldn't disagree.

"An honorary man."

"Listen, Smartie," she had said, "I'm five foot one. I gotta be fierce."

AS THEY WERE pulling into the driveway, her husband said, "Uh,
Patsy? There're some folks at the house. It was gonna be a surprise,
but you don't exactly seem in the mood for surprises."

"Hell, Magnum." She thought she had been very clear. She had
told him several times, both in e-mail and on the phone, "NO
goddamn homecoming." Unfortunately, he had assumed her edict was
of the particular feminine variety that was meant to be ignored: e.g.,
"You don't have to buy me anything for my birthday" or "Have a good
time with your friends."

She asked him if he could call the whole thing off, but it was too late. Her flight had been so delayed that the guests were already waiting.

"It's not like this big thing," he assured her. "Just Lacey, and the Pharm, and—"

"Not Mrs. Pastor, right?"

He shook his head.

"Or Pastor Dad, obviously."

"I . . . ," he began. "Your mom said she'd see you later, and your dad said he'd see you in church."

Her shirt was speckled with vomit, and the fly of her jeans was being held together by a safety pin. She was in no mood to see people. "I told you I didn't want no goddamn homecoming."

"Well, we ain't gonna give you a crown, Patsy."

Despite herself, she laughed. By then, she'd grown tired of busting her husband's balls anyhow, or maybe she was just tired. She told him to go in first and that she'd follow in about five minutes, after she'd changed her shirt. Once he'd left, she dug through her duffel bag, found a relatively clean T-shirt, and changed into it. There was nothing left to be done in terms of her beautification, but she still couldn't bring herself to leave the car. She just sat there, wishing that her husband had left the keys in the ignition, because then she'd drive somewhere and maybe she'd never come back.

After a half hour, her husband emerged from the house with arms raised in inquiry. She rolled down the car window and claimed she'd had a blackout, which wasn't true, but could have been.

As he moved to open the car door, she resisted the urge to lock him out.

"Nice shirt," he said.

The shirt had LET THE MOTHERF*CKERS BURN across the front.

"Nice sentiment."

"It was a gift."

"From who?"

"Some buddy of mine. He got his face blown off."

"I can send everyone home if you want, honey." She could tell he just wanted her to get the hell out of the car and go inside.

"That'd be great," she said.

"But it'd be better if you just came in for a few minutes and said hi. Then I'll tell everyone you're tired and that'll be that. Everyone's real excited to see you, Patsy."

"I am tired," she said.

Patsy among Friends

SHE THOUGHT THE festivities were a cross between a business meeting and a trip to a wax museum; perhaps, a wake. In any case, she felt conspicuously *not* the life of the party. For most of the evening, she was stilted and had trouble talking to more than one person at a time. Her eyes kept drifting to her wrist to rest upon a watch she no longer had. She had left it Over There, but she still had tan lines from where the watch had been.

"Jesus, Helen, thanks for coming all this way," Patsy said at the sight of her sister. She and Helen had never been close owing to the ten-year age gap between them, and she had not expected her there.

"Well, I'm not gonna be able to make it back for Thanksgiving or Christmas, but I still wanted to see you, Patsy."

"S'pose you want me to ask why you ain't coming back for the holidays," Patsy said.

"Really, Patsy . . . Must you speak that way? We all appreciate how tough you are."

"So, why *aren't* you coming back?"

"Well," Helen said with a knowing grin, "can't you tell?"

Patsy had no idea and was not inclined to guess.

"I'm pregnant, you retard," Helen said as she smacked Patsy playfully on the side of her head. "Five and a half months. In a couple of weeks, I won't even be able to fly." She lifted up her shirt and stuck Patsy's hand against the bare skin of her belly, which was soft and round. It occurred to Patsy that the belly was unlike anything else on Helen that had ever been or would probably ever be again.

"Goddamn, you're still skinny as anything. I'm probably bigger than you," Patsy said. She immediately regretted this comment as it potentially revealed more than she was prepared to discuss.

She needn't have worried. Helen was more interested in regaling Patsy with stories of her fertility woes than contemplating her little sister's subtext. According to Helen, she and Elliot had been trying to get pregnant nearly as long as they'd been married, but no dice. So, Helen had gone to a fancy fertility doctor ("Patsy, he was on *Good Morning America*!"), and it turned out that a four-pound cyst was blocking one of her fallopian tubes. She had had the growth removed, but even then, the television doctor hadn't known if she would be able to conceive. They continued with the expensive fertility treatments—"I honestly could have bought another house for what we spent!"—but still no luck. "I'd just about made peace with the idea of adoption. I'd started looking into the idea of getting one of those Katrina orphans, because, you know, they need homes, too. But then: a miracle!"

"Not for the Katrina kid," Patsy said.

"Seriously, Patsy. If you and Magnum ever try to conceive, you ought to get yourself checked out for this cyst thing, PCOS, first. It's hereditary."

"Uh, yeah . . ." Patsy suspected fertility problems were one more thing she and her sister wouldn't share.

"Mom and Dad wanted to come, but—"

"No, they didn't."

"Well, maybe not Roger, but Mom really did want to see you. And the Prodigal"—that's what Helen occasionally called their brother, though Patsy felt more deserving of the title than him—"was even planning to fly in from New York, but he had to work. He sent you those flowers, though." Helen indicated a box of tulips that were busily dying on the sofa.

At that moment, Patsy's sister-in-law, Lacey, arrived. Both Magnum and his sister had been named for 1980s television shows. Patsy supposed it could have been worse; she could have ended up married to the Fonz. "Hey, Patsy honey, welcome home! Sorry I'm so late. Had to stay at the Slick for the November push." Lacey was still wearing her orange Slickmart smock, which put Patsy in mind of the latest styles from Gitmo. "Someone ought to put those flowers in water before they completely expire. Hi, Helen! How you been? You're glowing, honey." Patsy admired her sister-in-law's efficiency—she had managed to kiss Patsy on the cheek, remove the flowers from the couch, and alienate Helen in under half a minute.

"I would have arranged them for you," Helen said, "but I wanted you to see what an expensive box they came in. Besides, it's rude to mess with people's flowers before they've even seen them."

At some point, Patsy became aware of the Pharm, formerly Marcus, still Magnum's best friend. Pharm had acquired the nickname because he was the number one drug dealer in Buckstop—he mainly sold marijuana, but he was willing to fill prescriptions, too. Pharm had also been responsible for introducing Patsy to her husband at Christian Soldiers Bible Camp. Eight years later, she had mostly forgiven him for that.

Pharm emerged from wherever he'd been hiding himself and whispered in Patsy's ear, "I got a little something for you after Helen drives Minnie home. A modest celebration now that you're out for good, you know?" Minnie, short for Minerva, was Pharm's little sister.

"Minnie's here?" Patsy asked.

"Turn around," the Pharm said.

The last time Patsy had been home, Minnie had still been more girl than woman, but in the intervening eleven months, that ratio had reversed itself. "Man," Patsy said to her, "you've grown up."

The girl laughed and said, "Well, I'm a junior now, Patsy. It happens."

During the first year or two of her marriage, Patsy had spent many an evening babysitting Minnie when Magnum and the Pharm were out being boys. Minnie's parents had died, leaving Pharm as the girl's primary caregiver. Though she had never wanted children of her own, Patsy felt almost maternal toward Minnie and assumed the girl was the closest she'd ever get to having a hand in raising someone.

She pulled Minnie over to the blue velour couch and said, "Tell me everything. Don't leave out the dirty parts, either."

Minnie giggled, which, in the manner of girls her age, was a perfectly suitable response to most anything. "I'm real sorry, Patsy, but it's a school night . . . And with your plane being so late . . ."

"Sure, I get it. Some other time."

Then the girl threw Patsy a bone. "I'm Mary in this Christmas thingy at the church. I know you're not much for the whole church-going business anymore, but you could come if you wanted. It's the Saturday after Thanksgiving."

"She's good," the Pharm added.

"He's just saying that 'cause he's my brother and he's being nice."

"Patsy knows I'm not nice, little sister," Pharm said. "I saw Minnie rehearsing."

Patsy promised the girl she'd attend. "I'm mostly nice," said Patsy, "and I'll tell you you're good whether you are or not."

Lacey returned with the arranged flowers. "Your brother must be doing well for himself," she said. "These are real pretty, Patsy."

"I told her that, too," Helen said.

"Yeah," Patsy said, "best thing that ever happened to him, being disowned."

"Oh hey, honey, I been meaning to mention. I could hook you up with a job at the Slickmart if you were interested. There're several different departments hiring right now."

Slickmart Superstore was the greater Buckstop region's answer to Wal-Mart. The store was a fifteen-minute drive from Buckstop, and it was where everyone from the town bought most everything. Need an inflatable dragon for the pool? Go to the Slickmart. Need a gun to shoot yourself in the head? Slickmart! They all called it the *Suckmart* because that's what it looked like in all caps with the *L* and *I* jammed up like a *U* on the sign:

SLICKMART
SUCKMART

They also called the Slickmart the Suckmart because popular opinion held that the store sucked. *Yeah,* Patsy thought, *I'd eff'n kill myself before I worked at the Suck.* Besides, she was planning to go back to college in the summer with the help of Uncle Sam and the GI bill, and she was reasonably sure that the last chunk of her earnings plus what she'd managed to save would carry her until then.

Lacey hugged Patsy again and then she sniffed her. "You smell like something sweet." Lacey sniffed Patsy more deeply and then her nose wrinkled. "Like barf, honey."

"I guess I had a little motion sickness on the way in," Patsy said.

"You guess?" Lacey's eyes wandered the length of Patsy's body. She paused rather too long in the midsection for Patsy's liking, and Patsy reflexively placed a hand on her abdomen.

It's too early for me to be showing, Patsy thought.

She knows, Patsy thought.

She wondered if Lacey would tell Magnum, then decided she didn't much care. *Go ahead,* she thought. *Save me the trouble.*

"Well, let me know about the Slickmart," Lacey said, her voice consciously light. "They'll be hiring extras through the Christmas season, all right?"

"Will do."

Lacey yawned. "I've been stocking since five AM, so reckon I'll head out now, if you don't mind. Magnum says you're real tired, too." She pulled Patsy into an embrace. "Take care of yourself, honey."

Not long after that, Helen and Minnie left, too. "Will I see you again?" Patsy asked Helen. No. Her sister was flying back to Texas the next day.

The only people left were Pharm and her husband. It occurred to Patsy that it was basically like her senior year of high school all over again. She was down a toe, but other than that, nothing had changed. Even the blue velour La-Z-Boy sofa was the same one from high school—it had formerly belonged to Magnum's father. She thought it might have been given to them as a wedding present and wondered if she still owed the man a thank-you note.

Pharm took the marijuana out of his fanny pack and started rolling a joint. "I got this special for you. It's government engineered, which is an irony I thought you'd appreciate, Patsy my dear."

"We thank you kindly, Uncle Sam," Magnum said.

"Guaranteed to give you a sweet high without any annoying paranoia. I'm gonna say a prayer, if you don't mind," Pharm said. He'd spent a semester or two in divinity school before having to come home to take care of Minnie and deciding to "pursue other opportunities." It was during that brief academic stint that he had acquired the habit of praying before getting baked. He set the joint on the table and bowed his head. "Dear Lord, we humbly thank you for the sweet sweetness of this high we are about to receive. We also thank you for the safe return of Patsy from Iraq.

> *We thank thee, Lord, for happy hearts,*
> *For rain and sunny weather.*
> *We thank thee, Lord, for this pot,*
> *And that today we are together.*

"Amen," said her husband. "Now, let's get stoned!"

Pharm lit the cigarette and, ever the gentleman, offered it to Patsy first. She shook her head.

"That ain't like you," Magnum commented. "I thought you'd be gagging for it."

She told him that she might have to take one last military medical exam, so she wanted to keep her system clean.

The Pharm looked at her. "Real sorry, Patsy. I thought you were through with all that now you're discharged and all."

"We can go smoke out back, if you want," Magnum offered.

"Nah, it's fine." While watching the boys pass the cigarette back and forth, she considered her options. She was two and a half months pregnant—not showing yet—but she knew she'd have to make a move soon, one way or the other. She only saw two alternatives: (1) seduce her husband and lie a whole lot or (2) become "one of them baby murderers," as her Grandma Fran used to say. In her father's church, the second was the worse sin by far. In her head, the first seemed harder to live with.

"Hey Magnum?" she asked.

"Yeah."

"Where's Scout?" Scout was her dog. He was part Jack Russell terrier, part Saint Bernard, and mostly of indeterminate origin. He had short legs and a thick muscular torso and had always seemed to her more donkey than dog. With all the homecoming business, it had just occurred to her that her dog hadn't yet put in an appearance.

Magnum inhaled deeply from the joint before he spoke. "He's dead."

"What?"

"He died about six months ago. I didn't want to tell you over the e-mail, babe."

"What?"

"He run out in traffic. He—"

"You let him run out in traffic, didn't you? You *know* he needed to be supervised."

"That's not what went down, I swear."

"Calm down, Patsy," the Pharm said.

"Were YOU here?" She turned toward the Pharm. "Were you two shit-bird losers sitting on this very sofa getting stoned while Scout run out in traffic?"

The Pharm shook his head.

"Jesus H. Christ! The only thing I fucking ask of you is to watch my fucking dog!"

She put her head between her legs and started whispering the military alphabet to herself, which was something she found herself doing during times of stress. "Alpha. Bravo. Charlie . . ."

"Don't cry, Patsy," Magnum said. "He weren't young, and he lived a good life."

"I'm not crying! I'm reciting the goddamn NATO phonetic alphabet!" she yelled. "And I'm just trying not to kill you is all. Delta. Echo. Foxtrot."

After a while, the Pharm put his hands on her shoulders. "We honored him, Patsy. We knew that'd be important to you. He's out back, if you want to go see."

"Golf. Hotel. India. Juliet . . . Juliet . . . Juliet . . ."

"Kilo," the Pharm added helpfully.

"I know what it is. I was just deciding if I wanted to go out back and pay my respects to Scout."

She decided that she did. Both boys offered to accompany her, but she wanted to be alone.

"He's under the apple tree. There's a little wooden cross," the Pharm called out. "You better take a flashlight."

She went out back to the apple tree. She turned on the flashlight and directed it toward the homemade cross that Magnum had fashioned out of two rulers. Patsy assumed he had stolen the rulers from the school where he worked. On a strip of tape, her husband had paid tribute to her cur in Sharpie: "Here lies Scout. He was a good dog."

He had been a good dog. Had she the ability to cry, she could imagine having done so then. She turned away from the grave and started heading back to the house. That's when she noticed the backyard.

What was left of it.

The hole was epic. More properly called a quarry, she supposed. So much sand and dirt and rocks everywhere that for one awful second she almost thought she was back in the shit.

"MAGNUM!" she yelled.

He came running. "Jesus, Patsy, what is it? It's after midnight. You're gonna wake all the neighbors!"

"Explain this." She gestured toward the hole.

"It was a surprise."

It had been that. "Explain why our backyard looks like goddamned Fallujah."

Her husband had been planning to build her a pool as a coming-home present, but the contractor had bailed in the middle of operations. Until all this was resolved, they were stuck with a big hole and a pile of rocks. He smiled at her bashfully and said, "I know how you love the water, babe."

She didn't bother pointing out the obvious: that there wasn't any water there, only rocks.

Patsy in Bed

SHE WAS SICK, sick of smelling herself—puke, stale air, marijuana, dirt, *swass and swalls*—so even though it was almost two in the morning, she took a shower, and after that was done, she took a bath, too.

If she could have chosen any job barring qualifications or the irritating impositions of reality, she would have chosen mermaid. While in Iraq, she had often reflected that she would have much preferred to have been in World War II. Then she would have been at Normandy and that was an "eff'n beach." In an e-mail to her husband, she had joked that she was so dry Over There, she worried she would turn into Lot's wife.

As she ran her bath, she thought what a miracle it was to just be able to turn a tap and have water come out of it. She almost felt Christlike. She was thinking of all the places in the world where one couldn't just flip a tap or pump a well, places where there wasn't any water at all. She hated to think of those dry, dry folks.

She sat in the bath, probably for an hour, but it might have been longer, and as her skin became increasingly wrinkled, she decided that if she could choose a way to die, she'd definitely want to drown.

Smartie had once said that there was a word for people like her: *hygrophilous*. At first, she had thought he meant something offensive relating to either her sexual preference or general butchness, but then she had looked the word up in her pocket travel dictionary. (The Buckstop SDAs had given her a gift set that included a dictionary and a Bible before she'd left for basic training.) It turned out that *hygrophilous* meant moisture-loving or a plant that grows best in the damp. Yes, that was her.

"Patsy, you fall in?" her husband called from the other room.

"I'm just taking a bath," she said. She stuck her head under the water and tried to calculate how long she could hold her breath.

Ninety-three seconds later she got out of the tub.

She put on what she thought was the least provocative outfit possible: an XL black T-shirt she'd had since the seventh grade, with the words JUST SAY NO splashed in a come-hither fashion across the front, and rainbow-striped woolen toe socks. It amused her how one of the toe shafts just hung there like a discarded condom, and she speculated how long it would take Magnum to notice that a part of her was absent without leave.

He was already under the covers when she got into bed, but he didn't start talking until she'd turned off the light. Patsy's lengthy ablutions had left him time to reflect and anticipate.

"Sorry about the yard," he whispered. "I'm gonna get it fixed ASAP."

"Great," she said.

"And the dog, too."

"OK, Mags. Let's just talk about it in the morning."

"You smell nice, Patsy. Real sweet." He spooned her and stuck his hand up her JUST SAY NO T-shirt.

"Hey," she said, "I'm tired."

"You don't have to do nothing 'cept lay there, Patsy."

She might have just let him have his way with her, but then he started running his foot up and down her leg.

"You're gonna get hot in those socks, babe," he said. With his foot, he pushed her sock down to her ankle.

"Get the hell off," she said. She would not be forced to take off her socks for the second time in twenty-four hours.

She flipped him onto his back, straddled him, and pointed her fore- and middle fingers at his eyes. "Make one more move and I'll blind you."

"You wouldn't do that," he laughed.

"Try me."

"You on top. Actually kind of sexy."

"I am not kidding, Magnum French."

He blinked, and his eyelashes grazed the tips of her fingers. "Fine," he said.

She rolled off of him and over to her own side of the bed.

"I just haven't seen my wife in a real long time is all."

She flicked on the bedside lamp. "Are we talking or sleeping?"

"Both, I reckon."

"Well, that ain't physically possible." She grabbed her pillow and told him she would sleep on the sofa.

She stalked out to the living room. The couch still reeked of pot, but she didn't care.

She had mostly fallen asleep when she was awoken by her husband. "You can't blame me for wanting to be with my wife."

"I'm asleep!"

"It's just . . . It's not right. You can't make me out to be some asshole for wanting to sleep with my wife!"

"OK," she said. "Your desire to fornicate is perfectly natural and understandable. Now, can't I please just go to sleep?" She was start- ing to feel desperate with tiredness.

"But why don't you want to? We always sleep together the night you come back."

"Because I been traveling all day. Because there's a big eff'n hole in my backyard. Because I just found out my dog is dead. Because we almost hit a deer with the car. Because I ain't used to sleeping with people no more. Because it's two in the morning, Magnum. It's two in the eff'n morning!"

He nodded. "So, it's definitely not 'cause of that thing you said before about me eating too many Betsy Rosses?"

She threw her pillow at him. "Oh, for God's sake, let me rest, will you?"

Like the deer of earlier, he stared at her in the darkness without moving. "Well, you have a good night, then, Miss Patsy," he said before returning to the bedroom.

She had to get back up to retrieve her pillow from across the room, and in so doing, she woke herself up.

She turned on the television. It had been a while since she'd been in command of a remote.

After circling through the channels, she settled on *E! True Hollywood Story,* "Britney Spears." The girl was everywhere.

Patsy hadn't realized that things had gotten so bad for Brit that the pop star merited an *E! True Hollywood Story.* One minute into the program, Brit was a Mouseketeer, the next minute she had a snake around her neck, the next minute she was kissing Madonna, and only one little commercial break later, she was barefoot and pregnant at a gas station. *And neither of us twenty-five yet,* Patsy thought, just before drifting off.

She woke in the morning with a crick in her neck from sleeping on the sofa. Her husband was standing over her clad in the green and gold Buckstop Academy gymsuit that constituted his business attire.

"Sorry about last night," he said.

"Gymsuit's looking a little snug there," she replied.

"Yeah, think I left it in the dryer too long."

"Maybe that's it, moose knuckles."

"You don't exactly look skeletal yourself, Patsy," he said.

She snorted at that. "It's all muscle."

"Mine, too."

"Wanna arm wrestle me?" She put her arm palm up on the coffee table.

"I don't want to have to crush you, woman."

"You won't."

"Seriously?" he said.

They both got on their knees and put their elbows on the faux wood coffee table.

He was stronger than she'd anticipated, so she fought dirty and twisted his wrist a little.

"Hey, you're fucking hurting me, Patsy!"

She twisted his wrist a little more and then she slammed his fist into the table.

"I win," she said.

AFTER HE LEFT, it occurred to her that it might have been wise to have slept with him the previous night, if only to have begun the charade that the sweet little parasite inside her might conceivably be his.

She meant to get off the couch that day—maybe take a drive or go for a run or call the VA office—but somehow it never happened. Instead, she watched all the morning talk shows and by the time that was done, it was afternoon, which seemed too late for the commencement of pursuits more ambitious. She made one more circuit around the channels, and found a show she'd never heard of called *Antiques Roadshow*. At first, she found it about as stimulating as watching her husband tweeze his nose hairs, but then, without warning, she was hooked. The segment that did it was a million-year-old guy with a million-year-old gravy boat. The gravy boat was worth $32,000 because it had belonged to none other than General William Tecumseh Sherman.

It occurred to Patsy that she, too, had a ton of junk—more than she knew what to do with, in point of absolute fact—and she wondered if she, too, might be harboring a $32,000 gravy boat. She roused herself from the sofa in order to go comb through her kitchen cabinets.

All she found was a collection of chipped Fiestaware, a bequest of Magnum's dead mother.

She hadn't eaten since yesterday, so she looked for rations instead. The refrigerator was empty except for a chunk of rapidly graying cheese.

Next to the fridge was the walk-in pantry, and what she found there disturbed her. Magnum was hoarding a lifetime supply of Betsy Ross snack cakes. There were All-American Bars, Chooey Gooey Brownies, Choco-Nutsy Bars, Sunny Plops, etcetera. He had the whole product line. If this had been his primary sustenance since her last trip home, it was no wonder he looked like the Michelin Man.

She had worked at Betsy Ross during the winter of her senior year. (Most everyone from Buckstop ended up working there at some point or another.) It was during that stretch that she and her husband had ended up getting back together for good.

Patsy had found several mouse droppings near the brownie batter machine, and she had told the supervisor, who, in turn, had told her to mind her own business.

"You really don't care that there might be shit in the brownies?" she'd asked.

The supervisor had shrugged.

"You won't even, like, investigate it?"

He wouldn't.

She quit. She was seventeen—it wasn't like she had a mortgage or car payments.

Magnum had overheard what had happened so he decided to quit with her. He offered her a ride home. They bitched the whole way about how disgusting their former employer had been.

"That time Arthur Proops lost his finger in the separator, and no one would even stop the assembly line!"

"I once saw some guys jacking off into the whipped cream machine! I tell you, there ain't a more disgusting animal by-product than that!"

"And those health bars are like seventy-six percent fat!"

At some point, she had asked him if he was going to regret quitting his job—unlike her, he *did* have car payments.

"Naw," he had replied. "I'd been looking for a reason to leave for a while." They were stopped at a traffic light, so he turned to look at Patsy. "And I knew you'd be needing a ride."

By then, she'd already broken up with him twice: once, because she'd been in "stupid puppy love" in Texas, and again, because she thought Magnum had gotten too clingy after she'd consented to relations with him at Bible camp. In truth, she'd always thought Magnum was not quite enough. Not smart enough. Not aggressive enough. Not impulsive enough. Not enough. That afternoon at Betsy Ross had forced her to reconsider her initial findings.

A year later, they were married.

She closed the door on Magnum's Betsy Ross stash and returned to the living room for another episode of *Antiques Roadshow*.

Around eight, Magnum came home with an entirely chicken-free meal from Kentucky Fried Chicken. Patsy still didn't eat meat, out of habit, not religious observation. After KFC, he went into the kitchen and called to her, "I'm having a Betsy Ross. You want?"

"No."

He returned with an All-American Bar, which was essentially a chemically preserved pound cake coated in patriotic-hued lard.

"Say, Magnum, what's with the pantry?"

"What about it?"

"Why do we got enough Betsy Rosses to get us through the end of days?"

"Just stuff I got for free." He delicately peeled off the cellophane wrapper.

"From your friend?" she asked.

"Yeah," he said. He started licking off the frosting. "About that. It's actually Pharm's girlfriend who works there."

"Jesus Christ. Pharm's got a girl! What's she like?" In all the years she had known him, the Pharm had never expressed much interest in that sort of thing.

"I don't know. She's, uh, a girl." He bit off the first half of the denuded pound cake.

"Yeah?"

"She, uh, works at the Betsy Ross factory." Magnum popped the rest of the cake into his mouth.

"Yeah, you mentioned that already."

"I don't know, Patsy. He don't like to talk about it that much. You know how secretive he can be."

At 11:35, *Letterman* came on, and the guest was Al Franken, who Patsy remembered from *Saturday Night Live*. Al did a bit about visiting the troops in Iraq. He described seeing a posting entitled, "Suggestions for Soldiers Making a Phone Call Home." "Number one," he read, "ask how your loved one is doing BEFORE you ask about your car or boat."

Magnum asked her if she had ever seen the list.

"Not that one specifically. But stuff like it, I guess."

"'Cause it's funny. You always used to ask about your car before anything else!"

"That ain't true, Magnum!"

"Yeah, it is. It was always, did you make the payment? Did you remember to get it washed? And you better not be driving it neither if you know what's good for you!"

"That's not true."

But she didn't know. It might have been.

After Dave, Magnum said he was going to bed. "You coming?"

She told him that she thought she'd stay up a bit longer.

"You going for some sort of TV watching record, Patsy?"

"Yeah, better call up the Guinness people," she said.

Patsy Pays the Bills

THE NEWS PISSED her off, but she watched most everything else, and her days became a series of agreeably anesthetic sound bites:

Leshawn, you are . . .not . . .the father.

Jerry! Jerry! Jerry!

Come on down!

You teach people how to treat you.

John Tra-Vol-Ta!

Gimmee Gimmee Gimmee.

In other Brangelina news . . .

She nearly dropped *her baby.*

The tribe has spoken.

What's next for the Boy Wizard?

It might have gone on like that forever, except one morning she was interrupted while watching the 11 AM *Maury Povich* (there was also a 1 PM). About four times a week, Maury did shows featuring paternity tests, and these tests had become Patsy's favorite thing in the whole viewing universe. She appreciated the black-and-whiteness of the tests—someone was either the father or he wasn't. Mystery solved. She also appreciated Maury's showmanship, particularly the dramatic pause he took before revealing whether a man was a father or a fool.

She was in the middle of watching such a program when the cable cut out. The interruption happened at a most inconvenient time for Patsy—just as Maury was saying, "ANFERNEE, YOU ARE—" Though she knew the gesture was likely futile, she banged the side of the television just in case it was the kind of problem that responded to force.

She tried to call Magnum on his cell, but the phone went straight to voice mail. She dug around the house until she found the number for the cable company, and after spending an age on hold, an operator came on the line and informed her that no one had paid the cable bill for three months.

"There's got to be some sort of mistake," Patsy said. "Can't I just put a check in the mail right this instant?"

"No." The account was "seriously delinquent," though Patsy was welcome to pay by credit card. "You'd best do it today on account of the holiday weekend 'cause otherwise your cable'll be turned off through the Friday after Thanksgiving," the operator said.

How had it gotten to be Thanksgiving. "You didn't happen to be watching *Maury*, did you?" Patsy asked.

"No, ma'am. I've been working."

Patsy found her credit card, and about a half hour later, service was restored. Anfernee and his paramour Ayesha were long gone by then—he was either the baby's daddy or another goddamn cuckold; she would never know now. Although Patsy was a mere twenty-three minutes from the second *Maury* of the day, she didn't feel her usual enthusiasm. The whole episode with the cable company had left her uneasy. She wondered what else her husband had been neglecting to pay.

She decided to dig around the house a bit. The usual: mortgage, car payment, and credit card statements. Magnum had taken no pains to hide them. If she hadn't been in such a foul mood, she might have even been touched by how organized he had left things. After skimming the documents, she concluded that Magnum had indeed been experiencing financial difficulties. Although he was current on most everything (except cable which he must not have considered a neccessity), he had made several late payments across various accounts over the last year. She found a credit card bill that said they owed $17,000 and another one where they owed $13,000. She found the paperwork for that stupid pool he'd been trying to build for her. He had paid a $3,000 deposit on it in January, right after she'd last been home, but then he'd never paid the rest. A letter detailed the whole fiasco: the pool was going to cost more than the original estimate due to an "unanticipated number of rocks in the backyard."

She located their bank statements last. All her money from the military—her paychecks (paltry though they were), her enlistment bonus money, the re-up money that she'd been paid to date—should have been in there. Approximately $24,000 from her added to whatever Magnum had managed to save from his job at the school.

The account was nearly depleted. They had $997.97.

By the time she'd gone through all of this, she'd missed the second *Maury,* and it was well into the 2 PM *Antiques Roadshow.* She watched that, but again, did not feel her usual enthusiasm. A little girl brought her great-grandmother's paper doll collection, and the paper doll collection was worth . . .

Eleven hundred dollars. Nothing spectacular, but more money than she and Magnum had, put together. The paper dolls would have been worth a whopping $1,500 if the girl hadn't been such a fool as to have played with them.

Where had the money gone? Aside from the hole in the backyard, Patsy detected no physical improvements to the house. If anything, it was more of a wreck than the last time she'd been home: soiled and mismatched furniture, cracks in the ceiling, a kitchen that had been the height of modernity fifty years prior, a sinister black mark underneath the apple-printed bathroom wallpaper, etcetera. If he was going to spend all their money, she thought the least he could have done was purchase a new couch.

At 3:00 PM, Dr. Phil stuck a person who hated thin people with a person who hated fat people in a house together, and although this should have been a most intriguing scenario, Patsy could derive little enjoyment from it. She decided to pay a visit to her husband at school.

Since she'd been back, she hadn't yet attempted to leave the house. In the garage, she found another surprise.

Her car was gone.

For the next thirty seconds, she lived up to her reputation as an honorary man.

The car had not been anything special: a baby blue 1999 Toyota Corolla. Four wheels, a hood. But it had been her car.

It had been hers.

She found it difficult to imagine her husband selling the car behind her back and then not informing her. Not to mention, he'd had just about the perfect opportunity for confession when they'd been watching that Jewish comedian on *Letterman*. No wonder he'd never bothered her about sitting in front of the television, she thought. He'd probably liked her that way. All fat and docile and unquestioning.

She decided to run over to the school. She wasn't sure if she was supposed to avoid running while pregnant, but she didn't really care.

The school was only a mile from their house, but she was sucking wind by the time she got there. She threw up on a patch of daisies and took a moment to marvel at how quickly her body had gone to hell. She then went straight to the gym to have it out with her husband.

"Where's teacher?" she asked. All the children were looking at her, and they seemed impossibly young, even though she was only twenty-two herself. "Where's your eff'n teacher?"

After a while, a little blonde girl, who might have been the Ghost of Patsy Past, replied, "Mrs. Poker stepped out, but we're supposed to be stretching. And you really shouldn't curse in front of children, ma'am."

Since when did tiny Buckstop Academy have TWO gym teachers? Only 150 kids went there. Patsy asked if someone could tell her where the other gym teacher, Magnum French, was?

The kids snickered.

"What? What?"

Finally, one said, "He doesn't work here anymore, ma'am."

HER HUSBAND CAME home around seven o'clock dressed in his gymsuit.

"You have a good day teaching gym?" she asked.

He shrugged.

"What sports the kids doing this time of year?" she asked.

"Basketball," he replied without even a moment's thought.

She'd been planning to play it cool. Basically, give that shit bag enough rope to hang himself. But the word *basketball* triggered something in her. She jumped off the couch and tackled him to the ground. "WHERE THE FUCK'S MY CAR? WHAT HAPPENED TO THE NEST EGG? WHY HAVEN'T YOU BEEN PAYING OUR BILLS?" And other things of that nature.

At some point, he said to her, "Patsy, honey, stop choking me. Just let me explain."

"If you can speak, you're not choking," she said. Still, she removed her hands from his throat, and he coughed a bit as prelude to the story of their financial woes.

January, right after her last visit home, Magnum had been watching either *Dateline* or *60 Minutes*—he couldn't remember which for certain. It had been a show about how kids were getting fatter and fatter. As a physical education teacher, Magnum had observed this to be true. The show got him thinking, though, and thinking had always been a dangerous thing for her husband. The show got him thinking that maybe he could do something about all the fat kids in his own classes. He hatched what he thought was a brilliant plan to stop teaching sports and start working on weight loss. At this point, he was imagining himself getting written up in the newspapers and receiving a medal from the president.

Magnum went back to school all riled up, and he gave a speech to each of his classes about how America was getting fat, but Buckstop Academy was not America, and *he*, Coach French, would not let Buckstop Academy get fat, not on his watch. By seventh period, he'd given the speech six times and felt it had been refined into an honest-to-goodness thing of beauty.

The trouble began the next day. Magnum had decided he would start by getting all the kids' measurements—their heights, their weights, etcetera. Lacking this information, how could he track all the progress they were about to make? Unfortunately, some of the kids did not take too kindly to being weighed. There were tears, flat-out refusals, and someone even punched him.

By evening, irate calls had started coming in from the parents: Coach French had traumatized their chubby children. Coach French needed permission to take measurements. Coach French had deviated from the accepted teaching methods. Coach French hated puppies and Jesus Christ and firemen and babies and all that was good in America.

The next Monday, they asked him to resign.

Magnum refused, feeling that he had done nothing wrong. "How could such a little thing as weighing a bunch of kids cause such a ruckus?" he asked. He also felt rather put upon. He had given them *an honest-to-goodness thing of beauty,* after all.

As he would not resign, they fired him in the last week of January. Magnum looked for another gym teacher job, but gym teacher jobs were few and far between in the middle of the school year and even further between for someone who'd been fired from his prior post. Summer came and went, and Magnum had yet to find a new teaching job. In September, he took a position outside of the physical education field—*way* outside of it—at the Betsy Ross factory, which, at the very least, settled the question of the bounty in the cupboard.

"Fuck, why didn't you tell me?"

"At first, 'cause I was ashamed," he said, "but then I didn't want to worry you. You seemed pretty . . . uh . . . uh—"

"Spit it out."

"Wound up. So I decided I wouldn't tell you till you got home. That's why I brought the Betsy Rosses in the car to the airport—visual aid, you know?—but you didn't seem to take too well to seeing them. So I just started wearing the gymsuit to the plant everyday, then changing in my car. I was gonna tell you eventually.

"And it's different there, Patsy, I swear! The Betsy Ross factory isn't the diabolical place we once believed it to be," he insisted.

She looked down at her husband. She was still straddled across his green and gold gymsuit-clad stomach. He had red finger prints on his neck from where she'd been grabbing him. He was looking up at her with something like hope.

She sighed. She could tell he felt bad about what he had done. She could also tell that he needed her to act like this was OK. And it wasn't like she wasn't a glass-house dweller herself. "So the old girl's changed?" she asked. "Tell me about it."

He smiled at her, and in that smile she could see what he must have looked like as a toothless little baby and what he would look like as a senile old man. "When I started there, Patsy, I had my doubts, too. But, I tell you, the company's changing for the better. Business hadn't been so good there for a while. What with people becoming more health conscious and stuff. That means there're advancement opportunities for people with good ideas. People like myself. My minor in college was in marketing, Patsy. Remember?"

She did.

"So there's this employee suggestion box, right? And they wanted people to submit ideas for promoting and extending the Betsy Ross brand. You know me, Patsy. I'm always coming up with ideas. I put, like, six things in the box and just about two months ago, they called me into the main office. And you'll never guess what they said?"

She could.

"They picked one of mine!"

It wouldn't have been much of a yarn if they hadn't.

Magnum's winning idea had been that Betsy Ross should try to get itself in the *Guinness Book of World Records* by creating the world's largest cupcake. Magnum had been named the head of the cupcake-building exploration and implementation committee.

"You know what that means, Patsy? It means more money! Eventually. They're hoping to do it before Christmas, and if it goes well, they might make me assistant director of marketing for all of Betsy Ross, Tennessee!" Magnum sat up, and she slid into his lap. He hugged her tightly, squishing her swollen breasts. "I'm sorry it had to come out this way, but I'm glad it come out, you know?

"And Patsy, I know I had to dip into our funds a little, but I swear to God, I'm gonna get you a new car, a better car, and replace all your money ASAP. I didn't want to tell you 'cause I just wanted to fix everything without you knowing. Probably kind of naive on my part, but I didn't want you to have to worry, babe. I know you got troubles of your own. Things you don't even tell me about."

She unstraddled her husband and sat back down on the couch. She felt heavy, and it wasn't just the unborn inside of her. It was the kind of heaviness that comes from knowing all your hopes are pinned on a cupcake contest, the kind of heaviness that comes from suspecting your husband is hanging on by a strand of spider web. If hope was the thing with feathers, she reckoned despair was the thing in armor.

She figured she was still owed a couple more beer vouchers from Uncle Sam, maybe totaling around $4500. If she was really careful, she could use that (plus the meager GI bill money) to pay for her first semester back at Chattanooga, but it wouldn't cover anything else. She'd been planning to use all her savings to pay for college so she wouldn't have to take some shit job while she was off bettering herself. She kept turning the math over in her head, but no matter what she did, the numbers would not resolve themselves to her satisfaction.

And, that wasn't even factoring the baby-or-abortion she was lugging around.

"Patsy? You been quiet a real long time."

"I'm just thinking . . . I got to call the VA office tomorrow," she said. "I'm still owed some money."

"Doubt anyone will be there," he said. "Tomorrow's Turkey Day. Besides, I don't want you to have to worry, hon."

"I'm not worrying. I'm just . . ." She decided to change the subject. "So, the Pharm don't have a girlfriend who works at Betsy Ross? Other than you, I reckon."

Magnum laughed and then he put his arm around her. She let it stay there, though it was damp and heavy on her shoulder. She was already so heavy, it really didn't add much additional burden.

To keep from thinking too much, she chattered about nothing and, in so doing, mentioned that she had missed the end of *Maury*.

Magnum exclaimed, "The eleven AM *Maury* rebroadcasts at two AM!" He had gotten familiar with the *Maury* schedule during his own time of troubles.

They stayed up until three watching *Maury*.

Anfernee was.

Not.

The father.

Patsy Attends Church

MAGNUM DIDN'T COME with her to see Minnie's Christmas play. Although he had once been a faithful enough churchgoer, he felt unwelcome since getting fired from the Academy and volunteered to spend the morning grocery shopping instead. Patsy had little interest in forcing her husband (or anyone else) to worship against his will, so she hitched a ride with the Pharm. Before they had even pulled out of the driveway, she informed him that she would be staying in the car for all parts of the service except Minnie's sketch.

They arrived early, which allowed ample time for watching the procession of God-fearers into the church: all the floral prints and white patent leather shoes and poly-blend light gray suits and baby girls dressed up like Shirley Temple and JonBenét and short-sleeved sky blue dress shirts with hopeless pasty arms sticking out and the strong gasoline scent of Brut and Old Spice and other colognes you could buy at the drugstore and old, fat women with swollen ankles and haircuts that looked like bad wigs.

She saw her mother, who had become one of those old, fat women, and Minnie a bit after that. Her father must have gotten there earlier, because she never saw him enter.

She could hear the service begin and the scuff of chairs as the parishioners rose. The Pharm thought the skit would happen approximately thirty-five to forty minutes in, so she closed her eyes and tried to take a nap.

Not long after joining the reserves, she had been excommunicated. The Sabbath Dayers believed in conscientious objection, though they still voted pro-life candidates as a matter of course.

Roger had said he was sorry, but that he had to do it to set an example for the flock. She was his daughter, and it was his church, and he'd only just become the pastor there. Of course, they would take her back if she gave a testimonial before the congregation, admitting that she had been wrong to join the military and reaffirming her belief in Jesus Christ and the Sabbath Day Adventists.

She sometimes found it hard to remember how it was that she had come to join the reserves in the first place. Not wanting to go to a Sabbath Day college—that had certainly been part of it. Pissing off her father had probably been an even more compelling reason.

The Pharm slipped out the front door and gave the agreed-upon hand gesture that meant it was time for the prodigal daughter to make her return.

She and Pharm snuck into the back pew. If her father saw them, he didn't acknowledge it. He just continued on with the introduction of a skit he called "a little something to remind us all about the true meaning of Christmas."

When the cast came out, Patsy had to stop herself from laughing. Someone had bought their costumes from the Slickmart, and it was clearly overstock from the Halloween just past. Minnie's Mary costume was Princess Leia's long white dress recreated in white polyester. Joseph, she was reasonably sure, was wearing Frodo Baggins's cloak. The three wisemen had on matching striped wool ponchos that made them look like a mariachi band that had lost their instruments. Every one of them was perspiring. It was one of those eighty-degrees-in-November Southern days. The AC in church was reserved for special occasions, and a Christmas skit was not considered one of them.

She knew that the actors were not necessarily aware of the costumes' derivations. Their religion frowned upon them seeing movies or watching television. The only people getting the joke were "bad" Adventists like Patsy and the Pharm.

She whispered to the Pharm, "When you think Yoda's gonna show up?"

He ignored her. The Pharm was very serious about his church attendance.

She had seen the play before and knew exactly how it would end. This gave her time to focus on Minnie.

She was a good actress, Patsy decided. Even in the stupid Princess Leia getup, Patsy found herself thinking that the girl really was Mary somehow. Every time Minnie spoke, the whole place hushed up. Even when Jesus was born and they brought out a genuine live baby, no one paid any attention to Jesus. And eventually God came out, too. (His costume was from *The Lord of the Rings*: Gandalf.) God was the worst actor ever—Patsy thought he might have been her old supervisor from Betsy Ross, but she couldn't tell under his fake Middle-earthling beard. No one was paying attention to God anyhow. They were all just looking at Minnie.

Patsy wondered what would have happened if they had all lived somewhere else and been other kinds of folk. Maybe Minnie would have been the lead in all the school plays, and maybe someone would have seen her in those plays and told her she was special. And she would have gone to drama school in New York or London or somewhere. And Patsy would have traveled to see all her plays. And maybe someday Minnie'd be a great actress—not some whore from the movies, either (Patsy's fantasy was specific on this point), but, like, a great stage actress. Patsy saw what the girl's whole life might have been, if she'd only been born to different folks.

The Pharm nudged her. "Patsy, show's over. If you want to slip out without seeing your parents, we best be on our way."

She was about to agree with him when she had another bout of morning sickness. She ran out the back to the church bathrooms, which were still empty as the service wasn't quite over.

On her way out of the bathroom, she encountered Mrs. Treadwell, who had once been a friend of her mother's. Mrs. Treadwell was a big lady with upper arms like fishing nets. She was hard to sneak past.

"As I live and breathe," Mrs. Treadwell said, "is that who I think it is?"

"That depends," Patsy replied.

"Well, you've not changed a bit, Patsy. Your mama didn't mention you were back from your travels."

"I wasn't traveling, Mrs. Treadwell. I was fighting in a war."

"Oh, well, of course you were. A million apologies if I said it wrong. You children these days—all of you like to go so far from home. Well, here comes your daddy right now. Oh, Pastor Roger . . . What a wonderful sermon!"

Patsy could see Roger leaving the sanctuary. He was doing his rock-star-after-the-service strut—he even had a white terry cloth towel draped over his neck like Elvis Presley. Patsy wasn't ready to talk to him, so she tried to hurry Mrs. Treadwell along. "It was nice seeing you. I should really be on my way."

But it was too late. She had already been spotted. "Patricia," he said.

"Pastor Dad."

Her father paused to nod in her direction, then kept on walking. He didn't ask her how she was doing. He didn't say he was glad she'd made it back in one piece. Aside from her name, he said nothing.

George came out of the sanctuary next. Up close, her mother seemed even fatter than she had when viewed from the car. Patsy suspected the woman must have been nearing 250 pounds.

Her mother came up to her with fat tears in her fat blue eyes. She put her arms around her, then whispered in her ear, "I'm glad to see you, but you know you're not welcome here unless . . ."

"I know," said Patsy. "I came to see the show."

Like her father, her mother nodded and said nothing. *Typical response,* Patsy thought. *The party line.*

Minnie wedged herself between Patsy and George. The girl took Patsy by the hand and led her out to the parking lot. "Was I awesome?" she asked.

"I think you could be a real professional actress, if you wanted," Patsy said.

Minnie laughed and Patsy tried not to kill her.

"I'm serious," Patsy said.

"Yeah, I always been such a ham."

"I'm eff'n serious. You should go to school."

"All right, Patsy, whatever." Minnie smiled something wicked and asked, "What'd you think of Joseph?"

"Joseph?"

"The boy playing Joseph . . ."

"I hadn't rightly noticed anyone but you."

"Aw, you're sweet." Minnie lowered her voice. "Joseph's my boyfriend. His real name's Joseph, too, isn't that funny?"

The Pharm pulled his truck up next to where Patsy and Minnie were standing.

"Are you coming home with us?" Patsy asked.

Minnie shook her head. She had plans with Joseph-called-Joseph.

Patsy hugged Minnie and got into the passenger seat of the Pharm's car.

"You feeling better?" he asked.

"Just the flu, I think."

The Pharm nodded. "Maybe you ought to have that looked into."

"Yeah."

"You're quiet," he said.

"My stomach . . ."

"Yeah, but it's not that kind of quiet."

She told him that she wanted his sister to go to London to become a great actress.

The Pharm nodded. "Well, she's still young, Patsy. If she wanted to do something like that, she could."

"She's eighteen. By the time I was eighteen, my obituary was writ, you know?"

The Pharm didn't say anything.

"By the time you're born, your whole life's decided already." She paused. "There's no escaping the circumstances of your birth."

"That's not true."

"If she was gonna make a move, she'd have to do it now. *You'd* have to make her do it now." Then Patsy laughed because she didn't wish to discuss it anymore. It occurred to her that this might be the reason Minnie was always laughing. "Man, did you see those costumes?"

"I know. Seriously, Magnum should have come. I wished to God I was still smoking me a little Saturday weed."

"You're a drug dealer, Pharm. If God don't care about that, he's not gonna care about you doing pot on the Sabbath."

The Pharm shrugged. "I do what I can live with."

"You know what always kills me about the Nativity story? Like, Mary just tells Joseph she's a virgin, and he totally believes her. Immaculate conception, my ass. The world's first cuckold, more like."

"Well, Patsy. I reckon belief is one of the points of the story."

"Mmm-hmm."

"You know what always kills *me* about it?" Pharm asked. "How every inn is booked. Was there some kind of convention going on in Bethlehem or something?"

"I think it was 'cause they were penniless or whatever," she said.

"Well, not all of the accounts are clear on that point. I prefer to imagine a huge conference of real-estate agents or Trekkies or something," he said.

"Maybe it's 'cause it was Christmas Eve?"

The Pharm nodded. "Hotels do book up around then. This is quite true, Patsy my dear. But come on, don't you prefer my conference theory? The Bethlehem Marriott welcomes the Trekkies. No vacancy. And if they were penniless, why in the world were they going to all these hotels anyway? How about like the Greater Bethlehem Medical Center? Stupid Christians, right? Your mama's taking antidepressants, by the way," Pharm said. "She don't want your daddy to know, so she gets them from me."

She asked him why he was telling her this. Pharm shrugged. "Dunno, Patsy. Thought it might cheer you up."

Patsy Calls on Her Father
and a Sick Friend

HER TELEVISION HABIT cured by the knowledge of her abject pov-
erty, Patsy called the VA office bright and early the Monday after
Thanksgiving. Neither the final installment of her additional tour
bonus nor her last two paychecks (about $4,500 in total) had been
direct-deposited as scheduled. She also needed to determine how the
GI bill worked so she could get herself back on the road to Better-
ment and Personal Growth.

The VA hotline featured an intricate phone tree, and since her questions overlapped multiple categories, she really wasn't sure if she was
pressing the right buttons or not. When she finally came to the end
of the line, she was put on hold.

A half hour later, a human. "There's a problem," he said.

Alpha. Bravo.

It had to do with her discharge. Her departure from the army had
been somewhat abrupt, and there hadn't been time for her to do
everything properly. She thought she had managed things fairly well,
but what she had ended up with was a *general* discharge as opposed
to an *honorable* discharge. A general discharge wasn't as bad as, say,

a *dishonorable* discharge, but it wasn't good either. And apparently, or so the man on the phone would have her believe, it was enough to screw her bonus and disqualify her from using the GI bill. The news about the bonus she had anticipated—she had left a week shy of completing her tour and had suspected this could complicate matters—but it was the first she had ever heard about not being able to take advantage of the GI bill.

Charlie. Disco. Echo.

So, this was the situation she found herself in.

Foxtrot.

The man on the line informed her that there would be an investigation into the circumstances of her discharge before the rest of the bonus was paid out and also before they decided if she could take advantage of the free college money that had, of course, been her whole reason for enlisting.

Golf.

"When will I know the outcome of this investigation?" she asked.

Hotel.

"We'll call you," said the man on the line.

Indigo.

She hung up the telephone.

Juliet.

Then she picked it up again.

Kilo.

Then, she walked out back and threw the phone into the hole in the yard.

Then she returned inside.

But she needed to make a call.

So she went back outside, where she lowered herself into the hole to retrieve the phone.

It was harder coming out than going in, but she was strong and managed.

Then she went back inside, plugged in the phone, and called the church.

"Buckstop Church of Sabbath Day Adventists. Minister Roger Pomeroy's office," was how her father's secretary answered the phone.

"Is the pastor in? I mean, could I speak to him?"

"May I ask who's calling?"

It was an obvious enough question, but it baffled her. She didn't want to say who it was. She didn't want to have to ask, "Do you reckon the pastor has a moment for his estranged daughter?" And if he wasn't in anyway, she didn't want to leave a message and have the whole church speculating on what Pastor Dad's bad daughter wanted now. And she didn't want to wait for him to call her back. So instead, she asked what time his afternoon office hours were.

The secretary was out when Patsy arrived, and her father's office was empty. Patsy went in anyway and sat down. She looked at the pictures on her father's desk. An old photograph of her mother from when she was young and skinny and frame-worthy. The three kids from when they were little and pure-hearted. Patsy looked at the girl she had been and wanted to black her face out. Or, at the very least, draw a mustache and devil horns on her.

When her father arrived, he didn't acknowledge her right away. It was a sort of game with him, one she'd seen him play many times. He'd talk to a person when he was ready to talk to the person and not a moment before.

He took off his jacket and loosened his tie. Then he checked his e-mail. Then he watered a snake plant on his windowsill that had dust on it like it hadn't been touched in months. Luckily, it was the kind of plant that required minimal attention.

Finally, he sat down. He positioned himself right at the center of the desk, then rolled his chair back about a foot. He pushed up the sleeves of his white dress shirt as if he were saying, *I'm ready to get my hands dirty now.*

"Well," he said, a little laugh in his voice, like that *well* was some kind of great in-joke between them. "Well," he repeated, though she hadn't found it all that clever the first time around. "Well, I certainly wasn't expecting to see you at church."

"I'm sorry about that," she said. "I only went to see Minnie's play. She was good."

"She's a good girl," he said.

"No," she said. "I mean she was good in the play. A good actor, don't you think?"

"Good enough for church," he said.

The bastard just couldn't concede the point, she thought.

Her father nodded as if to indicate that the pleasantries portion of the conversation was over. "How can I help you?"

My whole life, she thought, *this man has never raised a finger to help me.* "I want the money Grandma left me to use for school."

"Will you be attending an Adventist college?" he asked.

She told him she wouldn't, that nothing had changed on that front, that she'd be finishing her studies at Chattanooga.

"We been through this before, darlin'. Your grandma wanted you to use that money to go to an Adventist school."

"No, she didn't. She only said it was for my Christian education, and seems to me I could still be getting that at a regular college."

He smiled but said nothing.

"Honestly, I don't want to have to do this . . . I don't want to have to make any trouble, but I'll sue for it if I have to," she said. "Grandma wrote that will when she was screw-loosed and senile, and she only added the Christian part in at the end . . . What she meant and the circumstances, they're . . ." She searched for the word.

"Contestable?" He shook his head in a fatherly and ministerly expression of extreme disappointment. "You do what you have to do, Patricia." He looked her in the eye, and she felt transparent and weak. He knew she wouldn't sue. "Thought Uncle Sam would be taking care of you anyhow," he said.

"The GI bill doesn't pay for everything, Dad!" She had considered lying, but she thought maybe he'd take pity on her and just give her the money if she admitted there were some problems with her bonus and the military in general. Her father liked to think he was saving people. So she told him how things stood. He seemed to listen. In any case, he nodded a lot, which gave her hope. At the end of her woeful story, she added, "And if you really think Grandma wouldn't want me to have that money for secular college . . . well, I'd even be sure to pay you back once my funds come through, all right, Dad?"

He laughed. "Well, Patsy, you raise some . . . points," he said. "I'm gonna have to pray on it."

She nodded. "Do you mean right now? 'Cause I'm just wondering how long praying on it will take."

He said he didn't know how long it would take—God was on his own schedule after all—but based on experience, God's schedule usually took no more than a week.

Her father's secretary knocked on the door. "Roger, do you have a moment?"

"For you, Megan, I've got all the time in the world," Roger said, his voice slick and bright. He didn't bother talking to Patsy that way. She had been immune to his charms for some time and was frankly amazed they worked on anyone.

The secretary stuck her head inside the office. Patsy had never seen her before. She was younger than Patsy, barely out of high school, and clearly had no idea who Patsy was. "Oh, I didn't realize you had company," the secretary said a bit jealously.

"We're all finished here." He waved his hand to dismiss his daughter, and Patsy let herself be dismissed.

On the walk back, she let herself best-case it. Maybe Roger would pray on it, and God would tell him to give her the money. And maybe everything would work out with Uncle Sam. And maybe even Magnum's cupcake contest would be a success. And maybe the unborn inside her would somehow work itself out, too . . . She didn't know how yet.

When she got home, the phone was ringing. She picked up the receiver, hoping to hear from either God (via Roger) or Uncle Sam.

"Patricia French?" It was a woman's voice.

"Yeah," she replied. "Who wants to know?"

She said she was the fiancée of that buddy of Patsy's whose face had been blown off. Buddy was in the VA hospital in Memphis, having some surgery on what was left of his visage. The fiancée thought it'd be "a real morale boost" to have some of his old friends visit. Not surprisingly, Buddy was pretty depressed about things.

"What kind of surgery?"

"Oh, nothing that major!" she said. Her punctuation mark of choice was the exclamation point, which made her sound like a cheerleader. Patsy was sure Buddy had shown her a picture of his fiancée, but she couldn't remember what the woman looked like. "They're taking some bone out of his hip and trying to graft it to his face so they can make him a new nose."

"Sounds kind of major," Patsy said.

"Not compared to what he's been through," Buddy's fiancée said. The woman had lost a bit of the cheer in her voice, but then it was back. "Anyhow, he heard you were in Tennessee, and he perked right up at the thought!"

"I'm real sorry," Patsy said. "I just don't know if I'll be able to make it this week. I'd come if I could, but a lot of things have sort of gone to hell on me here, and—"

"Please, Patsy. Do you mind if I call you Patsy? Please. He's been so low . . . I think it would help. I really think it would."

At that moment, Patsy didn't feel like feeling sorry for anyone but herself. Which was to say, she didn't exactly feel like driving all the way to Memphis and spending a million dollars she didn't have on gas just so she could see what was left of Buddy. But she agreed to go the next day. He had been her first real friend in the service, and she knew he would do the same for her. *He's one of us,* she thought.

She dropped her husband at work and then drove the three hundred miles to Memphis. She thought about other drives she had taken, which was something she always tended to do when driving long distances. It was strange, in a way, because she never felt like she was on the drive she was on. She was always on some other road, some road in her head.

The fiancée met her in the lobby of the hospital. "Patsy," she said. "I'm so glad you made it. How are you?" She did look like a cheerleader. She was curvy and compact and blonde-haired and ponytailed. She looked like she was built to be on the top of gymnastic pyramids and in football players' arms. *She looks like me*, Patsy thought. *What I used to look like.*

A doctor stopped the fiancée just as they were about to enter Buddy's room. Patsy stopped to wait for her, but she waved Patsy ahead. "He's waiting for you."

There were two patients in Buddy's room, and they were both, Patsy thought, pretty FUBAR. The one near the window had his head entirely wrapped in bandages, and he seemed to be watching television, though she couldn't entirely tell—he may have just been pointed in that direction. The guy near the door didn't have any bandages, but he didn't really have a face either. Guy number two was sleeping. He didn't have ears or a nose. He did however have a balloon on the top of his neck, probably to generate extra skin for an unimaginably excruciating future procedure. He had the kind of injuries that made Patsy want to get down on her knees and thank the Lord it wasn't her.

She concluded that Buddy must be the bandaged guy since the fiancée had mentioned him getting the bone grafted to his face, so she went over to the bed by the window.

"Hey, Buddy, how you doing?" Patsy asked.

Buddy didn't really reply. He just kind of grunted and nodded with what Patsy took to be enthusiasm.

It was depressing that her pal couldn't really talk. She tried to remind herself of the guy under all those bandages who'd been a damned good friend to her, and of other similarly unhelpful clichés.

"I'm sure you'll be talking again soon," she said.

The guy shook his head vigorously.

She had heard that when you met someone who'd had a stroke or some other head trauma, you should just keep talking naturally. She tried to do that, though she didn't find it to be particularly natural to engage in such a one-sided conversation. "S'pose you heard about me leaving the military," she said.

Buddy shook his head.

"Yeah, it was kind of abrupt, to tell the truth. I—I can't really explain it. I guess I just got fed up with being Over There."

Buddy cocked his head at her.

"Come on, Buddy, don't look at me that way."

Buddy cocked his head the other way.

"Aw man, you know me too well. I could never lie to you." She looked around the room and lowered her voice. "OK, here's the thing. You might have known I was sleeping with Smartie. Just like one or two times, that's it."

Buddy looked at her.

"Yeah, I know he was engaged! I'm married, you know. I'm not proud of what I done, but a girl gets lonely every now and again."

Buddy turned his head toward the window.

"So, I got pregnant."

Buddy shook his head.

"Yeah, I really don't know what I'm going to do about that either, but thanks for judging. And they were gonna put me on administrative detail. They were gonna transfer me to Bragg or I don't know where. And I got super depressed just thinking about it. Like, I'd served all this time, and you know me . . ."

Buddy shook his head again.

"Come on, you *know* me. I'm eff'n fierce. I wasn't some shit-bag private dickless who was always crying and whining and sleeping with people. OK, except with Smartie, but that was just like two or three times. I wasn't, like, Queen for a Year. I wasn't an eff'n

Desert Fox. I was tough. I hated the thought of everyone thinking I was some knocked-up loser at Bragg, having a kid that clearly weren't my husband's. So, I got my rifle. And I sat down on my bed in the barracks. And I raised the gun. Now, I just have to mention that, at this point, I wasn't really thinking straight. Like, you'd just gotten shipped home, and I'd been Over There for like eleven months, and I was knocked up to boot, so hormones might have come into play, I'm no expert. But for the record, my plan had never been to kill my—"

Enter Buddy's fiancée. "Hey, Johnny boy," she said, "how you doing today?"

Who the fuck is Johnny boy?

"Patsy," the fiancée said gently, "this is Buddy's roommate, PFC Jonathan Garcia. Buddy's over there." She pointed to the man by the door, the sleeping guy with the balloon animal in his neck. "Johnny boy can't talk just yet, but we're hoping he's gonna come around real soon."

For a second, Patsy worried that she had just told her entire life story to man she didn't even know. She comforted herself with the fact that he was mute and, thus, unlikely to tell tales.

The fiancée walked over to Buddy's bed, and she shook him awake. "Buddy, you got a visitor." In retrospect, it should have been obvious that this man, and not the bandaged man by the window, was Buddy. This man's hands were black; the other man's were white.

"By the way," Buddy's fiancée whispered to Patsy, "he can't really see you right on. He's kind of gotta look at you peripherally, but don't let that bother you."

Patsy sat down sidewise, so that Buddy wouldn't have to turn his head. "Hey, Buddy!" she said. Her voice sounded fake and tinny, like she was leaving a message for someone.

"Hey there, SweeTart." That's what they had called her over there because she was always eating SweeTarts. That was the only candy that was plentiful, and as a vegetarian, she could rarely find enough real food. Patsy's vegetarianism was not political, spiritual, familial, or otherwise. The fact was, having never eaten meat, her stomach had not acquired the knack of digesting it. She had complained about the lack of vegetarian options to her CO, who had responded that she ought to just start eating meat. Out of desperation/near starvation, she tried that tack for several days before being struck by an inevitable, though truly epic, case of diarrhea and deciding that malnutrition from a diet consisting of SweeTarts would be a preferable way to die.

"How you been, girl?" Buddy asked. Even though he didn't have much in the way of lips, his voice hadn't changed noticeably to her ear. And, as opposed to Fake Buddy by the window, at least Real Buddy had retained the power of speech.

The fiancée said, "You're just so happy to see Patsy, I can tell. You're like grinning ear to ear."

Patsy didn't know how the fiancée had determined this. The only expressions she could discern were injured and burned.

"I'll just leave you two alone," the fiancée said.

Patsy was about to tell her that that wasn't necessary, but the woman was already out the door.

"So, how you been?" Patsy asked.

"Ain't it obvious?"

"Guess so."

"Crap," he said with a laugh. Then he launched into a monologue about his health troubles. How he'd been in and out of the hospital for the last year. How he'd had some raging bacterial infection that you get from the dirt over there. How no one could even tell he was black anymore, his skin was so scorched and cankered. How no one would really talk to him or look at him either. How he scared his nieces and nephews. How he wouldn't have gotten through it if not for his fiancée. She might look like Barbie, but her head was screwed on tight.

And here Patsy thought he might have started to cry, though that was hard for her to tell. His eyes had a strange blue, glassy look any-way, and he might just have been sweating from the exertion of narrative. "The wedding's in April," he said. "You got to be one of my groomsmen, Patsy."

"Aren't groomsmen supposed to be men?" she asked.

"Damn, SweeTart. You're an honorary man, you know that!"

She had always been proud of the fact that her best friends from the service were guys, that no one ever said she was some weak, stupid girl. She agreed to be his groomsman. "If that's what you really want," she said.

The fiancée walked Patsy back to her car. "Thanks so much for coming."

"Weren't no bother."

"So, we'll see you at the wedding, right?"

Patsy nodded. "Say, did you used to be a cheerleader?"

"Yeah, in high school."

"Me, too," Patsy said. "Till they dropped me on my head."

FOR OBVIOUS REASONS, Patsy was in a reflective mood during the three-hundred-mile trip back to Buckstop.

Her time in the sandbox had sometimes seemed like one long truck ride. She could barely remember anything else except those trucks. She shared the truck with Buddy before he got himself blown up on Airport Road. And when she wasn't driving with Buddy, she drove with Smartie.

As a rule, she tried not to think about Smartie—she knew nothing good could come of it—but it was a long drive back to Buckstop, and so she permitted herself this exception.

He had made fun of her for listening to Britney Spears on her iPod and for having an iPod at all when it would have been a lot smarter to have something that took Duracells. But when he wasn't making fun of her, they had actually talked about things. He had wanted to know all about her vegetarianism, and he, in turn, had confided to her how the men under him didn't much like him. They were suspicious of him. He assumed that was because of his background. He'd gone to West Point and his uncle was a representative from Kentucky, but he was no elitist. And one time, he got her these vegetarian MREs because they were hard to come by. And he also taught her how to play chess. He had a little magnetic set in a zippered case. He used to make fun of her because she never liked to see the knight go down even if it meant sacrificing the queen and the king. "That's no way to play, SweeTart," he said, but he always got all crinkly around the eyes when he said it. She didn't really care about winning, she just liked the horse. And, well, that time in the truck with Smartie was sort of the happiest she ever was. Not just in Iraq, either. It was sort of the happiest she had ever been in her entire life. She knew that was a pretty pathetic state of things, but it was the truth. What she had said to Fake Buddy about sleeping with Smartie just because she'd been lonely? That had been a lie.

Smartie was getting married, too. Her name was Regan Graham, and she was studying in Chicago to be a curator. Patsy had never known anyone who became such a thing. It just wasn't something people from Buckstop (or even Big Rock) ever did. He had shown Patsy her picture once. Her teeth were on the big side, but Patsy couldn't find any other fault with her.

One time, while on leave and bored with nothing to do, Patsy googled Regan Graham. She wasn't a famous person, but there were still thirty-eight hundred links to her name. She had graduated from Harvard University, where she had been the rehearsal accompanist for the Gilbert and Sullivan Players. She had won a prize for a research paper entitled "Liminality in the Age of Distraction." She had been a bridesmaid in her older sister's wedding in Philadelphia. Her dress was made of black-and-white gingham. The picture ran in the society section of the newspaper in Philly, and Patsy had had to give her name and address just to see it. Regan had played lacrosse at some Quaker school, also in Philly. She had run in a 5K in Chicago just last February and placed forty-sixth. She had broken some boy's heart, and he had apparently responded to the blow by writing a long blog entry about what a bitch she was. For several months in 2002, photographs indicated that she had dyed her hair black. She cataloged all her books on one of those library Web sites. She liked art books, but they weren't the kind of artists Patsy had ever heard of. She had bridal registries at Pottery Barn and at Tiffany's. She favored dishes and linens in whites and beiges. She was five years older than Patsy—Regan's birthday was in October. Sometimes, Patsy felt like she should send her a present, knowing so much about her likes and dislikes as she did.

Not long after, Patsy had googled her own name. There were numerous links to Patricia French, but most of them had nothing to do with her. There was Patricia French, the real-estate broker in St. Louis, Missouri. There was Patricia French who painted animal portraits, specializing in equestrian. There was Patricia French who was an ombudsman in Leeds, England—she was probably the most popular Patricia French of all. There was Pat French, a youngish man who was into writing fan fiction about rather girly books; his friends liked to mock him by referring to him as Patricia.

However, she was the only Patricia Pomeroy French in the known universe. There were eight links to her full name. Three mentioned her first deployment. Two made reference to her being the pastor's daughter (with reference to her deployment). One mistakenly reported her as deceased. The final two were dead links, which meant they didn't lead anywhere at all.

UPON HER RETURN, the house was empty and the phone was ringing. It was Roger.

"Patricia," he said.

She walked over to the kitchen table, which was the one thing in the house that she liked, the one thing in the house that had been bought *brand-new* from Slickmart. The table and chairs were edged in silver chrome, like something from an old diner. She had purchased the set using money from the first installment of her enlistment bonus, and at the time, that had given her great pleasure. For once in her life, she had found it satisfying to have everything perfectly matched. As she sat and the cushion made a sympathetic sighing sound, she wondered if those chairs were to be the only thing she'd have to show for her entire military career.

"Patricia," he repeated, "are you there?"

"I'm here, Daddy. I was just thinking how you and Mom have never been over to the house to see my kitchen table."

"Patricia," he said, "I want you to know I prayed on your situation all day and all night."

She told him that she wouldn't have expected anything less. She looked at her face ever so slightly reflected in the Formica of the table. She was the moon on a cloudy night. She was spilled milk. She realized she hadn't been paying attention to Roger at all.

". . . But you knew the position of our church on the war when you joined up, so I'm gonna have to hold you to that."

"What's that supposed to mean?"

"You left your church and your family to join the military. You knew this was against our beliefs. You put your faith in the military to pay for your education, so you'll have to live with that decision and keep your faith with that."

She asked him what that had to do with Grandma's money.

"If I gave you that money, it wouldn't look right."

She noticed a tiny rip or burn in the vinyl of the chair to her left. Magnum and the Pharm had probably been getting stoned when it happened. She placed the tip of her little finger into the hole, which only made it bigger. This put her in mind of a story from her second- or third-grade reading textbook: upon being hired to patch holes in a blanket, a tailor comes up with the solution of cutting the holes out instead, leaving the blanket with bigger holes than ever. She wondered what the moral of the story was supposed to have been. Don't hire stupid tailors? Patch your own blankets?

"Uh . . . It wouldn't look right to who?"

"To the flock. It wouldn't set a good example."

"But, but no one would have to know!"

"I'd know. Your mother'd know. And God would know. I couldn't in good conscience . . . On the other hand, if you wanted to come back to the church and go to an Adventist college—"

"You can't do that!"

"Patricia, I'm only thinking of your immortal soul."

"I'm here now, Daddy. I'm alive now. I don't give a fuck about my immortal soul. I AM HERE NOW, AND I WANT MY FUCKING MONEY!"

"I won't have you cursing at me, Patricia."

"FUCK THAT! I've seen things. I've served in a war. I can fucking say fucking fuck if I want to! I have earned the right to use every fucking word in the entire fucking English language."

She wasn't sure if he'd hung up or not.

"Please, Dad, I'm sorry about the swearing; I'm sorry . . . I just . . . I really need that money . . ."

She continued begging until Roger cut her off. "Listen, Patsy, I know you don't think I've been the perfect father to you. I know you probably think I've made mistakes. But the reason I'm holding to this is because I don't want you to repeat any of the mistakes I might have made. And I want you to know that I'll be praying for you, Patsy."

She knew that *I'll be praying for you* translated to *FUCK YOU* in Christian. "DON'T FUCKING PRAY FOR ME! I DON'T WANT YOUR FUCKING PRAYERS!"

"I'll be praying for you anyway," Roger said and then he hung up the phone.

She threw the cordless across the room. It didn't break, but the battery came loose from the back and skidded under the oven.

All her destructive impulses usually just resulted in more work, and about a second later, she realized she was going to have to make another call.

After cajoling the battery from under the fridge with a long wooden spoon, she dialed Lacey's number. Her sister-in-law had mentioned jobs at the Slickmart.

She told herself that this would just be temporary.

Just until everything was resolved with Uncle Sam.

The unborn was banging her like a backward bass drum.

"Shhhhhsh!" she told it. "Be still, you."

But it didn't stop.

Patsy Gets a Job

PATSY CELEBRATED HER twenty-third birthday at the Slickmart superstore.

Her Slickmart interview was conducted by Abraham Slick, the owner of the store. Lacey considered this to be a big deal and asked Patsy endless questions about the meeting. Truthfully, Patsy could find little to say about Abraham Slick. He was one of the only Jewish folks she'd come across in the Buckstop area, and his hands had seemed uncommonly soft for a man's when they'd shaken. On the desk was a photograph of his wife, Esther, who was rumored to be crazy. Patsy knew that the meaning of crazy was variable in that part of the world. There was listening-to-rap-music crazy, or driving-your-kids-off-a-cliff crazy, or wearing-weird-hats crazy, or shooting-yourself-in-the-head crazy, or voting-liberal crazy, or worshipping-a-different-God-from-the-majority crazy.

"Patricia," Slick said, when he offered her the job, "we all in the Slickmart family are real proud to support our troops." Family was Slick's favorite euphemism for employees.

"Thanks, Mr. Slick," she said.

"And not only am I thrilled to be offering you a place in our family, I also have a proposition for you."

Slick leaned across the table. She could feel his breath on her forehead. "I was thinking, as our newest family member, you might like to star in a series of advertisements for the Slickmart superstore."

"Advertisements, Mr. Slick?"

"Well, not exactly advertisements. More like a picture of you dressed up in your uniform or fatigues or whatever costume would be appropriate, I'd leave that to you. We'd bring in someone to get your hair all fancy and do your makeup, don't you worry. And you might be stocking a shelf, right? Or maybe just a red, white, and blue background. And underneath it, the poster would say something like THE SLICKMART SUPERSTORE IS PROUD TO SUPPORT OUR TROOPS: PATRICIA FRENCH, NEWEST MEMBER OF THE SLICKMART FAMILY." Slick was staring like he could actually see it, like he was reading the caption off a cue card somewhere in the distance. He turned his focus back to Patsy. "So, Patricia, what would you think of something like that?"

It just about made her want to puke, but she figured she shouldn't say that if she wanted to be hired. "Hmm," she said, "that could be interesting. Let me pray on it."

Slick patted her hand with his too-soft one. "Well, you just pray as long as you like, darlin'. No rush." He put his arm around her and walked her out of his office. "'Course I'd be willing to pay you a little something extra for your trouble and the use of your likeness."

This did indeed make the proposition more appealing. She figured she might be able to wrangle more money if she didn't jump at the idea, though. She'd just keep her mouth shut and wait for Slick to approach her again.

"I'm expecting big things from you, Patricia," Slick said before leaving her with human resources to claim her Official Orange Slickmart Smock.

On her first day of work, she was assigned to the Slickmart sporting goods department, where the inventory included tents, fishing poles, and guns. Her job was simple enough. Help people find what they were looking for. Try to sell them the most expensive version of whatever they wanted and accessories they didn't need to go with whatever they'd come in for in the first place.

Two other men worked in her department. They were named Lenny and George.

"Like *Of Mice and Men*," she said when they were all introduced.

Neither had read it. They weren't really readers. But the fact that she'd said that gave them the notion that she was a big reader, and this embarrassed her. She considered herself to be pathetically not well-read. She had read most of the fiction books for high school English, and the Bible, naturally, and a couple birthdays ago, Magnum's sister had sent her a care package with *The Five People You Meet in Heaven*. Patsy had lent it to Buddy, who had reported it to be "pretty life changing." She'd not yet made the time to read it herself, but had found the paperback the optimal size and ballast for swatting flies.

"Also, my mother's named George." Though she rarely talked about her mother, she said this to steer the conversation away from her reading habits. "She isn't a dude, though."

Both men found this to be a perfectly hysterical observation.

"It's short for Georgia," Patsy said.

"Is she from there?"

"No, she's from Vermont." This, too, cracked them up. Patsy concluded that her new colleagues were easily amused.

"Georgia from Vermont!" said the tall, prematurely balding one she was pretty sure was Lenny.

"You're a funny one, Patsy," said the short, hairy, apelike one—George?

Because she knew more about arms than either Lenny or George, they agreed that she should work the gun counter. The only kinds of guns they sold were hunting rifles. When customers came in, she would act helpful and then quietly convince them to buy their guns somewhere else. She wasn't paid in commissions, and Abraham Slick wouldn't end up in the poorhouse because a couple rednecks had bought their arms elsewhere. And if a few less deer found themselves with a hole between the eyes, that wouldn't exactly be a tragedy either. If it got her fired, well, she was prepared to live with that as one possible exit strategy.

Her tenure at the Slickmart would be marked by a series of similarly futile acts of anarchy.

ON HER SECOND day of work, she began using a safety pin (the backup to the one used for fastening her pants) to punch holes in the store's stock of plastic water bottles. In so doing, she fancied herself something of a vigilante for the environment. The amount of waste at the Slickmart repulsed her. Every last item came in some sort of container, and then there were containers to contain the containers, and she suspected all of that crap was just going right into the ocean or onto some enormous toxic barge. In the truck, she and Smartie had discussed water bottles and SUVs and red meat and lightbulbs and how all this pointless shit was killing the planet, and them, too. How their lives would be different, if not for the oil. Smartie used to say how being downrange had made him even more concerned about this sort of thing than he'd been before. So she'd poke her holes and think of him.

ON HER THIRD day of work, Patsy was forced to get a ride home with Lacey. (Magnum and Patsy had settled on an alternate-day use schedule for their lone car.) Patsy had never found it particularly easy making conversation with Magnum's sister. Lacey said something about how much Mr. Slick had taken to her. Patsy said, "Yeah." Then Patsy said something about Magnum's cupcake contest, and Lacey said, "Yeah?"

But Patsy couldn't come up with anything more along that theme. At that moment, the unborn had unleashed a round of swift and adamant kicks.

Lacey dropped her off in front of the house. Patsy knew what the next logical step was: going inside. The door had a glass panel in the front, which had always struck her as rather obscene, as if the house were wearing a short skirt and no panties. Through the glass panel, she could see the yellow glow of the regular lights, the blue glow of the television, the red and white glow of the paper bucket, and the soft dark silhouette of her husband, pouring her a glass of diet soda. She could even imagine what she would look like once she got inside. All those other colors plus the orange glow of her Slickmart smock, and a smallish, dirty-blondish, orange-tinted woman who, though she wasn't even twenty-five, looked at least thirty.

She just didn't want to be that woman in that house.

She walked around back to visit her dog's grave.

She was not surprised to find the Pharm sitting on the edge of the big hole. He was smoking a joint and he offered it to her. Lord, how she wanted it, but she forced herself to decline.

She sat down beside him. Both of them dangled their legs into the dirt void where the pool should have been.

"You come here often?" she joked.

He took her question seriously. "Peaceful," he replied.

All the rocks and dirt and incidental pot started tending her mind toward blackness. "Pharm, is this how you saw your life going?"

He inhaled deeply. "I didn't see my life going at all," he said after a spell. "When we were kids, they always told us that the End of Days was imminent, so reckon I thought I'd be in heaven with Jesus by now."

"You believed all that crap?"

"Yeah, Patsy, I did. Mostly I still do." He inhaled again. "I'm royally screwed up, don't you know?"

She considered her oldest friend's face illuminated by his cigarette. He wasn't handsome exactly. He was delicate, almost like a boy porcelain doll.

"How's Vinnie?" he asked.

"Um. He's called me a couple times since I been back, but I haven't had time to return."

The Pharm nodded. "He still in New York?"

"New York and L.A. both."

The Pharm nodded again.

"Maybe you and me could go out to visit him some time?" she suggested.

"Yeah, maybe."

By then, he was finished with his cigarette. He threw the butt into the void. Then he helped her to her feet and walked her back to the house.

ON HER FOURTH day of work, she was heading into the break room when either Lenny or George said to her, "Not in there, Patsy." He beckoned her over and led her outside to the loading area and up an exterior staircase that ended at the Slickmart's attic space.

There wasn't much up there except panels and insulation, a tiny hole you could peek through and view the store from above, and a big bottle of Maker's Mark whiskey and several incriminating empties. "It's better up here, right?" Lenny or George asked, as he offered her the whiskey bottle.

"Different."

Lenny or George looked her up and down and said, "You look like a gal who can hold her liquor."

She shrugged. She didn't want to offend her colleague, so she said, "I think I'm coming down with something. Don't want to contaminate your stash." If she was having this unborn, she didn't want it to end up pickled and with webbed feet.

She peeked through the hole, and though it didn't seem possible, the perspective made the job even more depressing. All the little people became nothing more than ants gathering supplies for their personal dirt mounds.

"How you finding the work?" Lenny or George asked her.

"Had worse," she said.

ON HER FIFTH day of work, she spotted Minnie in the contraceptive aisle at the Slickmart.

Patsy called her name. The girl was holding a pack of condoms in her hand, which, upon seeing Patsy, she hid behind her back.

"Patsy," she said, "I didn't know you were working here."

"Just started," Patsy said. "How you been?"

They embraced, and the condoms dropped to the floor.

"You won't tell my brother, will you?" Minnie asked.

Patsy chuckled. "Pharm's not gonna care about you sleeping with some boy."

Minnie shook her head. "You don't know Marcus as well as me. And besides, it's not what you think," she said. "The boy I'm . . . we're getting married!"

"What do you mean?"

She told Patsy how she was in love with Joseph-named-Joseph from the church play, and they were going to get married, and neither of them believed it was right to sleep with a person before marriage, but they were going to make this right just as soon as they both graduated from high school. "It's a real relief to tell someone," she said. She put her arms around Patsy again, and Patsy wanted to weep, but not for joy.

"Minnie," she said, "you don't have to marry the first person you sleep with, you know."

The girl turned red as an apple and looked away. "I . . . ," she stammered. "I don't think it's right not to. 'Cause of God. And the Bible."

"The Bible don't know everything," Patsy said. "And God don't eff'n care who you sleep with."

"Stop yelling, Patsy!" The girl looked up and down the aisle to make sure no one was listening.

Patsy hadn't realized she'd been yelling, but now that Minnie had mentioned it, she could feel her heart beating quickly and sweat forming on her brow. She inhaled and thought a bit of the NATO phonetic alphabet. For a few seconds, the only sounds were distant rusty shopping cart wheels and the Muzak that was the store's liminal sound track—at that moment, "Top of the World," by the anorexic girl and her brother or husband, Patsy couldn't remember which. "Sorry," Patsy said. "It's just . . . I used to believe that shit, too. But they lie to you, Minnie. Every week, my dad lies to you. The church lies to you. You haven't been anywhere, so you don't know. You don't know anything."

For someone who didn't know anything, Minnie laughed in a most knowing way. Patsy could tell the girl pitied her.

Patsy offered to pay for Minnie's condoms using her 20 percent employee discount, but the girl declined, and Patsy had to get back to pretending to sell hunting rifles anyhow.

For the rest of the afternoon, she couldn't concentrate on not selling guns, and she accidentally sold one, which depressed her. She kept thinking about Minnie and how wrong and young the girl was if she really thought she had to marry Joseph-named-Joseph. Patsy had been guilty of that kind of dubious thinking when she'd married Magnum. She supposed she had married him to prove a point more than anything. Six years later, that exact point was sometimes hard to recall.

ON HER SIXTH day of work, the roof of the Slickmart began to leak. A persistent, menacing drip that escaped most everyone's notice.

*   *   *

ON HER SEVENTH day, the leak made a watermark on the ceiling. A customer commented that the stain looked like Jesus standing with His hands out. Patsy didn't really see it. To her, it just sort of looked like a stain. Upon squinting, she was willing to concede that the stain looked something like a man with his hands out, but she found no evidence to indicate that the man was Jesus in particular. She did think it looked rather like Magnum had the night he'd wanted her to get the hell out of the car.

She supposed it was timing more than anything—it was only ten days to Christmas—that made folks think the stain was a miracle.

ON THE EIGHTH day, Abraham Slick called the local television station, thinking a cute human-interest story might generate additional holiday traffic.

Unfortunately, it brought in the wrong type of business, too.

ON THE NINTH day, Patsy's mother made her first in a series of pilgrimages to the store.

Lacey went to discuss the matter with Patsy in guns, where she was busily not selling guns. Instead, Patsy was creating a Christmas rifle display—she wanted the guns to look like a Christmas tree, and this was turning out to be more challenging than her initial estimates. "Hiya, honey," Lacey said. "How's the arms dealing going today?" This was her one joke, which Patsy found rather edgy for Magnum's sister. Lacey looked at the gun display and furrowed her brow. "Is that supposed to be a tree?"

She nodded.

"Festive," she said. "So, Patsy, the thing is . . . Your mama's kind of at the store now."

"Yeah. Probably Christmas shopping."

"Uh-huh. The thing is, Patsy, she's kind of been here for the last six hours."

"Well, she's not gonna win any speed-shopping medals, that's for damn sure."

"Don't you want to go see her?" Lacey lowered her voice to a whisper. "She's in the condom aisle. You know, below the stain. If it were my mama—"

Patsy interrupted her. "Not really," she said and then she changed the subject to matters more pressing. "Lacey, do you think Mr. Slick would allocate some tinsel to guns? 'Cause the whole rest of the store looks like Christmas, and I think my little tree really wants for something."

ON THE TENTH day, Patsy's mother came again and though Patsy saw her, she chose not to say anything to her or even approach her. The Jesus stain was above the condom department, so Patsy really didn't have much cause to go there. But yes, she had seen her mother. She was hard to miss. She was 250 pounds and dressed for church. She would stand there in the middle of the aisle leaning on a shopping cart and just stare up at the ceiling. Sometimes her lips would be moving slightly. Patsy thought she was praying, but she never got close enough to find out. She wondered if the Pharm was still supplying George with antidepressants.

ON PATSY'S ELEVENTH day of work, her mother began moving condoms out of the row below the stain. George was overheard telling other customers that the prophylactics were disrespectful to Jesus.

Mr. Slick called Patsy into his office. He asked her if it was her mother in the condom row. She replied that although the woman in the aisle had certainly given birth to her, she hadn't been her mother for some time.

"You won't mind if I call the police, then?" Slick asked.

Patsy considered the question. She really didn't want to entangle herself with whatever spiritual/psychological breakdown her mother was having.

And yet . . .

She used the phone in Slick's office to call Roger, who she hadn't spoken to since he'd hung up on her.

Before she could even begin, her father said, "I haven't changed my mind."

"I'm calling about your wife," Patsy said. "She's in the Slickmart— I work there now—and she's about to get herself arrested, if you even give a crap about that."

Roger was momentarily speechless, and that gave his daughter pleasure. Patsy knew that the worst thing that could happen to the town's star preacher was one of his own making a spectacle.

He cleared his throat. "How long has this been going on?"

"'Bout three days."

"And you didn't think to call me sooner, Patricia?"

"Fuck that, Dad. I thought you knew. She isn't hurting anyone. They're only throwing her out 'cause she started moving the contraceptives."

Her father said he'd be there in fifteen minutes.

She went to see her mother below the Jesus stain.

"Hi, Mom," she said.

George was occupied throwing a bunch of K-Y Jellies into a shopping cart.

She was muttering to herself, "Now, I really only have to move the ones with spermicide. Because there's nothing wrong with a little lubrication. Nothing wrong with that at all . . ."

"Mom?"

"Oh, hello, Patsy," she said after a bit. "I've just got so much to do today, baby. It's crazy here."

For sure, Patsy thought. "Um, Dad's coming to get you in about fifteen minutes."

George paused for a second and looked at Patsy blankly. "Roger's coming here?"

"Yeah."

"Why would he do that?" Patsy thought this was said rather imperiously for a person who was making such a spectacle of herself in the Slickmart.

"Well, I . . . I reckon he wanted to help."

Her mother snorted. "You can tell him I got everything under control, Patsy-babe."

George held up a bottle of warming lubricant. "Patricia, do you know if this has spermicide in it?"

"I don't think so. I just think it makes things warm."

George smiled. "Then it can stay!"

When her father arrived, he pushed past Patsy and grabbed her mother by the meat of her upper arm.

"George, we are leaving."

"No," she said. "I'm not finished."

"You are," he said. She could see Roger pinching the adipose tissue under George's arm. *That will bruise,* Patsy thought. For years after, whenever she thought of her parents' marriage, this would be the image that came into her head.

Roger smiled tightly at the people who'd gathered to watch the family saga under Jesus. "Show's over, folks. Nothing to see here. Nothing to see."

"Dad," Patsy started to say.

"Not the time, Patricia."

Then he led her mother out of the store and Patsy watched George's round turquoise butt waddle away. Her mother kept muttering, "I'm not finished, I'm not finished, I'm not done."

"You're done," Roger said.

Her mother paused when they reached the automatic doors at the front of the store. "You'll come for Christmas, Patsy?"

"Probably not," Patsy said.

"Great, we'll see you then."

Patsy was not immune to the sight of her mother being escorted out of the Slickmart, to the pretty business of the woman who had raised her come undone. But she had seen some hard things in her life already and had learned to treat everything like the photograph of the thing instead of the thing itself. She could hang the picture in the museum and carry on. And that's what she did. That day was no more or no less than day eleven of Patsy's job at the Slickmart.

Patsy Gets Fired

ON HER FOURTEENTH day of work, she was fired. It was exactly one week before Christmas, and she was told that the timing represented quite an accomplishment as Mr. Slick preferred to wait until after the holidays for firings.

There were two official reasons for her dismissal.

One, she was caught on the security camera poking holes in water bottles. Upon seeing the tape, she thought that it was somewhat unclear what she had been doing. She told them that she'd been examining the bottles to determine why they were leaking, an explanation they seemed to accept. "I was plugging holes," she claimed. "Not making them."

"Why didn't you tell a superior?"

"Well, I wasn't sure if I was seeing what I thought I was seeing," she said.

The second incident occurred in the break room and was significantly more damning.

She'd been eating lunch with Lenny or George when a man she'd never met before came in. His hair was white blond and his arms were red, as was his neck. He worked in electronics, and the perception was that the electronics guys all thought they were the shit.

So, Electronics sat down with them. And Lenny or George said to him, "You know Patsy?"

Electronics kind of grunted in her direction. "Heard you were in the military?"

"Yeah." She said this with a definite period because she was not in the mood to entertain with old war stories.

"What was that like?"

"Hot," she said.

Lenny or George snickered.

"Also sandy," she added.

"Bet your crotch got all sandy," Electronics said.

What a wit, she thought, though she had certainly heard worse after four years in the service. "Yeah," she said, "my pussy's like sandpaper."

All of them laughed at that, and Patsy loudest of all. She had learned that this was a good strategy if one wished to get along with unpleasant men. Then she said she had to get back on the sales floor, but really, she just couldn't stand to be around the gentleman from electronics anymore.

Later that afternoon, she was on break by herself when Electronics returned.

"So . . . ," said Electronics, "what was it really like over there?"

"If you're so interested, why don't you sign up?" She took the lid off her yogurt container and started mixing the strawberries from the bottom to the top.

"Can't," he said. Then he lifted his sneaker and set it up on the faux wood table. "Flat feet. But you were lucky. 'Cause I bet you didn't see any actual combat over there or nothing."

She asked him to please explicate.

"I mean, 'cause you're a gal. And gals don't see actual combat."

An expert, she thought. She just shook her head. "Seriously, you don't know what the hell you're talking about."

"Naw," said Electronics, "now you're looking all upset, but I didn't mean nothing bad by it. It's still a good thing you done, going over there and serving your country and all."

"Thanks," she said. "Appreciate it mightily."

He wasn't finished. "But it ain't the exact same thing as when a guy does it, right? 'Cause the guys are the ones who see actual combat, and the gals—"

She set her yogurt down on the table. "You wanna see some actual combat right now?"

"I'm serious. I'm just trying to figure it. It's, like, different for girls over there. I mean, girls aren't on the front lines, so—"

"Honestly, I'm going to need you to stop talking now."

"Aw, Patsy, don't be mad. You're taking it all backward. I just meant—"

She'd had her fill. So she took her yogurt spoon, flipped it point outward, and aimed it at Electronics's throat. "Shut your cock holster, would you?"

Then, she jammed Electronics against the Coke machine.

"Am I talking to you?" she asked.

"Yes," he said.

"No, I meant before. Was I talking to you?"

"Um, yes."

"Seriously," she said, "I'm gonna need you to shut the fuck up, so I can eat my yogurt in peace. You reckon that's a possibility for you?"

Electronics was at least a foot taller than her, so she had to reach up to keep the spoon at his throat. He nodded a little, and she took the spoon away. She could see a dark red spot on his Adam's apple that would probably turn into a sweet little bruise.

She walked over to the sink and rinsed off the spoon, which she had brought from home.

"You're a crazy bitch, you know that?"

She sat down and tried to resume eating her yogurt. Something about the strawberries at the bottom repulsed her a little. It put her in mind of human flesh she'd smelled and seen, and animal flesh, and the acid of vomit and other things that should stay inside but had come out.

The unborn rewarded her with a kick to the gut.

Other folks in the break room were watching her, though no one was speaking. "Anyone want the rest of my yogurt?" she asked. "There's nothing wrong with it," she said. "I just don't want it anymore."

A roundish girl with apple cheeks spoke up. Her name was Lara, and Patsy thought she worked in cosmetics with Lacey. "Sure, Patsy," Lara said, "I'll have it."

Patsy gave her the yogurt, then returned to guns.

Mr. Slick fired her at the end of the business day. It turned out that Electronics was married to his daughter.

Patsy thought the boss's timing was either ballsy or stupid. At the moment of her dismissal, she had been holding a hunting rifle. It wasn't loaded, but Mr. Slick couldn't have known that for certain.

Slick put his arm around her shoulders and walked her out to the parking lot, and when she told him she didn't have a car, he drove her home.

"You're a nice girl, Patsy," he said after he'd pulled into her driveway. "You're just going through a bad time right now. Why don't you give me a call when you've had some time to sort yourself out?"

"I'm fine," she said. "I'm eff'n peachy. And hey, man, fuck you! You don't have any right to say that to me. You don't have any right to go acting like you're such a good guy after you're the one who just fired me a week shy of Christmas. Everyone knows your wife's crazy and everyone calls your store the fucking Suckmart. Did you know that? And your son-in-law's an asshole who don't know jack shit about the service. So which one of us is going through a bad time? You don't have any idea what kind of a time I'm going through."

Mr. Slick shook his head. He leaned over her and opened the car door.

She smiled, wide and awful. "What? You don't want to use me for your advertisements anymore?"

"Happy holidays, Patricia," he said.

Patsy Visits Her Mother and Does Some Last-minute Christmas Shopping

THREE DAYS LATER, she received a phone call from Helen.

"What's wrong with Mom?" Helen asked. Helen and George talked every Sunday night, and George had missed last Sunday's call. Patsy told her that she didn't know anything specific, but George had been escorted out of the Slickmart the prior Friday.

"And you didn't call me?"

"No, guess not."

"And you didn't think that Mom being carried out of the Slickmart was worth your further investigation?"

"Honestly, Helen, Dad seemed to be taking care of it—"

"Jesus, Patsy! You're such a baby! Don't you know by now that Dad doesn't take care of *anything*?"

Patsy continued, "And I basically got fired from the Suck 'cause of her. And I've got problems of my own, you know."

"Yeah, you've been away for five years. What problems do you have exactly?"

Patsy said nothing.

Helen sighed. "Here's what you're going to do now. You're going to drive down to Mom and Dad's, and you're going to see Mom and talk to her and find out everything that's happened since last Friday. Then you are going to call me back."

"Seriously, Helen, I've got stuff to do today."

"Yeah? Like what? Big appointment with *Dr. Phil?* You just told me how you got fired from your job. Seems like you should have some free time on your hands."

"Screw you. I'm a soldier, man. I'm an eff'n soldier, and I've got problems—"

"Patsy, I want you to know that I respect that you served your country, but you are not in Iraq anymore and you are not a little girl."

"FUCK YOU. You're not here. You're in your big fancy Texas house with your big fancy husband. You are not my commanding officer, Helen. You don't get to give me orders."

"Go deal with this, Patsy." Then Helen hung up.

Though Patsy was annoyed, she called the Pharm and asked him if he'd heard anything about her mother. He had. The rumor was she'd been put in some kind of a place.

"What kind of a place?" she asked. "You mean like a crazy-person place?"

He said nothing for a beat, so she knew that was likely his theme. "The Sabbath Day Hospital past county line," he said. "I thought you would have heard."

As it was Magnum's day for the car, she asked Pharm to drive her there.

They arrived around two. The receptionist asked if they were there for visiting hours, and Patsy asked why else would she be there. She and Pharm gave their names, and then they were led into an expansive, sunny room with bars on the windows. Most of the inmates were engaged in activities like macramé or painting, but not George. George sat by herself in the corner.

"Hi, Mom," Patsy said.

Her mother's eyes took a second to focus, but then she recognized her. "Patsy."

"And I brought my old friend, Marcus, with me, too. You remember Marcus, right? He's the old pastor's son."

"Oh . . . ," George said, and she averted her eyes and waved at him. Patsy told the Pharm to go amuse himself so that she and her mother could have it out alone.

"It's nice here," George said.

"Yeah," Patsy said, and then because she couldn't come up with anything else, she added, "lots of activities."

"Roger thought I needed a break."

"Probably not the worst idea Dad ever had."

"Yeah, that would have been getting his PhD."

George's reply surprised Patsy, and she didn't know if she should laugh. "Well, Helen wanted me to come and check that you were doing OK."

"I'm fine."

"Good. Then I guess I'll be on my way now."

"Wait, Patsy. Stay for a bit, would you?"

She sat back down, but her mother didn't seem to have anything to say. The silence made Patsy uneasy, so she said, "Sorry I didn't come help you that day at the Slickmart."

George waved her hand. "I was acting crazy. I see that now. I had gotten some antidepressants"—she didn't mention that they had come from the Pharm—"and I guess I was taking the wrong ones. Made me hallucinate a bit." She laughed. "Now I'm here, it's pretty much getting straightened out."

"Good," Patsy said.

"Patsy. You work at the Slickmart. I just want to know, what's gonna happen to that ceiling?" she asked.

"Well," Patsy said, "I guess they'll eventually repair it and put a new one up."

"Oh!" George's hands rose up to her face.

"I thought you knew it wasn't real," Patsy said.

"I do know. I just thought it was beautiful. It was something beautiful in this world, and even if it wasn't real, it was still beautiful and it was still a miracle and there aren't that many of those these days, I think."

"OK," Patsy said. "OK, OK."

"I just hate to think of that ceiling sitting in some Dumpster!" Pastor Mom grabbed her daughter's hand and looked her right in the eyes. "I'm so sorry," she said.

"Sure," Patsy said. "I'm sorry, too."

"No . . . For your father. For the way he's acted toward you. I told him to give you the money, but . . . And for when he sent you away in high school . . ."

Patsy laughed. "Mom, I don't even think about that anymore. It was so long ago."

George nodded and looked at her hands. "I'm proud of you," she said finally.

Patsy wanted to tell her to fuck off with her pride. She hadn't joined the military to make anyone proud, and if her parents had been any sort of folks to her, she wouldn't have joined at all. But she knew her mother was in a weakened state. So she just stood up and left. "See you around," said Patsy, and George turned back to the window.

ON THE DRIVE back to Buckstop, the Pharm stopped to make several "deliveries," and then they ate at a Fuddruckers. "This place is repulsive," he said.

"Pretty much."

About halfway through their meal, the Pharm said, "You know, I feel sort of bad about selling your mom those antidepressants since you told me they were the reason for her seeing things and all."

Patsy shrugged. She was in the middle of a bite.

"Maybe I could do something to make it up to her."

"Like stop selling pharmaceuticals?"

"Truth be told, I was already thinking about doing that. Drug lords are one thing, but those pharmaceutical companies are evil," he said. "But as far as your mom goes, I was hoping for something more personal."

While finishing her Diet Coke, she considered the question. She set down her glass. For the first time in a very long while, she knew exactly what action to take.

"What?" he asked.

"I know something she would really like." She told him, and the Pharm agreed to it. She had never found it hard to convince the Pharm of anything. He was predisposed toward breaking the law.

Pharm paid the check at Fuddruckers, and then they drove to the Slickmart, where Patsy French was no longer an employee.

Breaking in was easy. This wasn't a Wal-Mart, after all. The security system only worked from the front of the store, so they went through the back, through the loading area. The only thing holding the loading dock door in place was a combination lock of not much better quality than one found in a high school gym. Patsy sprayed it with liquid nitrogen (which they'd stopped to pick up at the twenty-four-hour Wal-Mart superstore), and the Pharm smashed it with a hammer. They were in.

They walked down to the condom row. The Pharm shined his flashlight on Him. Jesus was still beaming down on the contraceptives, though He was a bit blearier than He'd been when last she'd seen Him. "It really does look like the Messiah," the Pharm said somewhat reverently.

"Only when you're shining the beam that way," Patsy said as she grabbed the flashlight.

"What's your plan for getting the Nazarene down?" he asked.

"It's simple," said Patsy. She had spent plenty of time considering that ceiling in the brief time she'd been employed there. "See, those are all just separate acoustic panels. We just need a tall-enough ladder. And then we can take the three Christ panels down one at a time."

"Patsy, we're never gonna be able to reach that. The ceiling's like thirty feet up. We're gonna need an apple picker."

She thought that the store might have one. She and the Pharm searched around for a bit, but they both came up empty-handed.

"Now what?" he asked.

For thirty seconds, Patsy felt rather discouraged, and then she remembered Lenny and George's secret passage above the store. "We go from above," she said.

They went back outside and then up the metal staircase that led to the attic space.

"Sweet Jesus," the Pharm said. "There's a liquor store up here." He noted all the empty bottles of Jim Beam and Maker's Mark.

"Yeah."

The Pharm kicked over one of the empty bottles and a bit of liquor seeped out. "You suppose this is what might have caused the blessed miracle below?"

She thought it seemed like a reasonable theory.

They ascertained that the attic structure wasn't a weight-bearing part of the building proper, but more a freestanding loft space, like there might be in a church or a theater. There was an approximately two-foot gap between the floor of the attic and the ceiling of the Slickmart. They concluded that if they pulled up the floorboards they'd be able to reach the triptych of Jesus panels, no problem. So the Pharm pulled up one of the floorboards—they were pretty thin and warped—and that wasn't enough space, so he pulled up another. Patsy leaned over the new hole and found she could reach the middle panel that comprised the Jesus stain (basically, His nethers). The upper and lower panels were more challenging because her arms were too short. She pulled herself out of the gap and the Pharm said he would give it a go, though he was not particularly tall either. He stretched himself as long as he could. She said, "Hey, buddy, don't kill yourself. We can just open another board, and then I'll be able to do it." But the Pharm said he could reach. About twenty seconds later, he pulled out the panel that depicted the Savior's skirt and sandals.

Patsy looked down the gap. She could see the condom row that had so enraged her mother. From these heights, it was a long way down.

The Pharm returned for the final panel.

"You sure you can reach?" she asked. She offered to hold his feet.

"I'm fine," he said. His body stretched out long and catlike. "Got it!" he called.

That's when the horrible thing happened, though Patsy didn't see it. She just heard a whoosh and a clatter and a thud and a bang and a whimper.

"Pharm!" she called. "Marcus!"

There was no answer.

As she ran down the stairs back into the Slickmart, she was pretty sure she'd killed her last friend in the world. She thought of Magnum and Minnie and how aggrieved they were going to be and how much it was going to blow to have them on her conscience, too. She started a round of AlphaBravos just to keep herself together, but it didn't help. She kept forgetting what came after Juliet.

She ran to the condom aisle. Marcus was not moving, but his head appeared somewhat cushioned by several bags of menstrual pads that had fallen from the shelf. The final panel of the Son of Man, His crowned head, was lying beside him, smashed straight through.

Marcus was passed out, but still breathing. She couldn't tell which parts of him were broken.

"Marcus," she whispered. "I'm sorry. I'm gonna go call the ambulance."

"Don't," he said, then he opened his eyes and she almost cried for joy. "Just help me out of here." He reached for her, which she took to be an incredibly positive sign, because she was worried that if he was alive, he was going to go all Christopher Reeve on her. He reached for her again, and then he passed out.

"Pharm," she explained though he wasn't listening to her anyway, "I shouldn't move you. You could have, like, a back injury. And you shouldn't be moved." This was something she'd learned firsthand during her time in the service and also back when she was a cheerleader, though that seemed too long ago to even count.

She decided it was a far better thing that they both be arrested than that the Pharm be paralyzed because she so foolishly tried to move him. She left him on the floor and went into the employee break room, where she dialed 911.

She explained that she was a disgruntled former employee of the Slickmart and, due to her many grievances, she had gone into the store after hours and, long story short, her friend had fallen through the roof and was now in need of medical attention.

After an extended pause, the operator said he would send an ambulance. Though the man had chosen not to say, Patsy assumed there would be a cop car, too.

Patsy Makes a Phone Call

FIVE TIMES THE sheriff asked Patsy if she'd like to make her phone call, and five times Patsy told her no. The sixth time the question was posed, Patsy threw up, which wasn't by way of response, though she worried that the timing might have made it seem otherwise. "Sorry, ma'am," Patsy said. The sheriff was wearing one of those ridiculous empire-waist maternity uniforms and was significantly with child. Patsy hoped the pregnant cop wouldn't be the one to have to clean up the mess. "Really sorry," she repeated.

"Hate to break it to you, but it's not the first time that cell's been used that way and it's not the worst use it's ever been put to neither," the sheriff said. "You drunk?"

"Pregnant."

"Mmmhmm."

"I wish I were drunk," she said.

"Amen to that," said the sheriff.

"Do you know what happened to my friend?"

The sheriff shook her head. "Nope. You could call him if you want."

"I think he's probably on some pretty serious painkillers right now."

"You could call your husband or whoever, and they could probably find out for you," the sheriff suggested.

"It's late," she said. "I'd rather use my call tomorrow. No sense worrying all my folks tonight."

"Well, most people don't feel like you, that's for certain," the sheriff said. And then she picked up a book from her desk, probably because she'd decided that a person who didn't want to make a call was not worth bothering with.

Patsy could see that the book was an old copy of *To Kill a Mockingbird.* "I had to read that for school," she said.

The sheriff nodded. "Yeah."

"I didn't really like it at the time, but my dog's named for one of the characters."

"Boo?" the sheriff guessed.

"Scout."

"Good name."

"I'm sorry you have to be here on my account tonight," Patsy said. "Away from your family and all."

"It's my job and I thank the Lord for it."

"Truth is, I really don't know what the heck my friend and I were thinking."

The sheriff smiled and said nothing, and Patsy didn't feel comfortable bothering her anymore.

She lay down on the cot and tried to fall asleep. In the distance, she could hear Handel's *Messiah,* and though it was soft and sweet, she still found it difficult to sleep through. She couldn't really quiet her thoughts anyhow. She was thinking of Scout, and of Magnum and the Pharm letting Scout run off, and then she was thinking of dogs in general and how they were so much better than most humans, and then she was thinking how even Iraqi dogs have a hard time of it.

"Maybe I *will* call my husband," Patsy said.

The sheriff let her out of the cell and then pointed her in the direction of the phone. "I'll only be a minute," Patsy said.

The sheriff shrugged. "No one's timing you, honey."

Patsy dialed Magnum's cell phone. When he finally answered after seven rings, she could hear music and people talking in the background. A party.

"What's happening?" she asked.

"We did it!" he said. "We made the world's largest cupcake!"

"That was tonight?"

"Yeah, I told you about it. You should have come. Anyway, the local news was there, and my picture might be in the paper and on TV. Hey, could you tape the eleven o'clock news for me? It's no big deal. Just if you happen to think of it."

Patsy said she would try but that she wasn't sure if they had any blank tapes.

"Where are you?" he asked. He hadn't recognized the phone number that she'd been calling from.

"Just out," she said. "I'll be home soon."

"You sound funny," he insisted. "Is the Pharm with you?"

"No . . . No . . . I was just thinking . . . About this dog, of all things!" She tried to make her voice light and silly, but she couldn't quite manage it. "Did I ever tell you about this dog my unit adopted?"

"No, Patsy," Magnum replied. He sounded more sober than he had before. "You don't say much about all that."

"Well, we called him Old Yellow, 'cause he was yellow—pretty eff'n creative, I know. He was a yellow dog with a speckled gray belly that almost touched the ground and liquid brown eyes like molasses. He weren't of a breed you necessarily see in the States. Sad to say, but I remember this dog in greater detail than most any other non-American I met Over There.

"One day, we're disarming this old schoolhouse. They thought the Hajjis were stockpiling weapons, but it had mainly turned out to be a place where a bunch of folks were living. So, the people were confused about why we were there, and we were confused about why we were there, too, and one of them fired a shot 'cause people will defend what's theirs, no matter how shit it is, to the death. And we fired shots. And the dog had come along with someone, and that dumb beast got in the way, I reckon.

"I waited till I got back in the truck. I bit my lip right through, till my teeth were touching, but it didn't help none.

"I tried to hide it from Smartie—did I ever tell you about Smartie? He was probably the person I was closest to over there. You'd like him, I think. I tried to hide it from him, but he seen. How could he not?" She could hear Magnum breathing. It was quieter. He must have gone outside. "You still there?" she asked.

"I'm here, Patsy."

"You're quiet."

"I'm just listening is all."

"So what I told Smartie was that I was sweating something fierce. Pretty lame excuse, but it really was eff'n hot, by the way. I said I was sweating something fierce, but my stupid mouth failed me a bit on *fierce*.

"Smartie put his arm around me and he said, his voice all soft and sweet, 'Patsy. Patsy. What's a nice girl like you doing in a war like this?'

"I looked at him, Magnum, and I spoke my truth as I knew it, 'Just trying to get along.'"

PART III

A Relative Paradise

Six Years Later

2012

Helen before Dawn

IN A SENSE, she had picked the house for the trees. Most of the properties the Realtor had shown her, mainly new construction back in the latter-day boom time of 2003, had had little or no landscaping: just dirt or sod so fresh the lawn looked no better than a tiled bath; maybe a pile of anorexic saplings, unplanted and lacking promise, their roots bundled into cheap burlap sacks. "All this will be finished by the time you move in," the Realtor had sworn. "You have to use your imagination, Helen"—the Realtor had stopped addressing Elliot weeks earlier; it was clear who would be the decider—"Just close your eyes and imagine how it will look when it's done."

Helen would certainly not close her eyes, and though she did not say, she considered the suggestion ridiculous: telling a person to BUY something, anything, with her eyes closed! Helen had always made all necessary judgments with her eyes wide open, thank you very much, and it would be so with this and any other damn lawn she was asked to view. To her, such landscaping (or the lack of it) screamed nouveau riche. She had wanted *mature* trees, the kind that said generations had lived there (even if they hadn't been generations of her relations, generations of *somebody* at least), the kind whose branches gently tapped

the second-floor windows, the kind that provided shade in the summer and color in the spring and fall, the kind with tenacious roots
that the occasional Texas hurricane couldn't easily fell, the kind with
strong branches from which you could suspend a tire swing or a ham-
mock, the kind that her children (they had still been hypothetical then)
could climb.

"Trees like that require sacrifices in other areas," the Realtor had
said. "Old trees mean old kitchens and old baths."

But Helen knew better. All it took was money to redo a kitchen,
but you couldn't fake the trees.

So she had gotten her trees.

The children had taken longer, but Helen had managed to will them
into existence, too. Twins. Alice and Eli. Sturdy little elves of average
height, inclinations, maladies, and temperaments. Except that they were
hers—and this was a rather limitless clause—she supposed that they
were unexceptional in every way. And wasn't this a blessing really? Leave
the exceptional children, with their prodigious piano playing on the
one hand or their horrific birth defects on the other, to the exceptional
parents! Helen was a lover of the ordinary, the everyday, the world that
existed on the sweet, broad plain in the middle of the bell curve.

"Mommy," Eli said, "Mommy, wake up."

Eli tugged at her pajama sleeve. Helen glanced at the alarm clock.
It was 6 AM. "Mommy needs to sleep a little longer," Helen said. In
the afternoon, they would all be flying to Tennessee to visit her parents. An airplane trip with two six-year-olds entitled her to a half hour
more rest. And by her calculations, the airplane trip plus the weekend at her parents' impossibly tiny and stale house entitled her to at
least an extra hour.

"Mommy, Alice wanted me to tell you something," Eli continued.

"Mmmm, go tell Daddy."

Helen rolled onto her other side, away from Eli. She heard Eli sigh
and shuffle over to Elliot. She didn't feel at all bad about passing the
buck—Elliot turned retarded at the airport and was no help at all at

her parents.' He actually had the gall to act like a trip to visit her family was *vacation.*

"Daddy."

Elliot yawned. "What, kiddo?"

"Alice is stuck in the tree, and she won't come down."

"What tree?"

"The big one."

And just like that, they were all awake and in slippers and out the door, and there would be no extra sleep for anyone that morning.

The kids had been having a climbing contest. The rules were simple. The winner was the person who climbed to the highest point. Helen felt a passing swell of pride to hear that her brave Alice had won. Alice had won and, in a sense, she had also lost. She had climbed so high that she was scared to come down. On the way to the front yard, Elliot admitted that these predawn contests had been going on for some time. The kids had been told that they couldn't watch television before noon, so they had found other ways of amusing themselves.

It was the Friday before Labor Day weekend, and the dawn air was cool but damp. Helen scanned the yard but could not immediately spot Alice. She asked Eli which tree his sister was in. "That one," he said, pointing to a Southern magnolia, a particular favorite of Helen's for its fragrant white blooms in spring. For all Helen's mature tree reverence, this one was not a particularly tall Southern magnolia. Truthfully, it was a bit of a runt at twenty-two feet. As she tried to spot Alice, it passed through Helen's mind that large ones could run from sixty to ninety feet.

Helen peered up—she wasn't wearing her glasses and hadn't had time to put in her contact lenses. At the top was a small, reddish blob. She squinted a bit and could see (or thought she could see) a reluctant Christmas angel clad in pink footed-pajamas. The girl was sobbing softly. "Don't worry, cupcake. Mommy will come and get you," Helen called.

"OK," Alice replied. Her voice sounded as if she needed to blow her nose.

As Helen began walking toward the base of the tree, Elliot grabbed her arm.

"I think we should stop and think about this a moment," Elliot said.

Helen pulled away. "I'll be fine."

"I don't know, Hel. The branches on that thing are pretty weak. I don't want both of you getting hurt. I think it'll be better if I get my ladder."

"Mommy," Alice called. "I have to go to the bathroom!"

"I'll be there in a minute, baby!" Helen was annoyed. She turned back to Elliot. "Will your ladder even go that high?"

Elliot looked up at the tree. "Fully extended, yeah, it's just about twenty-five feet. We'll just lean it up against the top of the tree. One of us will stand at the bottom. Me, I guess. And you'll climb up and help Al down."

Helen sighed. "Fine. OK. Just hurry the fuck up, would you? I don't want to stand here all day discussing this."

"Mommy, I really have to go!" Alice called.

"Daddy's just going to get the ladder," Helen called. "Don't be scared, angel!"

Alice had begun to sob. "I'm going to pee my pants! I'm going to pee my pants!"

"Just try to hold it, baby," Helen said. "Mommy'll be up there in a second." Helen could hear Elliot banging around their three-car garage. "HURRY UP!" she yelled. A small hand gently tugged Helen's sleeve. Eli. "Mommy, can I help?"

"Just be quiet." This was said sharply, which Helen immediately regretted. She smiled at the boy in a way she knew was fake and likely terrifying. It was the best she could do. "Why don't you go inside and watch television?"

"But it's before noon," her boy replied.

"It's fine. Just for today," Helen said.

Eli went in the house just as Elliot returned with the ladder. "Everyone still okay?" Elliot asked.

"Yes."

"I need you to help me prop this up against the tree, OK?"

Helen nodded, and they went to work extending and arranging the ladder.

"Mommy, I don't wanna pee my pants!"

"You won't have to, Al!"

"Maybe I try to come down now!" Alice called.

Just as she and Elliot had gotten the ladder stabilized, Helen heard a thump. She thought the sound seemed too soft and light to hold any consequence for her. A laundry bag flung from a window, a fertilizer sack thrown into the back of a pickup truck, a sack of flour slipping off a modestly high grocery shelf. Something minor. Something distant even. Something happening to the neighbors and not to her.

George in the Morning

THE PHONE RANG while she was still in bed. She rolled across Roger's empty side to answer. A pretty, bruised voice wanted to speak to her husband.

"Roger's out of town," George said and then she remembered that you weren't supposed to tell strangers that you were alone in a house. Even if it was a woman. The woman might be a front for male criminals who'd come to rob or rape you, or worse. She had seen a television program where such things happened. "Actually, he's not out of town."

"So can I speak to him then?"

"What I mean to say is he won't be back until this evening. He's guest preaching in Chapel Hill." Why was she giving so much information? "I can take a message though."

"Could I have a cell phone number?"

Roger didn't keep a cell phone any longer. He said cell phones (and other devices of that ilk) bred secrecy in relationships. He had delivered a very popular (as such things go) sermon on the subject. George did have a cell phone—a prepaid one for emergencies that was a secret from Roger. "He'll be back tonight," George repeated. "Why don't you just call back then?"

The woman sighed. And then without warning, the sigh became a sob.

"Oh, I'm sorry," George said. "Please don't cry."

"My mother is dead," said the woman. "She's dead."

"I really am sorry," George repeated.

"Are you close to your mother?" the woman asked.

"She's been gone a long time," George said, "but no, not really. I wish we had been closer."

"Do you have children then? Are you close to them?"

"I think I am," George said. "I don't know what *they* would say." George laughed a little so that this last part would seem like a joke. "I've definitely made mistakes, but I've always tried to be close to them."

"My mother was my best friend," the woman said. "I feel so horribly alone. I didn't know I would feel this way. It's almost silly how awful I feel."

Despite herself, George yawned. "Oh, excuse me!"

"No," said the woman, "it's my fault. I shouldn't be calling this early. I'm just making my way through my mother's address book. I tried sending an e-mail to your husband, but it must have been an old address. There's going to be a memorial service for her next month at Texas University. I'm trying to invite as many of her graduate students and assistants as I can round up. Mom was always so close to her assistants. Plus she had a pretty healthy ego, you know, and she'd want the biggest service possible."

"I'll let Roger know. What was your mother's name, by the way?"

The woman told her and then gave George the details for the service. George dutifully wrote them down, though she felt quite certain Roger wouldn't attend. It was a lot of money to fly to Texas for some random professor's funeral, and Roger rarely spoke of that period in their life.

After hanging up the phone, George got out of bed. She was awake now, and she had many errands to run that morning anyway. Roger was coming home as she had recklessly mentioned, and both Vinnie and Helen were visiting for the weekend. Though Helen came home with dutiful frequency, Vinnie's last appearance had been more than ten years ago, for Patsy's wedding.

George took a shower and by the time she got out, the phone was ringing again. Roger, just checking in.

"What's on tap for you today?" he asked. He had been so gentle and sweet with her since her illness.

"Doctor's appointment. And I have to buy flowers and grocery shop. And then I have to pick out new eyeglass frames. You?"

"Mainly just the plane ride and then I'll go straight to the church, assuming I'm not caught in the usual delays. Either way, I'm going to work on that sermon they want me to give at that conference in Memphis. The one about Adam and Eve. It's such a cliché, right? Everyone knows it. You think it would be simple to hammer out a decent sermon. But George, the more I think about Adam and Eve, the more problematic that text becomes for me. If there had been no original sin, there would be no Earth, because Adam and Eve would still be in paradise. And there would be no us, because there would be no sex. So how can you tell people not to sin. Or . . ." Roger laughed . . . "Still with me?"

"I am," she said. It wasn't as if he'd said anything particularly complex. He always thought her a bit stupider than she actually was and himself a bit smarter than he actually was. It had taken her nearly thirty years of marriage to puzzle this out and another ten for it not to bother her. "I like hearing you talk."

"I sound like an eight-year-old in Bible class. Shoot," Roger said, "I'm late! I love you, Georgie. See you tonight!"

"I love you, too," she said. They both hung up, and George realized that she had forgotten to tell him that Carolyn Murray had died.

SHE HAD WHAT would probably be termed a schoolgirl crush on Dr. Charles. He was British and, unlike most of the doctors at the hospital, not Adventist. He was about her son's age—maybe a little older—and good-looking in a toothy, squinty kind of way, like the stuttering actor from the romantic comedies. He seemed shipwrecked, as if he belonged to a different (better) place and had a manner of entering his appointments with George as if he were surprised (though delighted, perfectly delighted!) to find himself among the savages of this particular island.

Incidentally, George's crush, like most of the schoolgirl variety, did not mean she wished to sleep with him. She certainly did not fantasize about him throwing her down on the examining table and pulling off her pants. No. She merely wanted him to find her pretty and pleasant and as nonburdensome as possible. Above all, she hoped he thought her a good patient, a good person, good, good.

"Mrs. Pomeroy," he greeted her holding out his hand for her to shake. "How are you, Georgia? Come in!"

She liked how he used her full name, and yet something in his voice did not sound delighted to her, and she suspected that the file he clutched in his lovely, cool, pale hands likely contained bad news.

There had been tests, you see. And the tests had turned up something. And now there would have to be decisions. And oh, how silly really to have the news of one's imminent passing delivered to you by a doctor who looked like a movie doctor! And at that moment, she thought, *It doesn't matter what or why or how or even when.* The point was that this body, no matter what abuses had been heaped upon it, had always unsentimentally gone about the business of healing itself, and soon it would not.

"I'm sorry," she said.

"I think I ought to be saying that to you," Dr. Charles replied.

At age seven, she had felt old. On Halloween, she had walked down the street in a cowgirl costume and thought, *I am too old for this.* At nineteen, she had felt old. She had a baby on her hip and thought, *Now there are people living on this Earth who are nineteen years younger than me: I am old.* At twenty-seven, thirty-two, forty-five, and fifty, she had felt old. At fifty-seven, when they cut off her breasts, she had certainly felt old. She realized she had felt old all her life. Until that moment. At sixty, upon hearing the news that she was likely dying, she felt young. Uselessly, stupidly young.

"It's not over yet, Georgia. I'd like to make another appointment to talk about options."

"Yes, of course."

"Your husband should be there," said the doctor.

"He's busy with work."

"I imagine he'd want to be there," the doctor insisted.

George shrugged. She loved her husband and acknowledged his limitations.

"One of your children, then?"

"Maybe." *Helen doesn't hate me, if she's willing to fly from Texas,* George supposed. "Dr. Charles? Could I ask you a question?"

"Of course."

"What will it feel like to die? I mean, how will it happen?"

"We're not there yet, Georgia."

George said nothing. And so he told her. An infection. Or one of the tumors would grow so large it would stop something vital—a heart, say, or a lung—from functioning. But—silver lining—with enough drugs, most people didn't feel this part very much. One was just there, and then one was not.

After this, Dr. Charles walked her back to reception, and George, despite the news of the hour, could not help enjoying the spectacle of being on the arm of the elegant physician. "Anything planned for the weekend, Georgia?"

"My daughter and her family, and my oldest, my son, are all coming to town. He's bringing his girlfriend."

"How lovely for you."

"Well, we haven't met the girlfriend yet," George joked.

Dr. Charles laughed a bit too loudly, a bit too long, a bit too horsily, and just like that George didn't love him anymore.

* * *

SHE HAD PLANNED the day so that all her city errands could be accomplished at one time.

On her way to the optometrist, George thought to herself, *I am dying.*

The driver in front of George, an old woman so small it looked as if her Cadillac were driving itself, had decided to go thirty miles per hour in a forty-five zone. George signaled and thought, *Oh, stop being dramatic. Everyone's dying. That lady in the Cadillac's dying. And besides, the doctor didn't say you were dying.* As she changed lanes, she cut someone off. It wasn't entirely her fault—that driver was doing about sixty and had come out of nowhere. The person honked and passed George on the other side. "FUCK YOU, LADY!"

George's heart was beating like mad—*something vital will cease to function*—and she thought, *I could have died just then.* Wouldn't that have been preferable, really? Quick and to the point. Avoid the business and the expense of it all. A commercial about death, not a miniseries.

George's errand at the optometrist was to pick out new frames. "Just point me to the cheap ones," George told the clerk.

"I hear you," the clerk replied. "But just try these first. They'd look great on you."

The clerk removed a pair from a case that wasn't the cheap one. George put on the frames. They were dark red (almost black), oval, with titanium arms.

"See, I knew it! I'm never wrong," said the clerk. "They go with your eyes."

After years of basically being ignored in stores, George had gotten cancer, lost seventy pounds (only six and a half of which had been breast tissue), and was suddenly the belle of the mall.

George looked in the mirror. "How much?" she asked.

The clerk quoted an insane number, and George set the credit card on the counter.

"Also," said the clerk, "they have to be special ordered, which means it takes a little longer for them to arrive. Is that all right?"

"Sure." When she thought about it, she supposed she had always been something of a gambler.

THE FLOWERS WERE purchased in town at Buckstop's lone florist.

"My, you're looking fit, Georgia!" said the florist. George was very familiar with the woman as she provided flowers for all of the happenings at Roger's church.

"Thank you," said George.

"I wish I knew your secret."

It didn't bother George that people from church speculated that she had had her stomach stapled at the same time she had had her mastectomy. It was flattering in a way and just showed how little any of them knew her.

"I want something kind of sophisticated. Kind of chic," George told the florist. "My son's coming in from New York. He's bringing his girlfriend. She's Indian."

"Like Native American?" the florist asked.

"From India," George said. "Her name is Mina. She's an actress."

"Fancy!" the florist said. "Would I have seen her in anything?"

George knew the answer to this because Helen had looked Mina Vaswani up on the Internet. "Do you know that movie about the terrorists who take over the cruise ship?"

"Yes! Yes, but I didn't see it." The movie had been R-rated and most of the church members didn't see (or at least claimed not to see) anything that wasn't PG. When George had first married Roger, the church's policy had been no movies at all. This had been hard for George as one of her favorite things in the world had been to escape to the cinema. She didn't mind going alone, didn't care about genre either. All that was really required was darkness and AC. Over the years, the church had relaxed—better to permit some things than run the risk of losing everyone—but by then, George had lost her taste for movies anyway. All the stars of her youth had died or had plastic surgery, and she didn't recognize anyone.

"She was one of the terrorists, I guess," George replied.

"Oh. Maybe birds-of-paradise?" The florist held out the orange and purple flower to George. The bloom struck George as vulgar somehow. Like looking at something poisonous. Like looking at a vagina. "No . . . I want something cleaner. Simpler, I guess."

"How about roses? You can't go wrong with roses."

George shook her head. The flowers had come to seem crucial somehow. She wanted—yes, she could admit it—she wanted Vinnie's girlfriend to like her. To like her and Roger, but mainly to like George. She wanted the flowers to say, *Despite what Vinnie's probably told you about his horrible parents—his crazy, thieving, weak mother and his religious, foolish father—we're all right, I swear. The things he thinks we've done, we had reasons for. The truth is, we're just regular old folks. Kind of corny, yes. But we buy flowers for our guests, and we cook nice, wholesome meals. Please tell our only son to come and visit us more than once every ten years.*

She looked around the shop. "How about those?" She pointed at the gerbera daisies that sat in a silver bucket.

The florist wrinkled her nose. "They're expensive, you know. And they don't last worth a darn. Petals all over the place before the weekend's out. Birds-of-paradise are much heartier."

"That's OK," said George. "That's what I want."

The woman sighed. "Well, it's up to you." The woman began wrapping the flowers in bright pink paper. "So, do I hear wedding bells?"

"My son, you mean? Um, I don't know." George handed the woman her credit card.

"When the gerbera start dying all over the place, tell the good pastor I advised against them," the florist said as she swiped George's card. "I'm throwing in a couple of birds-of-paradise on the house."

The drive home took George past the church. She saw that Roger's car was already in the lot, so she decided to stop to remind him that he was responsible for picking up their son from the airport.

His secretary, Megan, a bright, young thing, sat at her desk, but the door to Roger's office was closed.

"He made it back, I see," George said.

"Yes, Mrs. Pomeroy. His plane was early. The pastor's in there with Janet Phipps and Phil Harris. They're getting married next week."

"I know," said George.

"He'll probably be done in"—Megan stopped to look at her watch—"three and a half minutes."

"You know the pastor's habits to the second," George observed.

"Oh." Megan blushed. "No, I just . . . These things always take about the same amount of time."

"It's all right. He's lucky to have you." George studied the bright young thing more closely. She was pretty and freckled, leaner and older than Patsy. She wore a denim skirt, a modest white blouse, and pink lip gloss. Her hair was in a hopeful little ponytail. Without know-ing why and despite the fact that she had attended an engagement party for Megan Carlson only—when was it?—last year, George had the following thought: *When I'm dead, Roger will probably marry that girl.*

Megan worshipped Roger, that much was clear—*three and a half minutes indeed*—and Roger liked to be worshipped. And though George felt quite sure Roger would be appropriately devastated when she passed, she felt equally sure that he was not the kind of man who would tolerate the widower lifestyle very well.

"When's the wedding?" George asked.

"Next weekend," Megan said.

"I meant yours."

"Oh! Oh, we're still settling on a date," Megan replied.

The door opened—three and a half minutes, George noted—and Roger escorted the couple out of the office. George was still not immune to the pleasures of watching her husband enter a room. Knowing him as well as she did and as long as she had, she knew that she probably should be immune, but she wasn't.

"My, this is a surprise," he said.

"Missed you, I guess."

Roger took a moment to wrap things up with the couple. "Now, you know my services don't come without a steep fee . . . ," he joked. *He's good at this,* George thought. He had been a mediocre high school administrator and, though she had never determined the whole story, something of a disaster as an academic, but he really was an excellent minister. The job suited the worst and best of him somehow.

"Come and sit a minute," Roger said.

"No. I've got food spoiling and flowers withering in the car," she said.

"Just for a minute."

George followed him into the office and thought, *I don't want to die.*

No, it wasn't that. She didn't care about being dead. She just didn't want to have to go through with the dying. She had been hospitalized seven times in her life: three children, two miscarriages, her mastectomy, and the time she had lost her mind. And she had hated every single occasion. She had hated being on display and being in her pajamas when other people were wearing clothes and not being able to keep her own hours. It was all so . . . embarrassing. *I should kill myself,* she thought. But she knew that she was too weak for such things. In life, she had never been a person for the grand gesture, and she doubted she would be one in death either.

"What are you thinking?" Roger asked.

"Do you think Vinnie's bringing that girl to meet us because he's marrying her?" George asked.

"Well, unless he's already married her, they're not sleeping in the same bed. Not in my house."

"Oh, Roger," George said. "Who even cares? Vinnie's almost forty."

"I care," Roger said.

"I'm sure they sleep in the same bed in New York," George said. She didn't mention that with Helen, Elliot, Alice, Eli, Vinnie, and Mina all spending the weekend, in terms of the spatial limitations of their home, it would really be preferable for Vinnie and Mina to sleep together, Jesus notwithstanding. But this was her husband, and so it was pointless to argue. Over the years, she had learned that it was simplest to just do whatever she needed to do, even if it involved measures Roger would certainly have disapproved of. Vinnie and Mina would share a bed this weekend, and unless George was foolish enough to make an issue of it now, Roger would never even notice.

"All the kids'll be home, praise Jesus. That hasn't happened in . . . well, I don't rightly know *how* long it's been," Roger said. "Patsy still not coming, I suppose."

"Helen said she was going to try to call her and—"

Roger interrupted, "Talk some sense into her I hope. It's bullheadedness, pure and simple. Most of her troubles she's brought on herself, and the things she thinks we've done are mainly in her imagination. She only lives ten miles away from us. Why shouldn't she want to come? Why shouldn't she want to see her brother and her sister? That girl is . . ." Roger shook his head.

George took the opportunity of Roger's pause to remind him to pick up Vinnie and the girlfriend from the Chattanooga airport at 8 PM. (She resisted saying, "Be nice to the girl! Try to keep the Jesus talk to a minimum. Not everyone has the exact same opinions as you, you know?") Having accomplished her mission, she kissed Roger on the cheek, said good-bye to his secretary, and drove home to prepare for the arrival of the prodigal son.

It had been a day and then some already, she thought. The news at the doctor, of course. And the awful way it had begun with that poor girl crying on the phone about her mother. George wondered if her own daughters would cry over her that way. Probably not, she decided. She certainly hadn't cried for her own mother that way. She hadn't cried at all. Now that she was older, George felt a certain tenderness toward the woman that she had never come anywhere close to feeling in life. She imagined it would be the same for her own daughters. Years after George was gone, Patsy or Helen, probably Helen, would be driving down some road, and something would remind her of some small kindness George had given—*even though she was broke at the time, my mother knew the importance of a vellum overlay on a wedding invitation*—and she'd have to pull the car over to the side of the road, sick with missing her. *She wasn't so bad,* they'd think. *She did the best she could. She did the best she could when you consider what she had and where she came from.*

Her own mother, Grace, had gotten pregnant at seventeen. The father had been the married foreman at the hat factory where Grace worked in Smyrna, Georgia. He had given her five hundred dollars in cash and told her to either take care of it or get the hell out of town. Grace had chosen to leave. She bought a bus ticket to New York City. Somewhere around New Jersey, she fell asleep. For whatever reason, the bus driver didn't notice her, and she ended up at the bus's final stop in Burlington, Vermont. When she opened her eyes and looked out the window, there was a blizzard. Grace always told it the same way (and only when she was drunk): "I wiped the sleep out of my eyes and thought to myself, *So this is New York City. Guess I won't be able to see those skyscrapers until the snow melts.*" Once she got off the bus, Grace immediately realized her error but decided to stay anyway. Back then, Burlington was a snow globe of a town, and she reasoned that the four hundred or so dollars she had left would stretch a lot further there. "But I really thought I was in New York! What a dummy, I was," she'd say, usually as George was helping her into bed. "Promise me you'll never be that dumb, Georgie."

The image of the girl her mother had been, younger by far than either of George's daughters, looking out a bus window at the wrong city, made George feel as if her heart might break, and though she was only a mile from home, she had to pull the car to the side of the road. *I wish you had loved me,* George thought, *and I wish I could have loved you.* She gathered herself enough to continue the drive and resolved that, yes, she would have all three of her children in her house that weekend: no matter what it took, she would convince Patsy to come home, too.

Vinnie at Lunch and After

IT WAS NEARLY 1 PM, and Hamilton Banish, the producer Vinnie was to meet with, still hadn't shown up. The lunch had been scheduled for 12:30, which, considering that Vinnie's plane left from LaGuardia at 4:17 PM, had been cutting it close enough already. Banish had had no other time that week, or the next one either, and after that, the man was back to London, where he lived during half the year. Vinnie had been trying to get the meeting for months, so he had decided to accept the less-than-ideal time.

Vinnie called Banish's assistant on the phone. As far as the boy knew, Mr. Banish was on his way, nothing had changed.

He looked at the clock on his cell phone: 1:05. He decided to send Mina a text message: "take our suitcases and I'll meet you at the airport. big fish is late. no time to go home first. Love u." Mina would be pissed, but what could he do? There weren't exactly tons of people out there who were willing to help raise money for documentary films.

Thirty seconds later, Mina's reply: "go to hell. I'll see you @ lga. Xo, m"

Ah Mina. It had been her idea to take the trip to Tennessee. They had been together seven years, and she thought it was "positively disgraceful" that she had yet to meet his parents. About six months ago, she had accidentally (so she said) answered Vinnie's cell phone. Roger had been the caller. "He didn't sound so bad," Mina had reported later. "He was charming."

"How long was your conversation? Three minutes?" Vinnie's father could certainly muster three minutes of charm.

"He said your mother's been sick. You didn't tell me that," she had continued.

Vinnie shrugged.

"They won't live forever, you know."

Mina was a smart-enough girl, but Vinnie thought her obtuse in certain ways. Because her own parents (her father owned a chain of grocery stores, her mother was a therapist) had been tolerant and loving, she couldn't conceive of families unlike her own.

The discussion of whether they would visit had continued for the next four months. Vinnie felt terrorized by the topic. He had no way of knowing when or what would inspire Mina to resume talks. It might be an article she was reading online or a movie they had seen or a man pushing another man in a wheelchair. It might be nothing at all. "I don't want to move to Tennessee," Mina had said one day while she was sitting on the toilet. "I just want to go there once, get rubber-stamped, and that'll be that. We never have to visit again."

Vinnie shook his head. "Don't you get it? I don't care if *they* rubber-stamp you. *I* rubber-stamp you." She flushed the toilet, and he kissed her on her forehead.

"Vincent, I do not expect them to love me, if that's what you're worried about."

Of course, Vinnie knew that this was a lie. Mina expected everyone to love her. She wanted her yoga students to love her and her acting teacher to love her and the doorman in her mother's building to love her and the men who sliced the salmon at Zabar's and, sometimes, even her friends' boyfriends and husbands, too. It was her worst and best quality, Vinnie supposed.

Mina continued, "I know they'll probably loathe me because I'm not Christian . . ."

"No, my dad'll just try to show you the error of your ways," Vinnie joked.

"Your mother will love me, though. Mothers always love me."

"I don't care if my mother loves you," Vinnie said.

"I'm very lovable, you know."

Mina had booked the tickets that night.

"Should we stay at your parents' house or a hotel?" she had asked.

"Hotel."

"Hmmm," Mina had replied. "I think I'd rather have the full-on Tennessee experience if it's all the same to you."

That was what she would get, Vinnie thought as he waited in Le Pain Quotidien, which Hamilton Banish had specifically chosen for their meeting. Vinnie hated Le Pain Quotidien—not the restaurant itself, but more what it said about how important Banish considered their meeting. The place might have a pretentious French name and wooden tables, but it was basically fast food. *Le McDonald's*.

Vinnie checked his watch. It was 1:25 PM, and Banish was nearly an hour late. Vinnie wondered when it became acceptable to leave. Or rather, at what point did it make Vinnie seem pathetic to stay?

At 1:26 PM, Vinnie thought about taking that editing job in Canada and bailing on the whole idea of shooting another documentary feature.

At 1:27 PM, Vinnie thought about the tiny bump in his prostate.

At 1:28 PM, Vinnie thought about Mina and the likelihood that they would break up after their weekend adventure in Tennessee.

At 1:29 PM, Hamilton Banish walked through the door of the restaurant. Banish spotted Vinnie immediately, which suggested to Vinnie that the assistant had found his photo on the Internet—

probably from some second-tier film festival he'd gone to; maybe 2006 when he'd taken his first documentary feature to Slamdance? "I'm so sorry!" Banish unleashed a reasonably compelling cascade of mortification such that Vinnie almost believed the man was sorry. "I'm so, so, so sorry! I'm soooo glad you haven't left yet. I'm never this late. It's so rude. Don't hate me. I had a minor disaster on the way here, but don't worry, it's all good now. I'm starved."

Banish ordered quickly: a sandwich that the restaurant referred to by some vaguely Gallic word and a lemonade with mint. "Do you want anything?" Banish asked.

Vinnie had already eaten, but he ordered a cup of coffee. "Hamilton, the thing is, I've kind of got a plane to catch . . ."

"I'm so sorry. We're in a hurry," he told the waitress. Then, he turned back to Vinnie, "So, tell me all about yourself?"

Ah, the business of turning one's life into a series of charming narratives! Vinnie knew it well. He began with the story of how movies had been forbidden in his house growing up, but it was the only thing he'd ever loved, so he managed to find ways to smuggle them. He continued with the story of how he'd secretly applied to Yale, and how when his father found out he'd been accepted, the eighteen-year-old Vinnie had been banned from the house. "You don't have a home," his father had said, and he'd held to that, too. For all four years of college, Roger hadn't allowed him back for Christmases or summers. If his mother disagreed with the policy, she certainly had never said anything. And then, they'd all come to his graduation and had the nerve to act like everything was fine.

"Oh yeah, and I was excommunicated from the church, too."

"Sounds exciting. Like Henry the Eighth or Martin Luther. What'd that mean for you exactly?"

"That I wasn't allowed to go to the church anymore. Not much of a punishment really. I think my father had hoped it would serve as a cautionary tale to my sisters. Or improve his standing among other Adventists. Like, how hard-core a Christian do you have to be to advocate for the excommunication of your own son, right? I really don't know what his thinking was."

"What's he like, your dad?"

"Oh, you know. Your garden variety monster. No, he's . . . um, charming. If you met him, you'd probably like him. Most people do. For a while, at least."

Finally, Vinnie wrapped up with the story of how his mother had stolen his identity while he'd been in graduate school. How she had actually opened credit cards in his name and then not paid them.

"Wow," said Banish, "what's your relationship like with her today?"

"Nonexistent," Vinnie conceded. "She needs to act like none of these things ever happened. It's always been her way of coping, I guess. And I can't do that."

At this point, Banish was nearly finished with his sandwich. "I hope you won't mind a word of advice from a person a couple of years older than you, I think," said Banish. "At some point, Vincent, we have to overcome the disaster of our parentage."

Yes, Vinnie agreed, this was true. (*But really! How annoying of him to say! He was the one who had demanded the dog-and-pony show! It wasn't like Vinnie sat around stewing over this ancient history on a daily basis. He just trotted it out by special request.*)

"So tell me about this film project of yours. I'm very intrigued. Our mutual friend tells me it's about the treatment of women soldiers after the war."

Vinnie nodded and launched into another equally familiar narrative. "I don't know if I mentioned before, but my mother stole from my sister Patricia, too. Only, where Patsy ended up going to war, I just ended up with bad credit." Vinnie paused, and Banish laughed just as Vinnie knew he would.

At 3:30 PM, Banish reached across the table to shake Vinnie's hand. "I think we might be able to work something out," he said.

Outside the restaurant, it took Vinnie close to ten minutes to hail a cab. He checked his messages once he was en route to the airport.

There were three increasingly annoyed ones from Mina and one from his sister Helen. Apparently, Alice was in the hospital and this meant that Helen wouldn't be going home that weekend after all. "I'm sorry to stick you with our parents, but . . . I'll call you later, OK? When I know more."

Vinnie dialed Helen. "Helen, how are you? How's Alice?"

"Oh God, Vinnie, it's awful," Helen said, her voice soft and un-Helenish. "We don't know anything yet. She might have brain damage, she might be perfectly fine."

"What happened, though?"

"She and Eli were climbing trees. And she got stuck somehow. We were getting the ladder. But the kid didn't want to ruin her stupid Dora the Explorer pajamas, so she tried to come down by herself. The little idiot. She should have just gone in her pants."

"She was probably scared, Helen."

"It's the stupidest thing, though. I keep thinking back to the years when I worked as a speech therapist. I was so bad at that job. It sort of shames me to think of it. The way I . . . did that job with a sort of . . . I guess, you might say, a shameful lack of empathy. Because if Alice comes out of this, she might need a speech therapist, and . . . All day I keep thinking of that patient I had who killed himself and . . . I can't even remember his name now! He had a crush on me, Vinnie. Did I ever tell you that? And I start thinking about how this morning, everything, everyone was fine. And I was cranky and sleepy but happy, I guess. I just never realized my happiness was so . . . ugh, fragile? No, what's the word?"

"Gossamer?" Vinnie suggested.

"No, not quite. But something like that, I guess. Vinnie"—she began to whisper—"I've been going over it in my head all day. When she said she had to go to the bathroom, I think I told her to hold it. Do you think I'm horrible?"

"No."

"But if I'd just said to go pee!"

"Hel, you've got to stop torturing yourself. Focus on Alice, OK? I'm just getting to the airport. I have to pay the driver. Can I call you back?"

"Don't bother," said Helen, "I'm not supposed to talk here anyway. There're these no-cell-phone signs everywhere. I've just been pretending I don't see them."

The phone rang just as Vinnie's cab pulled up to the American Airlines terminal. It was Mina.

"We missed it," she said. "And I already checked. There aren't any more flights to Chattanooga until tomorrow."

"Shit," Vinnie said. "I'm sorry."

"I hate you," Mina said.

"No you don't," Vinnie said.

"A little bit," she insisted. "I definitely hate you a little bit. You never wanted me to meet your parents, did you?"

"Where are you?" Vinnie asked.

"Inside. Right by ground transportation. *Waiting for you.*"

"Hold on," Vinnie said. "I can see you already. We'll ride back home together."

Vinnie paid the cab driver and went into the airport to claim Mina.

"When you call your mother to tell her we're not coming, make sure she knows it's your fault, not mine," Mina said when she saw him.

Vinnie took the bags from his girlfriend. "I won't have to tell her. She'll know."

Magnum in the Afternoon

MAGNUM DRAGGED HIMSELF off the couch. He had considered not answering the door at all, but the visitor was persistent and had pressed the buzzer no fewer than fifteen times. It had begun to seem like more bother to ignore the person.

He had stayed home from work that day. The flu. Or, if not the flu, the usual assortment of symptoms that one might call the flu.

"Hello, Georgia," he said. "I'd shake your hand but I don't rightly know if I'm contagious." He paused to cough, and when he looked up, he noticed that she was carrying two rather ugly orange and purple flowers wrapped in paper. "Those for me?"

"No, um, I brought them for Patsy," his mother-in-law said.

"Yeah, I knew that. I was just joshing. She's out picking up Britt from, like, tap or something."

"Britt takes dance?"

"She's real good, too." He had begun to feel dizzy, so even though he knew his wife probably wouldn't approve, he invited George to sit down in their living room.

"What brings you to these parts?" Magnum asked. "We do have a phone, you know?"

"Well, I tried to call, but no one picked up, so I thought, what the heck? It's a nice Friday afternoon, I'll just drive over and see my daughter."

Magnum thought this explanation did not sound at all likely. "All right," he said. "I'll tell Patsy you came."

"Maybe I'll just wait until she gets back. Would that be all right?"

Magnum lay back on the couch and crossed his arms. "She might be a while. If you're in a rush, I mean."

"I got a little bit of time."

Magnum shrugged. He turned on the television and what came on was a cooking program. "This fine with you?" he asked.

"Sure. It's good."

"You know," he said during one of the commercial breaks, "until I started working at Betsy Ross, I never even thought about food at all. Like, you know, I just ate what was in front of me. But now, I'm like, damn! I had no idea food was such a fascinating subject. If I'd known how I'd take to it, I really think I would have been a chef, Georgia."

George nodded. "That's real . . . the thing is, Magnum, I was wondering if you could help me with something."

"Well," he said, "if it's something I have the ability to help you with."

"I want Patsy to come home this weekend. You could come, too, if you're feeling better." George explained how both of Patsy's siblings were coming, and how that rarely happened, and how, now that everyone was so much older, such opportunities were fewer and further between. "I already tried asking her once, but she turned me down flat. Magnum, I really and truly believe if she just thought about it, she'd see what a good thing it would be for everyone to be together one more time."

"Well, you know how she feels about that house from when she lived there with Fran."

"But that's silly! I changed everything! None of the furniture's the same or the walls or even the floors. It's not like it was back then."

Magnum coughed, then nodded, then coughed some more. "The thing is, Georgia, she don't really get on with your husband either."

"He's older. He's softened," George insisted.

Magnum took a moment to consider this. "You know Patsy. She don't let things go that easy, I reckon. The business with the college money and such still gets her all worked up, I guess."

George nodded. "In your opinion, what would it take to get Patsy to come to just one meal with her siblings on Saturday evening? Would Roger have to apologize? Would I? Because I've tried that, Magnum."

He thought about George's question. What did Patsy want from her mother? *At this point, nothing,* Magnum thought. Certainly not apologies. The truth was, and Magnum knew this from various discussions they'd had, Patsy just didn't want Britt raised around her parents. *Toxic people,* Patsy called them. Magnum wished very much that he hadn't answered the door. He wondered what he could say to get this woman to go away. "Money," Magnum said finally.

"You need money?" George asked.

"No. We got what we need," Magnum said. "But you know Patsy! She thinks that Roger and you stole from her. I'm not saying you did, I'm not judging, but that's what she thinks. And she cares, more than anything, about what's fair and what's not." *There's no way this woman will ever give Patsy that money,* Magnum thought as he was saying all of this.

George set the birds-of-paradise on the floor and took her checkbook out from her purse. "How much do you think it would take?"

Magnum looked at George, and George looked at Magnum.

"Ten thousand was what she was owed, right?"

Magnum nodded. George wrote the check, signed it, and set it on the coffee table next to the Vicks VapoRub. "Roger should have given her that money a long time ago," George said. "It was supposed to be for Patsy's education, if I remember right, but now that Patsy's near thirty, I think even my husband couldn't argue that it would be fine to reapportion it to Britt."

George stood up and raised her arm to shake Magnum's hand. He felt as if he had just concluded a business deal in which he would come out badly upon presenting the terms to his bosses. He wiped his hand, which was mainly clammy from illness, on his sweat pants. "Well," he said because he could think of nothing else to say.

"Please feel free to come yourself," George said. "And Britt, of course. Helen's kids'll be there. They're only about half a year older than Britt, I think."

"I'll walk you to the door," Magnum said.

George said she would show herself out. Upon hearing the door close, Magnum put the check in his pants pocket and went to the kitchen for some NyQuil. He drank a generous dose, then went back to sleep on the couch.

He was nearly (though not quite) asleep when he heard Britt and Patsy return. "Daddy," Britt yelled. "Daddy!"

"Shhh," Patsy said. "Daddy needs to rest. Don't wake him up. Just give him a little kiss, OK?"

Britt kissed him once on the nose. "What are these?" Britt held up the two birds-of-paradise that were lying on the floor wrapped in purple tissue paper.

"Flowers. Daddy must have got them for us," Patsy said. She imagined that he must have driven to the drugstore for cough drops or some such and then picked them up at the flower cart that was usually parked outside.

"It looks more like a plant than a flower," Britt observed.

"No, they're birds-of-paradise, which are a very rare, very pretty kind of flower," Patsy said, though she secretly agreed with her daughter. They were so the kind of flowers Magnum would choose for her and not at all the kind of thing she liked. Looking at the garish flowers, she felt an enormous, awful wave of tenderness for the man, and she nearly lost her balance. She steadied herself, then took her daughter by the hand. "Come on, Britsy, let's go get these in water before they die."

Roger at the End of the Day

AN HOUR REMAINED before Roger had to leave to pick up the prodigal son and girlfriend from the airport. The time should have been devoted to working on the sermon he meant to write about Adam and Eve, the one that had been giving him so much trouble. Instead, he was researching hair replacement methods on the Internet.

It was funny, Roger thought, how even a brief change of venue could be a revelation to a person. At the hotel in Chapel Hill, Roger had been shaving with the wall-mounted magnification mirror when he became aware of unwelcome and heretofore undetected changes to his hairline. He had gone entirely gray years ago, but the quality of the hair itself had been impervious to time, remaining thick and bountiful. According to the relatively superior lighting conditions of the Comfort Inn, however, this was no longer the case.

It might seem a silly thing, but good hair was important to a preacher, and having considered the matter on a good portion of the flight from North Carolina, Roger felt completely convinced that he would be a less effective preacher if he was bald. After all, he was a public figure. He reasoned that he needed to be attractive so that his congregation would find his message (God's message!) attractive.

It certainly wasn't vanity. He would never, for instance, have dyed his gray hair back to blond. That would have been ridiculous. Besides, gray hair gave a preacher a certain gravitas.

According to preliminary research he'd done, most hair loss therapies were effective when a person still had hair to work with. This meant that it was best that Roger take action sooner rather than later. There were creams to be tried. And combs with laser beams! And hormones and vitamins! And plugs and transplants, though he didn't know if he could take the time off required for that sort of procedure. Or, as a last resort, perhaps a discreet little hairpiece? George's wig had looked pretty good when she'd had chemotherapy a couple years back. Roger could even get a toupee made from actual human hair! (He would try not to spend too long thinking about where that hair had come from . . .) Some of the methods were pretty costly, but he'd been making a decent amount of money from all the guest preaching engagements. He'd even been asked to think about publishing a book of his sermons—just for a privately owned Christian publisher, but still! If it caught fire, those things could really sell! Not that he was counting his money before he'd made it. He'd learned a thing or two about that in his sixty years on this good Earth. The point was, if new hair made him a better vehicle for the Good Word, then it was, without question, a necessary expense.

A knock at the door. Roger quickly shut his laptop cover. "Who is it?"

"Oh, it's just me, Pastor," Megan replied. "If you're not too busy, I wondered if I might have a quick word before I go home for the night."

"You know I always have time for you, Megan. Come in."

The pretty secretary sat on the couch in his office.

"I feel bad. I know you're meant to be off to the airport," Megan said.

"I have a little time left. What's troubling you?" Roger asked.

The secretary clasped her hands and set them on her denim-covered lap. "It's sort of embarrassing," she said.

"You know you can tell me anything," Roger assured her.

"Well, it's not the sort of thing we usually speak of, but I wanted your advice. I so admire you, Pastor Pomeroy." She lowered her head and looked away from him. "I probably admire you more than anyone except Jesus. Even my own father."

"Thank you," Roger said. "I have a great deal of respect for you, too."

"Well. You know how I've been engaged a sort of long time?"

Roger nodded. It was well known that Megan had been engaged for five years, almost as long as she'd been working for him.

"At first, Ben wanted to set the date, and I didn't want to, because I wasn't, um, sure, I guess. And then last year, I started to think, Well, I'm turning twenty-five soon, maybe we should set a date, right? So I brought it up with Ben, and that's when we had the engagement party. But then, he started to hem and haw, and finally, I said, 'What's the problem?' And he said that he didn't understand why I didn't want to get married for so long and all of a sudden I do. And then he said I'd waited so long that now he was the one who wasn't sure about me. I guess I started to cry. I mean, in some ways, I didn't care and maybe I even knew I had it coming, but I guess it still hurt me."

"Of course it did. That's only natural," Roger said.

"But then he said he didn't mean it and that I had taken all of it the wrong way! All he wanted was a little proof that I really loved him and wasn't just going through the motions because I was getting on in years. And I said, 'What sort of proof?' And he thought about it a little, but the way he wrinkled his brow, I knew the thinking was just for show and he already knew what he was gonna say, had probably gone to bed the previous night knowing exactly what he was going to say. I said, 'Just spit it out, Ben.' And he said he wanted to sleep with me before the wedding."

"I see." Roger cleared his throat. "If you're asking me if you should sleep with him, Megan, I think you already know the church's position on that sort of thing."

Megan nodded. "I do, Pastor. Of course I do."

"I can't say enough how much Ben's in the wrong here, Megan. If you want me to talk to him, either with or without you present, I'd be glad to."

"No. It's not that. I *know* he's wrong. But I'm wrong, too. Because I think that if I really loved him, I'd do it. I'd *want* to do it. I mean, I'm twenty-five years old, and I've been dating Ben for eight years, and I'm still a virgin! What kind of twenty-five-year-old is still a virgin?"

"One who cares about the next life more than this one." The more Roger thought about it, the more he wanted to *kill* that boy. "One who cares about the spiritual quality of a union as much as the physical!"

"But Pastor, if you really and truly love a person . . ." Megan covered her hands with her face. "But I don't, Pastor! I don't love him one bit!"

"Then you shouldn't marry him, and you certainly shouldn't have sex with him." Roger put his hand on the girl's head. She was breathing heavily and her shoulders were heaving up and down. "There, there."

"I don't love him because I love someone else," she said softly. Megan looked up into Roger's face. She stood. And then she kissed him. Roger pushed her gently, but forcefully, away.

"Oh, I see," he said. "No. I'm afraid I couldn't. My wife. You understand."

Megan nodded. "I'm so embarrassed," she said. "I didn't mean to do that."

"Of course not," Roger said. "We were talking about very emotional topics." Roger cleared his throat. "Here's what I think we should do. With your permission, I think you and Ben and myself should have a meeting to discuss his, uh, proposition. I won't hesitate to let him know just how inappropriate I think it was. Sometime next week, yes?"

Megan fixed her ponytail and smoothed down her denim skirt. "I'll check the schedule to see when you're free, Pastor."

"Good girl," Roger said. "Would you mind closing the door on your way out?"

Roger sat back down at his desk. He opened his laptop. The information on hair loss was still on his browser. Roger ran his fingers through his hair and decided that he had probably overreacted. There was plenty of hair up there, after all.

WHEN ROGER GOT to the airport, he spotted George waiting in the arrivals lobby.

"The kids aren't coming," she said simply. "Vinnie missed his flight, and Helen's at the hospital. Little Alice fell from the roof or a tree, I don't have the whole story, but they ran some tests and they think she's going to be fine. Just a broken collarbone and a minor concussion. I was away all afternoon running errands, so I didn't find out any of this until late this afternoon. When I heard, I tried calling you at the church, but no one was answering so I thought you must have left already. I drove down here like a madwoman. We should really get cell phones, Roger."

"Yes," he admitted. "So, it's just us this weekend?"

George nodded.

"Well, in a way, I'm glad of it," Roger said. "All the travel. It's been a long week. A long day, too." He took his wife by the hand. "I'll walk you to your car."

"My spot's terrible," George warned him. There was nothing left in short-term, so she had been forced to park in long-term.

On the walk over, she told Roger that Patsy might come to dinner that weekend.

"How nice," Roger said, though he wasn't really paying attention.

"Oh, and I forgot to tell you. There was a message for you this morning. An old professor of yours died. Katherine something . . . Or Carol."

"Carolyn Murray?" Roger asked.

"Yes. That was the name. Were you very . . ."

In the middle of the airport parking lot, Roger sat down. "Oh, God. Carolyn."

"I'm sorry, Roger," George said after a while. "Was she very important to you?"

"No," he said and in that moment, he decided that Carolyn hadn't been. George offered him her hand, and Roger took it. He stood up and brushed the dirt off the back of his khakis. "I feel a little silly. I've had a very long day, and I was just tired and surprised, I suppose. She's only five years older than us, George." Roger laughed. "Makes me feel old." Roger laughed again. "What do you say we stop for dinner on the way back? There's a Chili's a couple of exits from here. You can just follow behind me."

GEORGE WAS STILL in the bathroom, but Roger was already in bed. In point of fact, eleven was way past his bedtime, and normally, having stayed awake this late, Roger would have fallen immediately asleep. What was keeping him awake was the topic he had specifically avoided all evening.

"George," he called out. "I'll never understand that boy!"

"I mean, honestly, what have we ever done that's so bad? We never beat him . . ."

This was not, strictly speaking, true, and even as he said it, Roger knew it. On several occasions, a belt had been used on Vinnie. In Roger's experience, though, a belt was not nearly the same thing as a beating. A belt was about discipline, and discipline was about love. No one ever got particularly injured from a belt. A beating, on the other hand, lacked control. Children emerged from them with broken fingers, swollen eyes. This had never happened to Vinnie. Not once! (By the time his two daughters were of age, Roger had retired the belt entirely.)

"We supported Vinnie's decisions even when we disagreed with them . . ."

Roger was thinking of the Yale graduation, of course.

"Maybe there wasn't always much money, but he never lacked for food or clothing or any of the basic needs. I mean, George, you grew up poor! And so was I until my mother married my stepfather! And that man beat me silly—not that I didn't probably deserve it, but still. I mean, *that's* beating." Roger laughed, and then he stopped.

"So, what is it George? Why do they hate us so much? Because it's not just Vinnie. It's Patsy, too! I've prayed over it, and I've asked God, and I just don't understand. All our parishioners love me, you know. Megan always says how she *wishes* she had had a father like me! So, why?"

George came out of the bathroom. She was wearing a smart pair of cotton pajamas (a Christmas gift from Helen). "I don't know, Roger. I wish I did."

George Just before Sleep

BUT SHE DID know, of course. It was just pointless to tell Roger these things. She got into bed.

"Tell me, Georgie, is it so wrong that I wanted our children to have a rich spiritual life?"

"No," she said. "I don't think so."

"Me neither," Roger said. He turned onto his side, flipped off the nightstand lamp, and closed his eyes. "Maybe I shouldn't have belted Vinnie," Roger whispered. "I mean, had I to do it over again, I probably wouldn't have belted him. But we were so young when he was born."

"You were twenty-one," George whispered back. "I was only twenty."

"You were a baby!" Roger said.

"What did we really know about anything?" George looked at the digital clock. It was nearly midnight. In the glow of the clock, she noticed the phone, and she was reminded of the phone call that had begun her day. She tried to remember if she'd ever met Carolyn Murray. She could vaguely recall a tall Jewish woman with curly hair. Nothing more. George's memory had been more than a little selective since menopause, cancer (and its various treatments), and her experiments with antidepressants.

Even though Roger had only been gone a week, she had missed his body in bed. His warmth and his heft and his scent. She pressed herself against him. *Above all things, this,* she thought, *I will miss.* She suspected that heaven was probably a long shot for her, and though she would never confess this to her husband, she had never really believed in the place. But if she should make it to heaven, it could only ever be a relative paradise. At this late date, she was willing to admit that paradise was this man in this bed, and that there could be no other. This was the paradise for which she had cheated, lied, and blinded herself. The other didn't exist.

"Roger," she whispered. "Are you still awake?"

There was no reply, and so George felt emboldened to continue.

"You know what you were saying this morning about Adam and Eve? I have an answer now. Sin is good, in a way. I mean, we need sin," she said. "Because without sin, there wouldn't be any possibility for redemption."

There was still no reply.

"Roger," she said. "I'm dying."

A snore.

"And I don't want a Christian doctor either," George said. "I want an atheist doctor or anyone who doesn't believe in the possibility of an afterlife."

Another snore.

"Roger, I don't believe in Jesus. The closest I ever got to Jesus was under that ceiling in the Slickmart. I wasn't exactly in my right mind at the time, so that ought to tell you something about my relations with him. But I don't believe, Roger! And I have never believed. When we first met, I just said I believed because I wanted you. I fell in love with you, and you were so certain. *Are* so certain. And what I wanted was to be certain like you."

More snores.

"And I have never liked being called George."

PART IV

○ ○ ○

Baby One More Time

TEN YEARS LATER

THE FUTURE

Closing Time at
the Hoot and Holler

THE WAITRESS KICKS off her clogs and leans her elbows into the counter. "Tom, lemme give you a hypothetical," she says.

"Shoot," replies Tom, the greasy spoon's owner and chef.

"My daughter goes to school with this girl," says the waitress. "Guess you'd call the girl a good friend."

"Uh-huh."

"The girl's got herself in the family way, if you catch my drift."

"Uh-huh."

"And the family's not rich. They can't afford another mouth. And . . . Well, what's your opinion?"

"My opinion is that sucks," says Tom.

The waitress laughs a little. "Big time. But what would you do?"

"Well, supposedly, there're some doctors that'll do it off the books 'round here," says Tom.

"That's what I'd heard."

Tom looks around the diner. Just one customer left. An ancient man who's been eating the same piece of cherry pie for the last two hours. Tom's pretty sure the guy's asleep. He takes off his apron and drapes it over the oven handle. "But you can't count on those illegal guys. Like, they could take your money and not do it just for spite. Or they could have monkey-business tools—a wire hanger and a bottle of schnapps. And the girl could get sick. Or die. And they'll know at the hospital what happened. *They'll know.* They can tell. And the girl could even get hauled into court. The parent, too. It's a bad situation is what it is."

The waitress nods.

"It's a bad situation is what it is, is what it is," Tom repeats.

"You said."

"How old's the girl?"

"Like I said, she's a friend of my daughter's. So, same age as Britt."

"How old's Britt these days?"

"Fifteen," says the waitress with a little sigh.

"They grow up right quick," he says. "But back to your hypothetical. Wait, is it a hypothetical or an anecdote about someone you know? 'Cause it can't be both."

"I guess the second, then."

Tom nods. He puts his hands on the waitress's shoulders. "You be wanting any company tonight, Patsy?"

"Yeah, Tom. You know anyone?"

Patsy wakes the old man with the pie, and Tom shuts off the lights. They drive in separate cars to Patsy's little two-bedroom house, of which the best thing that can be said is that it is not on wheels. They tiptoe past the bedroom where Britt's sleeping, and then they go into Patsy's bedroom. They both smell like French fries and the sex is comfortable and dull. She likes the taste of him and she surprises him by sucking his cock for a spell. When it's done, Tom embraces Patsy from behind.

"You're quiet," he says.

"Just sleepy is all," she replies.

"You know what we were talking about before?" Tom whispers.

"Yeah."

"Well, if it were my daughter . . . ," he says, "if it were my daughter, Patsy babe, I'd fly up to Canada. It's legal there, and you can get it done in a real hospital or clinic. Somewhere nice and white and clean. I'd do it over the girl's spring break—assuming that worked out timing-wise. I'd tell everyone we were going on a little vacation. We'd stay a couple of days, make sure it all come out OK, then we'd turn around and fly back."

"Flying's expensive," Patsy says.

"You could drive."

Patsy nods. "Driving all the way to Canada's expensive, too."

Tom shrugs. He gets up to go to the bathroom. "That's what I'd do."

Second Opinion

THE LITTLE WAITRESS calls her sister-in-law, Lacey, on the phone and presents the same hypothetical situation to her.

Lacey sighs, then says, "I heard of a place just outside DC that does it."

"A nice place?" Patsy asks.

"Well, I haven't been there personal, but a woman I worked with, her cousin I think it was, had a similar situation to . . . And I think she just drove up there, got it taken care of, and drove back."

"Do you have any idea how much it cost?" Patsy asks.

"A couple thousand. Maybe it was less than that, I'm not sure. I remember that she had to use cash."

"And you're positive it's a nice place?"

"I really don't know, Patsy. Like I said, I've never been."

Patsy thanks her for the tip.

"I wish I could do more," Lacey says.

"It was just a hypothetical," Patsy says.

"Oh God, it's all turned into such a bad business." Lacey sighs. "It used to be so easy. I mean, it was never easy, but it was so much less awful than—"

Patsy interrupts her. "It was just a hypothetical, OK, Lacey?"

"I understand," Lacey says, and then, because she adores her niece and because she can't help herself, she cries out, "poor Britt!"

Preparations

THE NEXT AFTERNOON at work, Patsy tells Tom that she's going to need a couple of days off.

"How long you reckon?"

"Three days. Little trip to our nation's capital," she says brightly. "Heard they just broke ground on that stupid Iraq memorial."

"Take a week," Tom insists.

"Nope," she says, "only a couple of days." Patsy wants to keep the trip as tight as possible. She and Tom are in the middle of flipping a house—it's only a cheap little nothing in DeLand, but it's still a big deal to them. They bought the property "as is" for a steal in a foreclosure auction. Tom thinks they'll be able to double their money just by cleaning the place out, repainting, planting a tree or two, and not much else. She wants to be back in time for the weekend so that she and Tom can start the process of clearing out the house's interior. "I plan to be back for the weekend."

"Honestly, Patsy babe, I can take care of this part of the flip without you being there."

Patsy shakes her head. "I'll be there."

Tom nods. Patsy's a hardheaded little gal, and when she sets her mind to something, there's no convincing her otherwise. For instance, Tom would very much like to be married to Patsy, but she's against it. He would settle for living with her, but she's against that, too—she thinks it would set a bad example for her daughter if she lived with a man to whom she's not married. "You need any extra money?" he asks.

"I'm OK."

"You want I should come with you? I haven't been to DC for a while."

Patsy shakes her head. "We'll be fine. I'm gonna stay with an old war buddy in Bethesda. And you gotta look out for our business interests, Tom."

"Call me on the road," he says.

"Will do."

"Take care, Patsy."

She kisses him on the cheek even though they're at work and Patsy doesn't like to "parade" their personal relationship. Incidentally, all the other employees know perfectly well that Tom is Patsy's beau, and none of them cares at all. Tom is a kind boss; Patsy is a hard worker; both have had their share of hard times; everyone wishes them well.

Patsy kisses Tom hard on the mouth.

"Whoa," he says. "What was that for?"

"I gotta take off early," she apologizes.

Tom smiles at her. "You should take off early more often, darlin'."

PATSY'S FIRST STOP is the bank. She has been saving money for her daughter's college since the day Britt was born. Every week, no matter what was happening in Patsy's life—e.g., the death of her mother, the death of her husband, the time she got fired, the time she got laid off—no matter how little money she had or how meager the deposit, Patsy put whatever she could into Britt's college account. Today, for the first time ever, she makes a substantial withdrawal, $3,600 cash, and she tries very hard not to hate herself for it. She feels ill, thinking of both the penalties she'll pay and the violation to the account's spirit. But what can she do? Most of her own cash is tied up in the flip.

She stops at the grocery store on the way back from the bank. She buys sandwich makings and drinks for the road. At home, she packs all of it into the cooler she and Tom take on weekend trips to Daytona Beach, and Patsy thinks to herself, *It's almost like a mother-daughter holiday.*

She sends an e-mail to her war buddy, Charles Scott, in Bethesda, confirming that she'll be staying with him for two nights. She closes by writing, "Thanks to you and Cherie for the hospitality. Looking forward to catching up, Buddy. It's been too long. Yours truly, SweeTart."

Before she goes to bed, she plots a map on the computer that starts in Orange City, Florida, and ends at what she hopes will be a "nice place" in Maryland. By the program's estimates, the drive takes twelve hours if conditions are optimal.

Orange City

THE BOY WHO done it (as Patsy thinks of him) shows up at the house to see them off. "Mrs. French, I'd like to come with you," he says.

This is the one my daughter loves, she thinks. *This half-formed weed of a boy.* She wants to say, *It's you who got us into this fix.* But she knows he means well. "We can't afford to take you, Kip."

Patsy wants to run into the house and get a banana from the basket in the kitchen and a condom from her nightstand and make both Britt and the boy unroll the condom onto the banana. She wants to see with her own eyes that they know how to do it properly.

"I could pay my own meals. I could maybe even get some for fuel. I could contribute," Kip argues.

Patsy shakes her head. "If you were gone, your folks would wonder where you were. It's better if no one knows. It's better if Britt and I can just disappear for a spell, all right?"

The boy nods. "I'd really like to go," he says dumbly.

His earnestness is touching, but there's no way she's driving that boy to DC with her. "I'll make sure she calls you from the road, OK?"

Britt comes out of the house. She's carrying a large stuffed tiger, a gift from the One Who Done It, and the toy makes her look like a baby, which, in point of fact, she is. Patsy gets in the car so that Britt and the boy can say their good-byes in relative peace.

There are tears and tongues. After five minutes, Patsy honks her car horn. Britt shoots her a look of pure evil.

Patsy rolls down her window. "We have to get going! I want to make it to Bethesda before nightfall!"

Britt nods. She kisses the boy one last time, then gets into the backseat of the car.

"You're not gonna sit in the front?" Patsy asks.

"I'm just gonna be sleeping anyway, Mother."

"What'd I do?" Patsy asks.

"You know what you did. Like all this isn't hard enough on me already."

It's hard on Patsy, too. It's hard financially. She's gotta miss work. And the flip. And then there're all the fuel and tolls and meals. And she isn't even sure what the abortion will cost. After perusing several relevant online destinations, she'd come up with the figure $2,500, but things always have a way of costing more than you expect.

Patsy hears her daughter crying quietly in the backseat.

"I'm sorry about honking the horn," Patsy says.

Bethesda

CHARLES SCOTT ANSWERS the door. "Aw man," he says, "you're a sight for sore eyes, SweeTart."

Patsy holds out a bottle of wine. "We brought this for you and Cherie, Buddy."

"You shouldn't have. I'm just happy to see you. And this is Miss Britt, I presume?"

Britt holds out her hand. "Nice to meet you, sir."

"Good manners on this one," Buddy says. "Reckon the apple *does* fall far from the tree." Buddy laughs, and so do Patsy and Britt.

The wife emerges from the kitchen. "Well, don't leave them standing in the foyer, Charlie." Cherie kisses Patsy on the cheek. "It's good to see you, Patsy." Cherie's even blonder than the last time Patsy saw her.

For dinner, Cherie serves turkey and mashed potatoes. For dessert, there's apple pie.

Charlie's a lawyer, but he mainly works as a lobbyist for veterans. It's a nice house. During dinner, Patsy finds herself imagining how the listing would read: *Custom kitchen with granite countertops and a stainless fridge! Bonus room upstairs,* etc. He's done well for himself. Two

twin boys, age six. A pretty blonde wife who teaches tenth-grade bi-
ology. *Not bad at all,* Patsy thinks. *Buddy's really done it.*

After dinner, Charlie's sons take Britt to see their room, Cherie
excuses herself to grade papers, and Charlie and Patsy retire to the
den to tell old war stories and a few new ones.

"Whatever happened to Smartie?" Patsy asks after a second round
of drinks.

"He wrote a book."

"Yeah?"

"Yeah. It won some big-deal prize for nonfiction. It's about . . ."
And Charlie describes it for Patsy, which is completely unnecessary,
because she's already read it. Patsy just feels like talking about Smartie
with someone who knew him. "He did a reading in DC, and me and
Cherie went to it. Same old Smartie . . ."

She closes her eyes and enjoys hearing a story about a man she used
to love.

IN CASE HER daughter's fallen asleep, Patsy tiptoes into the guest room
that she's sharing with Britt. She's awake, though, and is on her stomach messaging with Kip.

Patsy grabs Britt's phone.

"Hey!" Britt says.

"It's late, and we've got a long day tomorrow. You can text Kip all
you want once this whole business is over."

Patsy flips off the lights and gets into bed next to her daughter.

In the darkness, Britt whispers, "What's wrong with him?"

"What's wrong with who?"

"Mr. Scott. You know, his face. It sort of looks like a mask."

A Nice Place in Maryland

THE PLACE IS only a twenty-minute drive from Bethesda, and Patsy chatters inanely the whole way to distract them from the task at hand. "Look, birds!" she says. "I didn't know they had birds in Maryland!"

"Yes, Mother," Britt replies, "they do have birds in Maryland."

"Look, a Payless Shoes! I could use some new flip-flops. Maybe on the way back?"

"Uh-huh."

"I think you could use flip-flops, too. And while we're on the subject, where do you think you might want to eat later? Because Cherie was telling me about this wonderful little tea house—"

"I don't think I'll want to eat."

"Well, the tea house only has finger food. So, it might be good—whenever you're hungry, no rush—just to eat something light. Just to get something in your—"

"Honestly, Mom. I don't want to hurt your feelings, but could you just try to be quiet?"

"Sorry," Patsy says.

* * *

THE PLACE HAS no official name. There's a sign out front that says YOUNGER'S STONE FRUIT FARM, and Patsy knows that's where she's supposed to make her turn.

She turns onto the dirt road. There's a large building that looks like a barn. Patsy hopes that it doesn't look like a barn on the inside, too.

Patsy gets out and walks up to a window in the front of the barn. A skinny red-haired, red-faced man asks Patsy if she and her daughter are here for the tour.

"No," Patsy replies. "We're here for the hayride." Patsy feels rehearsed and awkward, like she's in a school play.

"Can you pay for the hayride?"

"Yes."

"We only take cash."

"I know." Patsy looks around. She wishes she'd thought to bring a firearm with her.

"One thousand up front. One thousand when it's done."

Patsy nods. It's slightly less than she was expecting. She counts out a thousand dollars and is about to push it under the window when she stops herself. "Can we look inside first?"

He tells her that she can look inside after she's handed over her money.

"Could I talk to the doctor?"

He shakes his head.

Patsy looks around the "stone fruit farm." It's a pretty place. The grass is just coming in and there are leaves on the birch trees. The barn is freshly painted. When they were driving in, she had noted several metal trash cans lined up along the side of the gate, but they weren't bloody or anything. No one's screaming. Birds are chirping. Patsy pushes the pile of cash under the glass window.

"Go around to the side," the red-haired man says.

"That man was wearing a wig," Britt whispers to Patsy on the walk over. "Did you notice?"

Patsy hadn't noticed, because she'd been too wound up to notice much of anything. But now that Britt mentions it, his hair had pretty much looked like Ronald McDonald's. *A disguise,* Patsy realizes. *So we can't identify these people later if something goes wrong. How could I not have noticed?* Patsy takes a calming breath: *Get yourself together, girl.*

Around the side, they are met by an extremely overweight woman who is also wearing a wig—a big blonde one like Dolly Parton or Mae West.

"Red only gave me money for one," Dolly says, annoyed.

"There's only one today," Patsy says.

"Which one of you?" Dolly looks from Patsy to Britt.

Britt raises her hand like she's in class.

"Come on, then."

Britt and Patsy move to enter the barn.

"No," Dolly says to Patsy, "you wait outside."

"I'm her mother. I want to come in with her," Patsy says.

"Only people having the procedure go inside."

"That man"—Patsy gestures to the front of the barn—"that red-haired man told me I could go inside once I paid my money! I want to go inside with my daughter! She's underage!"

"Calm down," Dolly says. "If you're upset, there won't be any procedures at all today."

Patsy takes a very deep breath and thinks a little of the NATO alphabet to herself. "OK," Patsy says. "OK, OK. Now I'm gonna beg. Woman to woman. We drove all this way from Florida. This is my only daughter. My husband, her father, is dead five years . My mother is dead, too. I do not speak to my father. This girl is my whole life. Please, just let me go in with her. I won't disturb anything. I'm not a cop, if that's what you think. I'm a waitress. I'm just a woman. I'm just—"

"I don't need your life story. Just no hanky-panky in there, all right?"

* * *

THE FIRST THING Patsy notices is the smell—like fecal matter and rust. For the record, she cannot see any fecal matter or rust, but then the lighting is not particularly conducive to seeing much of anything. Several dim fluorescents. The bulbs aren't in fixtures either, just cords that swing from beams. There's a low-pitched buzz, which Patsy thinks is the lightbulbs but might be something more sinister—flies, maggots (do maggots buzz?), she doesn't know.

"Mom?" Britt says.

Patsy wonders if the dirt is just a front to conceal what really goes on here. That once this filthy curtain is pulled back, there'll be the sparkling clean clinic of Patsy's dreams.

"Mom?"

Patsy's eyes adjust to the dim lights and she discerns a row of folding lawn chairs. A girl about Britt's age with a bruised eye sits in the first chair. She's clutching a wad of cash. A woman near Patsy's age, wearing an old velour sweat suit, leans on the wooden counter for support. Patsy thinks she sees a blood stain on the back of the woman's pants—it's hard to tell on account of the dim lighting and also because the word *JUICY* is embroidered across the seat pockets of the pants.

"Mom, I've got to throw up." And then Britt vomits on the floor.

An orderly hears Britt's retching sounds and comes out to see who it is. He looks from Patsy to Britt. "I'm not cleaning that up," the orderly announces to no one in particular.

In an instant, Patsy decides. She takes her daughter by the hand and leads her out of this place. They run out the side of the barn, past Dolly, who says nothing. They run past the front of the barn, past Ronald McDonald, who yells, "Don't expect your deposit back!"

Patsy doesn't.

Ramada

PATSY CHECKS INTO the first hotel she can find. "I got to make some calls," she tells Britt. "Why don't you go out to the pool?"

Without a word, Britt puts on her swimsuit, slathers on some sunblock, and leaves.

Patsy calls Tom and tells him what happened. "I don't know what to do," she says. "I'm going crazy here."

"Canada," Tom repeats. "Your brother's still living in Toronto, right?"

"Yeah." Vincent is an editor for Canadian television.

"Call your brother," Tom says. "I don't need you for a couple of days, and you're halfway to Toronto already." Tom doesn't bother saying that this is what he'd told Patsy to do in the first place. "Get some rest, then run for the border, Patsy babe."

Patsy hangs up with Tom and then calls her older brother on the phone. They aren't particularly close, owing to the ten-year age difference between them, but Vinnie is still her brother and he's glad to help.

* * *

IN THE MORNING, Patsy wakes before Britt, so she decides to use the hotel's hot tub. The only other person there at this hour is a very old man who is wearing very old swimming trunks. Patsy herself is wearing a towel and, under that, an old bra and her underwear, as she hadn't considered she might want to go swimming when she packed for this trip.

Patsy thinks the old man is black, though she isn't quite sure. He's at that age where all old people start to look the same color—shades of gray. The underwear and bra she's wearing are the same color as the man, more or less. She says to him, "Sir, I hope this won't offend you, but I got nothing on under here." And then she corrects herself. She hadn't meant it to come out that way—provocative-like. "That didn't come out right. I meant to say, all I got is my underthings on. I mean, I'm not wearing my swimsuit. I didn't think anyone else would be using the hot tub this early."

He laughs and says, "Come on in, darling, the water's fine."

She takes off her towel and slips into the hot tub, and he says, "See, I wouldn't have even known you weren't wearing a proper bathing suit, if you hadn't told me. You jumped the gun, missy."

"Yeah," Patsy concedes, "story of my life."

Patsy reads a tabloid that someone had left in the hotel room. The names change, but it's always the same old stories. They're taking some pop star's baby away from her. A movie star yelled at the paparazzi and the so-called journalist suspects the movie star may have done something to her face.

"What brings you to these parts?" the gray man asks.

"Nothing," she tells him. "I'm just passing through."

"Where you on your way to then?"

"Nowhere," she says. "Somewhere up north."

"Mmm-hmm," he says. "I hope you don't mind my mentioning it, but I couldn't help but notice you're missing a toe."

She isn't missing the whole thing. Just half of what used to be the longest (the second) one on her right foot. "Lost it in the army."

"Bet there's a story there," he says.

Patsy smiles and shakes her head. "Yeah, the story is very short. The story is, I accidentally shot it off."

He wants to know what she did in the army, other than shooting off appendages, ha ha.

"I was a thief," she says.

He raises an eyebrow.

"I went around parting the natives from their weapons."

"What do you do now?"

"Waitress," she says. "Amateur real-estate baron."

He laughs. "So, what really happened to your toe?"

"It won't make any sense to you," Patsy says.

"Try me."

Patsy shrugs. She'll never see this man again anyway.

"I got pregnant. I didn't want to go on administrative detail, so I shot off my toe instead of shooting myself in the head. They discharged me for being nuts, which I pretty much was after two tours Over There. I came home spitting fire and tacks and eventually I got some help in a PTSD place and that was that. A lot of folks have it worse than me."

"That's not a short story at all."

"Maybe not," Patsy concedes.

"So, what happened to the baby?"

Toronto

THE ABORTION LIVES up to all of Patsy's expectations. Actually, the abortion exceeds Patsy's expectations. Things had seemed so terribly bleak when Britt told her she was pregnant. Patsy hadn't known what to do. She couldn't afford another baby, and even if she could, that wasn't the kind of life she wanted for her only child: single mother at sixteen. And then, once they'd all decided an abortion would be the thing, the question of where and how and who. She had been picturing rusty tools and mustache-twirling men. And that's what she'd more or less gotten a preview of in Maryland. Except there'd been women, too. Patsy had never imagined that a woman, someone's daughter, could participate in such a bad business. In any case, it had been an excellent suggestion to go to Canada. Because here, for once in her life, no one is making anything hard for her.

Vincent presents his ID and explains that this is his niece from America and they have come for an abortion. The nurse smiles, and Patsy and Britt are shown into a beige room with a series of reassuringly dull nature lithographs on the walls. They are presented with brochures, and a female therapist comes in to consult with them. Does

Britt understand? Yes, she does. They make an appointment for 9:30 AM the next morning.

The abortion is over in an hour. Britt is given painkillers, and Vincent drives them back to his apartment.

"How was it?" Vincent asks.

"It was a goddamn Mardi Gras," Britt says woozily.

"I shouldn't have asked that," Vincent says.

Vincent rushes to help Britt out of the car, and Patsy lets him. He leads the girl into the guest bedroom. He tucks her into bed and closes the door.

"She's a trouper," he says to Patsy.

Patsy shrugs. "It doesn't mean anything to her yet."

Some day, Patsy thinks, this will all mean something to the girl. Britt will think about what that baby might have been like and whether it could have been the One Who Changed Things for the World and other speculations of this nature. But today it only means a dull pain and relief. This is as it should be.

Vincent needs to finish editing the documentary he's working on. "Will you be all right by yourself?" he asks.

Patsy nods. "Please. Go. We've disturbed you enough." At the clinic, Vinnie had surprised her by paying for the abortion, telling Patsy to put her money back in Britt's college fund. Patsy hadn't needed to be asked twice. "Thank you," she says again.

Vincent hugs Patsy. "Have an orange," he says. He points to a red colander on the white tile countertop.

Patsy sits down in the sunny breakfast nook of Vincent's house. It's one o'clock, still early. She peels an orange and the skin comes off easily. Nothing sticks in her fingernails; the peel is in two long strips. She worries that the orange will be dry or bitter when she bites into it, but it isn't. It's sweet and good.

She finishes the orange, then throws the peels into Vinnie's compost bin. *Good people compost,* Patsy thinks, *I should compost.* And then a sort of joke occurs to her: *All people compost eventually.* She wants to tell someone, but it seems too hard to relate (*So, I was looking at this compost bin . . .*) and not phone-call-worthy anyway.

She thinks what a beautiful day it is—*I could do anything today*—and then she yawns and decides that the thing she would most like to do in the whole world is stay perfectly still.

Around four-thirty, Britt comes down from the guest room. Patsy asks her if it hurts, if she's bleeding very much. No on both accounts.

"Can I do anything for you?" Patsy asks.

"I'd . . . I'd like to go to the movies maybe."

So Patsy takes her daughter to the cinema. The only thing playing near Vinnie is an old war movie. Patsy loathes war movies, but not for the reasons you'd think. She doesn't hate their schmaltziness or their inaccuracies or their fakeness or their slickness or their oppressive generalities or that she can never see herself or anyone else she knew in them. She hates that they are all those things and yet they can still make her feel.

About ten minutes into the movie, Patsy starts to get antsy. She tells Britt she's going to the bathroom, but instead she decides to call Tom. She wants to see how it went with clearing out their flip property.

"Hey there, little lady," Tom answers the phone. "How'd it go?"

"Beautiful," Patsy replies. And then she feels her eyes grow hot and wet. It's tension, more than anything, and the release of it. And love—so much love for that surly fifteen-year-old in the movie theater that the heart can hardly stand it. It is lucky, she thinks, that we don't feel all the love inside us every moment. We couldn't breathe or walk or eat. It is lucky that it just flares up every now and again then resolves itself into a manageable dormancy.

"Are you all right?" Tom asks.

"Happy, I s'pose," she says. "You know, babe, what I really want to hear about is the flip."

"Aw, Patsy, you're not gonna believe it. You remember that shitty old blue carpet?"

"Yeah."

"Well, it was covering the sweetest patch of hardwood you ever seen in your life. I almost cried, I ain't ashamed to say it. We're gonna be thousandaires, darlin'."

Patsy laughs. Then Tom laughs because Patsy is laughing. "What?" he asks. "Is something funny?"

"Well," she begins, "I was looking at this compost bin . . ."

She and Tom talk for a brief while longer, and then Patsy returns to the movie. The main character in the film, a female soldier, is having her leg cut off below the knee. Patsy can see that Britt's eyes are tearing up.

"Mom, you want me to catch you up on what's been happening?"

Patsy shakes her head. "Nah, I been there before."

Detour

THE NEXT DAY, they're on the road back to Florida. They pass over the border with no problem. A guard asks her what her business in Canada was, and Patsy replies, "Just visiting my brother." She points to Britt. "Her uncle."

"My spring break," Britt adds cheerily. And in that moment, it's as if the whole real reason for their trip to Canada has been erased. Patsy can see what the guard sees—a mother and a daughter out to visit Canadian relatives over spring break—and somehow Patsy and Britt magically become those people. Patsy can almost imagine what that trip might have been like.

Britt sleeps until around noon, when she announces she's hungry. Patsy is, too, so they stop at a Friendly's in upstate New York. Patsy's feeling a bit flush, so she tells her daughter to order anything she wants.

While they're waiting for their food, Patsy says, "When I was a girl—a little older than you, I guess—I was in love with this guy. He was black, like Kip, and my parents didn't exactly love that—"

Britt interrupts. "Truth, Mom? I don't want to talk about this kind of stuff today."

Their food arrives then. The waitress is a pro. She has remembered to put Patsy's tomato on the side and toasted the bun as requested. Patsy decides to leave her a ridiculously big tip. That's the kind of thing you do when you're on vacation with your teenage daughter.

They are just passing into Washington, DC, when Patsy's cell phone rings.

It's Patsy's sister. "I've been trying to call you all morning," Helen says, "but your cell phone's been off."

"I was visiting Vincent. I don't have service there," Patsy explains. "And then I forgot to turn it back on."

"You went to Canada?" Helen asks. "Why didn't you tell me you were going to Canada? Maybe I could have come."

"It was last minute. Britt's spring break. Why are you calling anyway, Hel?"

"Dad passed away," Helen says. "I guess he hadn't been feeling well for about a week. He thought it was the flu, so he didn't even go to the doctor. But on Monday morning, he just didn't get out of bed. He died before he even got to the hospital." Helen starts to cry, but Patsy does not. "Can you believe it, Patsy? He only just turned seventy-two. And he was always so fit! Megan called me this morning. I'm going to get a flight to Tennessee as soon as I can. Where are you right now?"

"Virginia," Patsy says. "I guess I could start driving to Dad's house."

"Good," Helen says.

Patsy presses the hang-up button on the phone.

"What is it?" Britt asks.

"Your grandfather's dead."

"Oh," Britt says. "I didn't really know him. Are you sad?"

Patsy shrugs. "Not exactly."

Buckstop

MEGAN POMEROY, ROGER'S second wife, answers the door to the little white house that used to be George's, which used to be Fran's. Megan is five years younger than Patsy. It had seemed like a big deal at the time Roger and Megan married, but it doesn't anymore. Patsy will be thirty-nine in December; Megan is nearly thirty-four. *We're all so fucking old,* Patsy thinks.

"Patricia! Britt! I'm so glad to see you both!" Megan embraces them. "I have to keep saying to myself that the pastor's gone to a better place," she says tearfully. "He's really gone to a better place."

Patsy knows that Megan has been a good companion to Roger, that this woman is the wife that George never quite was. Megan is devout, for one. Her house is spotless and smells like cinnamon potpourri. The checkbook is always balanced. Her hips are slim, and her breasts are pert. This is the home of a perfect Christian wife but for one thing—Megan couldn't have biological children. She and Roger tried for a while. Five miscarriages and one stillborn carried to term. They have one adopted son, Mintuk, a refugee from some disaster or another.

"Come in," Megan says. "You both must be hungry."

"Not really," Britt says.

"We ate on the road," Patsy explains.

"Maybe just something to drink?"

Patsy and Britt sit primly on the beige, flower-embossed sofa in the living room. Patsy thinks that the couch in a prior upholstery incarnation might have belonged to her mother but she can't tell for sure. "It was so lucky you guys happened to be on the road!" Megan calls from the kitchen.

"Yeah!" Patsy calls back.

"What were you doing in Canada?"

"Visiting my brother!" Patsy says.

"My spring break!" Britt adds her part of the routine.

"Oh, how nice. I spoke to him this morning. He won't be able to come to Roger's funeral, but he sent a very beautiful flower arrangement."

Patsy thinks that she, too, wouldn't have come if she hadn't been on the road already.

Megan returns with three tumblers filled with lemonade. "I squeezed it myself," Megan says. "Our lemon tree's blooming in April. It's so weird."

"Signs of the apocalypse," Patsy jokes.

"The burial's going to be tomorrow. It's quick, I know, and it's probably silly of me, but I didn't want Roger to be just left out rotting. I know it's just a body, but . . ."

Patsy shakes her head. "That doesn't sound silly."

"I'm so glad you're here," Megan says. She takes Patsy's hand. "When Magnum died, just tell me one thing. How did you ever stand it?"

Patsy's sweet, dumb, beautiful husband is now five years gone. He had been good to her. He had cared for Britt when she was an infant and Patsy was away at the PTSD rehab center in San Diego. He had loved their little girl like his own blood, though he definitely knew otherwise. They had only discussed the subject of Britt's paternity once, on the day Britt was born. Magnum had said, "Just tell me he's dead. Tell me he died Over There." And Patsy had replied, "He's dead, Magnum." But Magnum is the one who's dead now, and Britt's biological father is alive and well and winning prizes.

When he passed, the depth of her feeling for the man had astonished her. At times during their marriage, she had felt that she barely liked him, let alone loved him. She had loved Harland; she had loved Smartie. She had been transported by love for those men. But Magnum? Sweet, dumb Magnum? Yes, he was good and—what was it they had called Joseph?—a just man, but . . .

Then he had gotten sick, and she had shifted into the role of caretaker, dutifully and without much reflection. One day, his big body was gone and it felt as if a great trick had been played on her. The space in her bed was almost too much to bear. The hole in her life, unexpected and maddening. In the three months following his funeral, she quit her job, put the Buckstop house on the market, got a U-Haul, and drove from Tennessee to Florida. This was how she and Britt had come to live in Orange City.

During this latest adventure, she has never once allowed herself to long for him. She has not imagined Magnum driving Britt to Canada. She has not imagined him turning the whole ordeal into some sort of educational road trip—how he would have taken their daughter to Graceland or to colleges, for God's sake. She has certainly not imagined Magnum calling her from the road to say, "Don't worry, Patsycake. It's done. It's all taken care of," and Patsy sobbing with relief and gratitude for her sweet, not-so-dumb husband. "We bought you an Elvis shower curtain," he would say. "We'll see you in three days."

How had she stood the grief? She hadn't, not really. "I didn't," she says to Megan. "I just do my best to ignore it."

Megan apologizes. "I shouldn't have asked that. It's not like you're not mourning Roger, too."

"I doubt as much as you."

"He was your daddy. Of course it's as much as me," Megan insists.

Patsy says nothing.

"He loved you, Patsy. All I can tell you is he loved you kids. I wish you could have been in church two Sundays ago. He gave this beautiful sermon about grace, about how he'd never been able to give it to himself or the people he loved best, and how he found it so much easier to say all the important things from the pulpit," Megan says.

"Sounds like a good speech," Patsy says.

"I tell you, Patsy, there wasn't a dry eye in the house. But later, I was reflecting how it must be hard for you and Vinnie, 'cause you two never go to church. So you never got to hear what a wonderful man your daddy really and truly was."

The next afternoon, in ill-fitting black clothes borrowed from Megan, Patsy watches them lower her father's coffin into the ground and a funny thought occurs to her: You spend your whole life trying to get out of holes. The hole you're born into because of who your parents are. The hole you dig yourself trying to get out of that first hole. The hole your children are born into is the saddest hole of all. It occurs to her that she has spent most of her life digging herself out of or into one hole or another. And then, in the end, they just lower you into the ground anyway. She whispers a question, kind of like a prayer, if she were the praying sort, to no one in particular, "How in the world do you ever get out?"

After the funeral, Patsy and Britt go back to the house. Helen is there with her husband, the dentist. So's the Pharm, who is known as Marcus once again though mainly as Mr. Jones. Mr. Jones is the eighth-grade history teacher at Buckstop Academy; sometimes the kids make fun of his limp. And there's Marcus's little sister, Minnie, who did indeed marry Joseph-named-Joseph and has, by all accounts, a deeply happy, deeply ordinary life. And Lacey, too, though Patsy talks to her several times a week anyway. Lacey keeps threatening to move to Orange City to be closer to Patsy and Britt.

"How did it go in DC?" Lacey asks.

"Just fine," Patsy replies. "In the end."

Britt and Patsy go into Roger's office to get away from all their well-meaning relatives. On the desk is a copy of a book entitled *God's Classroom: Revised Edition* by Carolyn Murray. The name is familiar, but Patsy cannot quite place it—she certainly doesn't associate it with the nippleless woman who had been the inadvertent architect of so much of her life. In any case, her father had not gotten very far. There's a bookmark between pages 12 and 13, and what Patsy thinks is, *he'll never finish it now*.

Britt sits under the window in front of a small teak bookshelf that had once belonged to Patsy. She busies herself flipping through a pile of old family albums.

"Mom," Britt asks, "is this you?"

Patsy sits on the floor next to her daughter. It's a picture of Patsy in a cheerleading costume, standing in front of the old Texas house. It had been taken before the disastrous red paint job, back when the house was still yellow.

Patsy nods.

"Your house was nice." Britt comments. "You must have been rich."

Patsy snorts. "It was all for show."

"What's that supposed to mean?"

"I mean, my parents didn't own any of it. They were in debt up to their eyeballs. My mother stole money from your uncle. She stole money from me."

"But, their house . . . it's way bigger than ours."

"I know what it looks like. I know. But if you want to know the difference between me and them—and well, there're many—but if you want to know the biggest, it's that I don't owe nothing to no one. For better or worse, I own my own life."

Britt nods and puts the photo album back on the shelf. She hadn't wanted a lecture on self-reliance, only to poke fun at her mother's ridiculously skimpy cheerleading skirt.

Megan comes in from the other room. It's a small house, this house Roger died in. It's a small house, good for eavesdropping and not minding your own business. "You say you own your own life," Megan says, one hand on hip. "Well, what about God?"

Patsy pushes herself up off the floor. She wipes the dust and travel grit from her palms then replies, "What about Him?"

Acknowledgments

For a variety of services, my thanks to Stuart Gelwarg, Seth Fishman, Janine O'Malley, Sarah Odedina, Jean Feiwel, Drea Peters, Jessica Monahan, Caroline Trefler, Michael Hornburg, and, as always, my parents. My special thanks to Doug Stewart, Hans Canosa, and my editor, Lauren Wein.

ZEV   Zevin, Gabrielle.

        The hole we're in.

3C